DANGEROUS DEEDS

LIZZIE ~ BOOK 1

THE WESTPORT ROMANTIC MYSTERIES

BETH PRENTICE

BOOKS BY BETH PRENTICE

The Westport Romantic Mysteries

Lizzie

A Sinister Sign ~ The Prequel

Dangerous Deeds

Give Murder A Hand

Deathly Desire

The Christmas Gift – A Mini Lizzie Mystery

Molly

Wicked Little Lies

Gracie

The Ivory Veil – a novella

Chloe

Killer Unleashed

Deadly Tails

Alexandra

Invitation to Murder

The Aloha Lagoon Samantha Reynolds Mysteries

Deadly Wipeout

Lethal Tide

Fatal Break

Tidal Wave

The Dandelion Ponds Mysteries

In High Spirits

The Hollyday Spirit - novella

That's the Spirit

The Dun Roamin' Romantic Mysteries

Tilly ~ Before Dun Roamin'

Matilda's Wish

Author: Beth Prentice

Website: www.bethprentice.com

Copyright 2017 Beth Prentice

First Published in Australia in August 2017

EBook ISBN: 978-0-6481306-0-4

Paperback ISBN: 978-0-6481306-1-1

❀ Created with Vellum

CHAPTER 1

It's probably important that I start this story by telling you who I am. My name is Lizzie Fuller and I'm the tallest female member of my family, measuring in at 5' 2". I'm average weight with a small waist and hips. Unfortunately, I was at the front of the queue when God handed out breasts. I got my brown eyes and long, dark, curly hair from my mum's side of the family. I also have dimples. I don't know who I inherited those from. Grandma Mabel was a bit of a wild card, so we don't really know what's hidden in the family gene pool. As far as intelligence goes, I'm not stupid but I'm not a genius either. Today I'm debating that.

I'm standing here trying to turn the sticky lock preventing me from opening my new front door. Well, new is a stretch of the imagination, but it's new to me, so I guess it's okay for me to say that. About a month ago, I had a premature mid-life crisis and realized that at the age of thirty-one, I didn't own anything of significance. Sure, I own my car and a collection of high-end fragrances, but if I was to take an unscheduled trip to the Pearly Gates, I had nothing that stated this was who I was. True to form, I rushed out and bought a house. No time like the present, hey?

Now, I'm wondering if I should have had an affair like every other sane member of society having a mid-life crisis. It would have been much easier…and cheaper.

"Hurry *up*. It's freezing out here," complained my sister Molly. Molly had come along today to help me move, but I was about to ask her what her definition of 'help' was. So far, I'd yet to see it.

"It's stuck," I grumbled, rattling the door in the hope that it would miraculously unlock itself.

"Use your shoulder," she suggested. "Give it a good shove."

The timber door looked pretty solid from where I was standing. "You're welcome to give it a go."

"Sure, but you're wearing jeans, whereas I'm in a skirt. Jeans are much more appropriate for the job." I'm not sure what occasion Molly had come dressed for today. It definitely wasn't moving house. Her skintight jumper, mini skirt and high heeled boots looked amazing, but that was all they were good for.

Looking at the door again, I reached out and picked at the peeling paint, considering my options. I'd never rammed a door before, but maybe Molly was right—it just needed some encouragement. And the condition of the house was pretty decrepit so maybe the white ants might have weakened the frame for me.

"Stand back," I warned Molly before I changed my mind. Taking a couple of steps backward, I then ran at the door. My aim was perfect, my shoulder hitting the door above the lock. I'll admit to not being the strongest person on the planet, but I gave it my best shot. Unfortunately, the door was stronger than I was and it held firm, causing me to bounce off it, landing on my butt on the timber boards of the porch.

Molly stared down at me, her hands on her hips looking thoughtful. "Maybe you should have just climbed the drainpipe and gone in through the open window up there," she said, nodding in the direction of an upstairs window.

"You couldn't have mentioned that before I threw myself at the door?" I snapped.

"I know you don't like heights."

I sighed and accepted her outstretched hand, getting back onto my feet and rubbing my shoulder as I moved.

Negotiating the couple of front steps, I stood on what was left of the front lawn, squinting up at the window Molly was referring to.

She was right. The timber casement window was ajar.

"Why don't you climb it?" I asked. "You were good at scaling drainpipes when you were a teenager."

Her smile beamed at the memory, before she looked down at her skirt and boots.

"What exactly did you come dressed for today?" I asked.

"Lizzie, it's important to always look your best." I sighed. "Come on, I'll tell you how to do it," she encouraged.

I knew it wasn't a good idea. I knew it. But I did it anyway.

"Take your shoes off," she suggested, "You get a better grip with your toes that way. Then you just grab the drainpipe and start to climb."

The window wasn't that high, and it was directly next to the drainpipe, so if I didn't look down, surely I could do this.

Doing as Molly instructed, I kicked off my sneakers and started my ascent. The plumbing creaked and groaned, but before I knew it, I was nearly at the top.

Once the window was within reach, I stretched to grab it. The bolts holding the drainpipe to the wall didn't seem too happy with the extra strain put on them, and with an almighty snap they gave way, allowing the drainpipe to fall away from the building.

I screamed and held on to the rusted metal pipe with all my might.

Molly yelled, but I didn't hear a word of what she said. The only noise that my brain was receiving was the loud groan of the metal, the sound of rust flittering past my ears, and my blood pounding through my veins.

I said a quick prayer that this would all end well, as the pipe gave its final groan and succumbed to my weight, plummeting to the ground with a mighty crash.

The descent had been much faster than the ascent, and as the air gushed from my lungs, I saw Molly's anxious face peer over me.

"Are you alive?" she cried. "Oh, please tell me that you're alive!"

I blinked.

As relief washed over her, she succumbed to an uncontrollable fit of giggles. By the time I had managed to roll over, push the rusty drainpipe off me, and sit up, she was on the grass next to me holding her sides as tears of laughter dripped off her chin.

"That was so not funny!" I cried.

"Oh yes it was. You should have seen your face."

Bloody sisters.

As I was considering if I'd actually broken any bones, a man walking his dog down the street, looked over the tiny fence toward us.

He gave me a small smile. "Afternoon ladies. Is everything okay?"

Brushing the rust and grass off my top, I smiled at him and explained that I had just purchased the house and couldn't get in.

"Oh, well I'm Edward. I live at the end of the street."

"Pleased to meet you."

"You should just go in the back door," he suggested. "It's never locked."

"Pardon?" I asked, as the heat raced up my neck.

"The lock doesn't work on the back door and the previous owner never bothered with it. Everyone in the street knew that if they needed to get in to her, that was the way to do it."

"Oh. Okay. Well...thanks then. I'll try that." Just why I hadn't thought to do that before listening to Molly's hare-brained ideas was beyond me.

WALKING through the knee length grass toward the rear of the house, I struggled to remember what the hell possessed me to buy the very first property I'd seen. The house was a tiny, detached two-bedroomed Victorian. Probably the best way to describe it is a dilapidated cross between a gingerbread house and the house of horrors. It's a money pit. I know that. But my rival buyers wanted to knock it down, and I couldn't let that happen. All I saw was the memories the house would hold, and knew that now was the time to protect it. It needed to be restored to its former glory. But why I thought I had the skills necessary to do such a thing is beyond me.

"Why didn't you buy one of those new apartments they've just finished overlooking the river?" complained Molly, looking around the overgrown yard.

To be honest, I was now wondering the same thing myself.

Pushing my hands deep into my pockets for warmth, we walked to the back porch. The morning had started with the sun shining and not a cloud in the sky, but as the day had rolled on, the clouds had moved in and the wind had picked up. Typical Westport weather. I'd lived in Westport most of my life, only moving to the city ten years ago for work. But I'd had enough of working in the city, so I'd made a deal with my boss and would now be working from home.

I looked up at the old house and groaned. I really should have bought something with a usable office.

Reaching the rear timber deck, we negotiated the few steps. My first attempt to push the door open was unsuccessful, but with the use of my hip and a bit of force, we finally made it inside. Finding the light switch, I flicked it on and waited until the dim 60-watt bulb illuminated the room. I looked around and bit my lip. The excitement I'd felt when I awoke this morning was fading by the second. I surveyed the room, biting down on my disappointment. Molly followed me in. As she stomped her feet to warm herself up, I watched the dust rise and nearly consume her.

"Bloody *hell*," she coughed, waving her hand in front of her.

The smell of a stale, damp room hit me. I looked around at the dirty old kitchen cabinets and scarred timber flooring, and felt a lump form in the back of my throat.

"Leave that door open, will you Molly, and for goodness' sake *stand still*."

Once the dust had settled, we silently walked through the house. I don't think either of us could find the right words to say. It was only as we were walking back down the stairs from the attic that Molly finally broke the silence.

"Who the hell thought this wallpaper was a good idea?"

It's funny, but I don't remember seeing the wallpaper the day I bought the house. To be honest, I don't remember the house looking this bad at all. That day, all I could think about was how it would look revamped.

The house had a simple floor plan. There was a main hallway with the staircase off the front door. To the right of the stairs was the lounge room and to the left was the kitchen. It's the same on the second floor, only to the right was my bedroom and to the left was the bathroom. The second set of stairs led to the attic, which was home to a second bedroom. The amount of work needed before this house was even livable made me feel queasy. The butterflies in my stomach were going crazy, telling me to run, but what the hell did they know? This was going to be fun, right?

"It's going to be great. A bit of a cleanup and you won't recognize it," I said, not daring to look Molly in the eye.

"A bulldozer would be better, but if you're insistent on sprucing it up then you'll need a hot handyman to help you." Her petite nose wrinkled as she glanced around her. "What is that smell?"

"Rodents, I think." I blinked against the sting of tears. I hated rats. I mean, *really* hated them. Like phobia-hated them.

"Don't worry," said Molly. Sensing I was about to cry, she placed a hand on my shoulder. "The cat should help with that."

"What cat?" I looked at her, surprised. "I don't have a cat."

"Well, maybe he came with the house. He was sitting on the window seat in the lounge when we walked in and looked quite comfortable, if I may say so. Didn't you see it?"

"No. But there are a lot of things about this house I don't remember seeing," I said, feeling a weight on my chest. "How could I be this stupid, Molly?"

Molly pulled me into a big sister hug. "You can come and stay with me if you like."

"Thanks, but no. I got myself into this so I have to see it through," I said sniffing. I took a minute to enjoy the warm, safe feeling of Molly's hug before I stepped back and pulled myself together. Feeling sorry for myself was not going to improve this situation. "Now, where was this cat?"

I followed Molly to the lounge, and there, sitting on the window seat, was a particularly large, fluffy ginger cat. Damn, she was right.

"But I don't want to own a cat," I whined, thinking I have trouble looking after myself. I should never be allowed to own any animal. You see, I did fish-sit for my mum once and—between you and I—the results were disastrous.

"I don't think you have much choice."

Okay, the cat did look quite at home sitting there, leg in the air, licking his privates. It stopped mid-lick, tongue sticking to its fur and gave us the once over. Deciding we were of no interest, it resumed what it was doing.

"Do you think it wants food and then it'll disappear again?" I *was* hoping it had the wrong house.

"It's worth a try."

"There's enough bloody rodents around here it could have a

smorgasbord." Maybe a cat wouldn't be a bad idea. This last thought was actually encouraging. I mean, a cat isn't like a dog, is it? You can forget to feed a cat and it will find food itself, won't it?

"I think you should go and get it some real cat food. It looks far too lazy to actually catch anything."

Bugger.

WE SPENT the rest of the afternoon cleaning. Not that you could really tell where we'd been. The solicitor who'd handled the sale of the house told me it was empty for about six months, and prior to that an elderly lady had lived there. I guess that explains the three inches of dust on every surface.

Molly helped a little in the end, but not without complaints. By the time my dad arrived with the truck full of my belongings, we had dusted and vacuumed every inch downstairs. Now all I had to do was clean the bedroom and bathroom before I could go to bed tonight.

"Why don't you sleep at my place until you get this place straightened?" offered Molly.

"Thanks, but I'll see how I go. It's going to take forever to renovate this place, so I'll have to get used to it at some point."

"Yeah well, the offer stands. Even if it's midnight, just get in your car and head over."

I smiled. On the surface, Molly may look shallow and self-obsessed but it was all an act. On the inside she was a big softy.

After Molly and Dad left, I improvised a lock on the back door by pushing a chair under the handle, and made a quick trip to the local grocery store, which meant I could now feed not only myself, but also my squatter. I had a feeling Cat belonged with the house and that even after feeding him the best Kitty Kat food money could buy, he was not going anywhere. I'd also purchased every mouse and rattrap the store had in stock because my faith in Cat was pretty low. There was no way I wanted any of those little rodents crawling over me in my sleep.

Feeling tired and irritable I drove back to my new home. I was exhausted, everything I owned was in boxes and there was no way I was unpacking them until I knew all furry creatures had moved on. Most of the house was still filthy, I was responsible for a cat, and now the sun was setting, I was starting to feel Molly was right. I was pretty creeped out.

As I drove to the house, it looked dark, scary and lonely. Carefully driving around the black sedan parked opposite my driveway, I parked my car and contemplated spending the night in it. I could lock the doors and not have to face going inside the house until morning when it was bright and sunny again. But no, I had to stop being stupid and get inside. There was nothing in there that could hurt me. I had personally checked every cupboard for dead bodies and scary creatures earlier in the day. Checking again would probably put my mind at ease, but there was no freaking way I was going to check in the dark.

Entering the house, I turned on every light in every room, all except the attic which—as that particular light switch was at the top of the stairs—was way too creepy for me to even think about.

I stood outside my bedroom door and looked toward the darkened staircase, terrified. I probably should have ventured up there and turned it on. Peace of mind is a powerful thing. Oh well, I'll just lock the door, jump into bed and pull the covers over my head. That would work just as well.

CHAPTER 2

I'd been dreaming. Someone was standing over me, watching me while I slept. It wasn't a reassuring-angel-watching-you kind of dream. It was a scary, some-lunatic-wants-to-kill-you kind of dream.

I woke with a start.

The hair on my arms and back of my neck stood on end as I sat up and had a good look around. Everything was the way I'd left it. Everything except the bedroom door. It was wide open, swinging on its hinge.

Fear ran through me, ending its journey in my stomach, where it swirled around, mixed with anxiety, and left me feeling sick. I looked out onto the darkness beyond the hallway, knowing I'd left every light in the house burning. So why was it dark?

Thankfully my bedroom light was still on, so I reached for my phone and pulled back the covers before allowing my toes to curl into the dirty carpet as I stood. Grabbing my handbag, I quickly searched for a weapon.

I came up with a can of deodorant.

Oh well, it's the best I was going to get right now. I shook the can, and walked toward the door, my heart pounding against my chest. What I really wanted to do was run. Run through the door, down the stairs, out to my car, and drive as far from here as I could get. But I guess I should grow a set and deal with whatever opened that door. The closer I crept, the harder my heart pounded.

With the dream still lingering, I peeked into the hallway. The staircase leading up to the attic looked darker than ever, and not for the first time I wished I'd turned the light on up there before going to bed.

Standing still, I held my breath and strained to listen for any unfamiliar noise. Unfortunately—as this was my first night in this old house—every noise was unfamiliar.

I couldn't see anything or anyone that shouldn't be there, so I relaxed a little bit. Not too much though. I still needed to walk down the stairs to check the kitchen and lounge. Shit, I hated this.

Hearing the wind rattling the old windows, I wondered again why I hadn't bought a brand-new house.

The stairs creaked under my weight, alerting any intruder I was on my way. I also forgot one of the treads was loose and nearly sped up my descent as it slipped when I trod on it. Grabbing the railing I regained my balance, but not before a small scream escaped my lips. Well, I guess I could cross *Spy* off my ideal career list.

"Hello! Is anybody there?" I yelled, giving up on the creeping bit. I'm not really sure what I expected to get back. I didn't exactly think any intruder would jump out yelling, "surprise!", but I'd never been in this situation before, so who knew?

Waiting for what felt like an eternity, the only response I got was the sound of the wind. Reaching the bottom stair, I paused. I didn't know which way to turn. Should I check the kitchen or the lounge first? I decided on the kitchen as it contained the only other exit. I could see the lock on the front door was firmly in place, so that was comforting, at least.

Pushing myself as close to the wall as possible, I slowly peered around the corner. The light, thankfully, was blazing. Well, blazing was a bit of an over-statement, but it did give me enough light to see the room was empty and the back door was closed.

I let out a shaky breath when I saw it was locked. Now all I had to do was check all the windows in all the other rooms and I could go to bed and back to sleep. Maybe. Oh, who was I kidding? Sleep was something I figured would evade me.

Taking a deep shuddery breath, I entered the lounge. Thankfully, the only thing I found there was Cat snoring loudly on the couch. He didn't seem upset by anything so maybe my door was only open because the house was old. Timber moved, didn't it?

Picking up Cat, I walked into the hall and checked the switch for the upstairs light. No matter how many times I flicked it, it didn't work. I guess the bulb had blown.

My knees shook as I continued my rounds of the house feeling the loneliness creep in, threatening to smother me. Earlier in the day I thought it was because the house was unfamiliar, but now I feel like the house was watching me, letting me feel its sadness. I hugged Cat closer to me as a lump sat in my throat and I made my way back to bed, once again shutting and locking the door behind me.

I DID MANAGE to doze just as the sun was rising, but woke with a start and let out a scream as something big, ginger and fluffy jumped onto my chest.

Cat.

Sitting there, yellow eyes staring into mine, he started to howl. Obviously, it was breakfast time.

Jumping out of bed and shaking myself off I looked at Cat,

fighting the trembling threatening to take over my body. The sun was streaming in through my open curtains and even though I thought I had closed them last night, after the dream and then my early morning search of the house, I wasn't sure of anything anymore.

Shaking off the remainder of the night, I checked my alarm clock and saw it was already 6.20am.

"You scared me," I said, patting Cat and listening to it purr. I should pick it up and check what type of privates it had and then give it an appropriate name. Maybe after I'd had breakfast, as looking at a cat's genitals was not something you should do on an empty stomach. Deciding a shower would probably make me feel much more human, I put my brave girl pants on, opened my bedroom door and headed to the bathroom.

It wasn't the most pleasurable experience I've ever encountered, but after a quick finger scrunch of the hair and a five-minute make-up routine, I dressed in jeans, T-shirt and my comfy flat shoes, and called my sister Molly to ask if she would meet me in town to help me buy some furniture.

Of course she would, she loved spending other people's money.

OKAY, I admit it. I wasn't really paying as much attention to the road as I should have been as I reversed out of my drive and only narrowly missed the black sedan parked on the opposite side of the street. For some reason I couldn't fully shake the dream and it had left me feeling anxious. I probably shouldn't have had the three cups of coffee either. Caffeine is not the best thing to have when anxiety levels are high to start with. Slamming my foot on the brake pedal—my handbag sailed off the seat spilling all its contents on the floor—I put my hand to my heart as I felt the shot of adrenaline surge through me.

Bugger, that was close.

But seriously, what idiot parks there?

Swearing under my breath, I put the car into forward and planted my foot, heading off in the direction of the shops, thinking how I would have to be more careful.

By the time I got there, Molly was already in the store and well ahead of me. Finding her, I quickly realized that she had a trolley full of household items that seemed to be for me.

"Molly, do I really need all this stuff?" I asked. She turned and glared at me. Today she was dressed in a tight-fitting dress and had her long dark hair piled on top of her head so nothing obstructed the view of what was concealed inside her Victoria's Secrets.

"Well hello to you too, Lizzie."

"Sorry. Hello Molly. But what is all this stuff?" I asked, my voice rising into the stratosphere.

"It's necessities, Lizzie," she said, placing her hand on her hip and raising one eyebrow, almost daring me to argue with her. "Are you questioning my ability as a housewife?"

"Molly, you're a photographer who lives alone and who doesn't know how to cook. Of course, I'm questioning your abilities as a housewife." Maybe I should have called my brother Danny for help instead.

"I will have you know I am very capable of looking after myself. And of course, you need all of this. I mean, just look at this really cute stripy bowl. How could you possibly own a cat and not allow him to eat out of something so cute?"

"Well, he didn't seem to mind the old Chinese container I fed him with this morning." I huffed. This was easy for her. It wasn't her budget she was spending.

Sniffing indignantly, she turned her back on me and marched to the next section of the store, leaving the trolley for me to push. I could almost feel her rolling her eyes, even from back here.

By the time we reached the registers, I was only narrowly

avoiding a breakdown. It was with shaking hands and unsteady breathing that I handed over my credit card and asked for all the big stuff to be delivered, putting all the smaller stuff back in the trolley, ready for me to take home.

"Molly, I need a drink." My shoulders drooped and a headache started behind my eyes.

"There's a coffee shop over there," she said pointing toward a large food court.

"No, I need a real drink. Caffeine just isn't cutting it today."

Laughing, Molly walked ahead of me as I was left to push the huge shopping cart through the crowds of people milling around.

"I'm not joking." I called after her. "Remind me to come alone next time," I sulked, speaking to myself, as Molly was way ahead of me already. Molly walked with an air of authority and somehow the crowd just parted as she approached, so it was no surprise that by the time I caught up, (sadly, I did not inherit her ability to part the seas) she was already seated.

"Thanks for waiting for me," I moaned as I sat down.

"What? And miss out on a table. Snoozers are losers, Lizzie."

"Christ, Molly, have a bit of sympathy. My back is killing me from all the cleaning I did yesterday. I thought holidays left you feeling refreshed and relaxed, not sore and cranky," I said, rubbing the knots out of my shoulders.

"You know, you would think you would be grateful for my help. But all you've done since you got here is whine. What the hell is the matter with you today?"

"I'm sorry," I grouched. "I'm just tired. I had a bad night's sleep last night. I swear that house is watching me. If houses had feelings, I'd say this one is depressed," I said, thoughtfully. I could see Molly roll her eyes but her tone softened.

"Lizzie, houses do not have feelings. You have an over-active imagination." She sighed. "Anyway, how long are you on holidays for?"

"Two weeks. But as I'm working from home now, it won't feel

like I'm going back to work at all." This was a scary thought. Looking at the attic this morning, I doubted my ability to get it finished in time. "I'm excited about not having to make the trip into the city every day and I'm not really going to miss the people there. Scott can keep me up-to-date on the gossip." Scott's my boyfriend. He's not the perfect boyfriend but he is mine. "Plus, I get to work my own hours and best of all I won't have to attend those stupid bloody leadership days our boss is always organizing," I said with a smile. This last thought totally energized me and I could feel my irritability start to fade.

"Two weeks isn't much time to get your office organized. Have you found a cute handyman to help you yet?" She wiggled her eyebrows, smiling.

"Geez Molly. You keep going on and on about this handyman. What's with you? Have you been having erotic dreams again?" Judging by the color her face went, I'd say I hit the nail on the head. "I'll tell you what, if I do hire someone, you can come over and watch him work."

"Yeah, well make sure you do. I need a bit of excitement in my sad life," she replied, sipping her coffee which had just been delivered to our table.

"I thought you'd sworn off men for a while?"

"Yes, but I'm not blind. I can enjoy a good look, can't I?"

"Speaking of men, I plucked up the courage this morning and checked out Cat's privates. And he's definitely all boy." I grinned.

"Gee, you really do live an exciting life, don't you?"

"I bet it's more action than you've had for a while."

Sticking her tongue out at me, she asked, "Have you given him a name yet?"

"Yes. After much debate and deliberation, I've decided his name will be Cat."

"Wow, I'm impressed by your creativity."

"You know, as much as I didn't want a pet, he does make the house feel less lonely."

"Honestly, I don't know how you stayed there last night. I was expecting a knock on my door about midnight because you got too scared to stay there alone."

"I wasn't scared at all." Terrified was probably closer to my actual feelings. Molly just looked at me, eyes narrowed.

"Yeah? Whatever."

CHAPTER 3

*W*aking the next morning, I decided it was time I started on the attic. My mood was much more positive today after a better night's sleep with no nightmares, and even though Cat had somehow miraculously opened my locked bedroom door, he did not sit on me this time demanding food.

Standing in the attic, making a list of all the things needing to be done, I started to imagine what it was going to look like when it was finished. It had been an easy decision to make it my office as it was the smallest of the two bedrooms, but to make it workable the lovely shag pile carpet had to come up, the floral wallpaper had to be removed and then I needed to paint.

Easy. I could do this without any help as I had watched many, many TV renovating shows and it all seemed so simple.

Okay, now this is the point where I could bore you with all the details of how I attempted to get the carpet up, but in all honesty, I'm too embarrassed. So, let's just say it involved several broken nails and a lot of swearing. Two hours later I sat back and looked at my effort and decided I needed to find help. Fast.

Oh, and also cheap.

I thought back to my conversation with Molly yesterday, and decided maybe a handyman was just what I needed.

Remembering I'd seen a hand written ad on the notice board at the local shop, I made a quick trip and got the handyman's number and name. Giving the number a call, I found out I was a lucky girl (you honestly have no idea just how lucky, but I'll tell you about him soon), as he was in-between big jobs so he could come over right away and have a look at what needed to be done. I wasn't feeling very confident about this 'in-between big jobs' bit. After this morning's effort, I was thinking I needed him for quite a bit longer than that. But true to his word, he knocked on my door in no time.

However, in my hurry to not let him get away, I ran down the stairs. The old rotten wood creaked under my weight as I took them two at a time, and I remembered about the loose tread just as I put my foot on it.

I felt it slip, but it was too late for me to do anything about it. I didn't even have time to grab the railing as I fell forward, hands out in front and the wind rushing past my face. Hitting the ground face first, my body followed, propelling me forward toward the front door.

Oomph.

Silence followed. I could hear the ticking of the clock as I lay still, mentally checking myself for injuries. Tears threatened an appearance, but I could feel my legs and arms, so no spinal injury. That's a good start, right? My face was burning, probably from embarrassment, and my elbow was killing me. Pulling myself into a sitting position, I looked down at the ugly red mark that had started to appear. Apart from that, all seemed to be intact.

Okay, job number one—fix stair tread.

Looking toward the door I could see a silhouette of a man through the opaque glass, standing patiently on the doorstep waiting for me to open it. I would have liked to run and hide in a hole for a while—at least until my cheeks stopped burning—but with him standing outside the door, I didn't have time for that.

Okay, deep breaths. In and out, in and out.

I wiped the moisture from my lashes, pulled myself to my feet and took a step toward the door. My knee ached but I reached out and turned the door handle.

Plastering a fake smile to my red face, I looked out and blinked. Several times. Just in case my eyes were playing tricks on me or the fall had actually caused head injuries and I was hallucinating. I felt my eyes go wide and my lashes flutter uncontrollably. Tentatively, I reached out my hand and touched his arm— you know, just to make sure.

Nope, no tricks. He was real.

OMG.

All thoughts of my aching knee gone, I stared up at a man so good-looking, I thought it was Adonis himself. Now, I think I should tell you I'm not very eloquent around good-looking men. Add that to my fall and embarrassment, my brain felt like it couldn't cope.

"Oh…um…hi," was the best I could do.

"Hi, I'm Riley. Would you be Lizzie, by any chance?" His gentle, deep, smooth and extremely sexy voice stirred a memory, but I shook it off as I subtly scanned him, noting his voice pretty much matched the rest of him. He stood very tall—I'd guess about 6'3"—looked to be about my age, with blond hair, and the most amazing blue eyes I had ever seen (think of the sky on a brilliant day). But what had me all aflutter were his eyelashes. They weren't overly long, but they were dark and thick. Slowly lowering my gaze, my mouth hanging open very unattractively, I noticed he was wearing a white T-shirt over jeans and, from what I could tell, had a pretty damn good torso underneath.

Oh…he was looking at me expectantly. Bugger, what did he ask me?

"Lizzie?" He extended his hand for me to shake.

"Um… Yes. I'm Lizzie." I shook his hand, noticing my voice sounding remarkably like one of the chipmunks. Wow, his hand felt amazing. It was strong and kind of rough, not like Scott, whose hands were baby-soft.

"Are you okay? I could see you through the glass and it looked like you fell down the stairs." Damn, he noticed that, did he?

"Oh, ha ha ha. Yes. I'm fine, thank you. Just took the express route down." I laughed self-consciously. Geez, I sounded like a moron. His left eyebrow rose, but he continued on.

"You were saying on the phone you need some help getting this place livable again. Like I said to you before, I'm in-between jobs at the moment, so I would be able to give you a few weeks to get most of the bigger jobs underway." He smiled.

Oh, *wow*. Great smile, too. That was really important in a man. I mean who wants to look at someone's face for the rest of your life if they have a crappy smile? I was, at present, giving him my best sexy smile. But honestly, if you asked me what he was talking about, I couldn't tell you. I hadn't actually heard a word of it. Right now, the only things my brain was receiving were his gorgeous blue eyes and his super white smile.

"Maybe you should show me around," he suggested helpfully, giving me a kind, yet sympathetic look, almost as if he was trying to weigh up if I was sane or not.

"Hmm? Oh, show you around. Yes…that would be… umm…great. Maybe we should start in the bedroom." I giggled, thoughts still not quite coming together in my brain.

Oops. That didn't sound right.

I watched his eyebrows disappear into his hairline.

"I mean that's the room I want to start work in," I stammered. Oh my, what did I say that for? He must be thinking I'm a nymphomaniac who wanted to get him into bed. Although that wasn't such a bad idea.

Riley stepped inside the door and closed it behind him as I started to walk up the stairs.

Bad move. Now I had him behind me and all he could see was my backside which certainly wasn't my best attribute. Today I'd thrown on an old pair of jeans that were slightly on the tight side and made my backside look three times bigger... like it needed that sort of help. Maybe if I found that broken stair tread, I could hide underneath it.

Looking over my shoulder, I could see Riley making mental notes as he walked toward the bedroom. I thought the look of *my God, what the hell have I got myself into?* crossed his face, but I couldn't be sure. I was just hoping I'd remembered to make my bed this morning.

"In this room I want to take up the carpet. As you can see it's awful. I can live with the wallpaper for now, but I think the carpet is causing my nightmares," I blabbered, tugging at the neck of my T-shirt. I was feeling quite flushed all of a sudden. It felt like all the air was being sucked out of the room. Funny, this room never felt this small before. Maybe it was the shock from the fall.

"That won't take long." I watched him as he walked around the room taking notes. I actually loved this room. It's an exact copy of the living room underneath it. It's the length of the house and has a big bay window in the front. On a clear day I would be able to see the river from here.

"I notice you don't have any wardrobe space."

Yeah, that was pretty obvious by the mountain of boxes scattered around the room. I had absolutely nowhere to put my clothes so leaving them in their boxes seemed like the best idea. Now I felt embarrassed by the mess.

"Yeah, a wardrobe is on my ever growing To Do list." I let out a long sigh.

"Old houses are a lot of work." Riley smiled, looking at me through those incredible lashes. "But they are worth the effort. This one is something special."

Heat rushed to my face. I don't know why, but it felt like Riley was paying me a compliment. I mean, that's what I'd thought when I bought it, right? It was something special.

"So, I'm not as stupid as everyone keeps telling me, then?" I saw the puzzled look cross his face.

"No, you're not stupid at all. I wanted to come to the auction and put a bid in myself but got called away at the last minute. I was hoping it got passed so I could make an offer later. According to the agent a lovely young lady bought it before I had the chance." Now I really did blush. "Looks like he was right."

Oh boy. The temperature in here must have risen about a hundred degrees judging by how hot I was feeling.

"I could get this started tomorrow if you like," Riley continued. If he noticed how red I had gone, he thankfully didn't mention it.

"That would be great." I smiled. "But really my priority is the attic. I have to start work up there in less than two weeks and right now, it's a mess."

We turned and headed for the stairs. Reaching the top, I stepped back and allowed Riley to enter the room first. His eyes immediately dropped to the carpet and I could see the look of amusement cross his face.

"What happened here?" he asked, smiling at the mess I'd made.

With all the blood rushing to my face, it's a wonder I hadn't passed out. Absolutely no other body part was receiving oxygen right about now.

"As you can see, I have no idea what I'm doing," I said. "I'm thinking my mother was right. I've bitten off more than I can chew." I hated admitting my mother was right. Riley looked at me and gave me an absolute killer smile. It was so amazing I actually felt brain cells die as I basked in its glow.

"It's okay. That's what I'm here for." Oh damn, he's talking again. I'd better listen so he doesn't think I'm an idiot. "How about I go home and get some tools and come back here after lunch. I can have the bedroom carpet out in an hour or so and then I can get started in this room in the morning."

"Really? That would be fantastic," I said gratefully, my brain rejoining the conversation. "Oh, and if it's not too much trouble, could you change the lock on my bedroom door? I keep locking it, but I wake up every morning to the door wide open."

After lunch Riley came back, complete with new door lock and headed upstairs to my bedroom. I followed him this time and must say the view was spectacular. He fitted those jeans well. Even before I'd seen the quality of his work, I knew he was more than worth the money I was paying him.

With my help, we had the bed and various boxes out of the room in no time and as I left him, the doorbell rang. It sounded more like someone was standing on the cat, but as Cat was sleeping on the stairs, I knew he was safe. Cat had settled in with me pretty damn quickly. Running down the stairs—this time skillfully avoiding the broken tread—I opened the front door.

Standing on the doorstep was my boyfriend Scott.

Oops, with Riley around I'd actually forgotten about Scott.

"I thought I'd come over and see your new house," he announced, handing me a bottle of wine with a small frown between his eyes.

That bottle's not going to be near big enough.

"Well, are you going to invite me in, or am I just going to stand out here?" he asked, his jaw clenching.

"Sure, come in," I said, stepping aside. "I'm surprised to see you. You don't normally pop over without ringing first."

"Elizabeth, I don't *pop* anywhere," he said, the frown deepening.

He actually looked quite tired with his tie loosened at the collar of his white shirt and, if I'm being totally picky, his shirt wasn't tucked into his black trousers properly.

Scott and I first met at work where he was a senior accountant.

I had just started at Bradley and Sons and noticed Scott straight away. As I was a lowly bookkeeper it took him a while to notice me, but eventually he asked me out after the staff Christmas party.

We've been together for about two and a half years now and I was hoping for a more permanent commitment on our anniversary, but Scott said he wasn't ready for that. This had ticked me off a little bit but I guess if he was not ready, then it was best not to push him.

Apart from the dark circles under his gray eyes, he did look kind of cute. He was not in Riley's league, but then again, not very many men were.

"Sorry. I'm very happy to see you." I gave him a quick kiss on the cheek which was a feat in itself. His head was moving from side to side so fast as he took in the mess that was my home, I thought it might fall off. He didn't look happy with what he saw. Not surprising though. Scott liked everything to be neat and tidy and believed everything should be in its place. Including me. I know it was wrong, but I always felt like I was not good enough for him and that if he stopped to think about it for too long, I knew he'd dump me and find someone who deserved him. So, I tried really, really hard to be my best whenever he was around. Looking down at what I was wearing, I knew that today it was mission failed.

"I know it's a mess at the moment but it's going to look amazing when it's finished," I said hurriedly. If I explained myself to Scott quickly, I might be able to avoid the look of disappointment in his eyes.

Damn, I wasn't quick enough. "How about I show you around? The house has a great feel to it when you give it some time." I started easing him up the stairs and away from the disaster that was my kitchen. As he reached the top, he stopped when he saw Riley.

"Who's this?" he asked, turning his back to him and looking at me, his manhood clearly threatened. Fair enough. Riley did exude an awful lot of testosterone.

"This is Riley. He's helping me with all the work that has to be done. Riley, this is my boyfriend Scott."

Riley extended his hand, which Scott glared at, then turned and walked out of the room. With a quick apologetic look to Riley, I raced after him.

"Scott, that was rude. Riley's a great help."

"I bet he is." If I didn't know better, I would think that was jealousy, but Scott didn't believe in jealousy. He thought it was a wasted emotion.

"What's that supposed to mean?"

"Never mind," he said with a sigh, looking at me with a critical look. "You remember tomorrow night is the meeting I have with Donald Shepherd, don't you?"

"Of course, I do," I smiled reassuringly. Shit. I'd forgotten.

Scott had this big meeting with a client he was hoping to win, and I had promised I would go with him. My job was to make Scott look like the perfect man. Not sure if I was the right person for the job, but I was happy to give it a go. That meant, instead of spending the day helping Riley rip my house apart, I would be spending it waxing, bleaching and plucking my little heart out.

"Make sure you wear the red dress I gave you. And remember to be on your best behavior."

Sometimes I felt like I was in a relationship with my mother.

CHAPTER 4

I was woken the following morning by the wretched doorbell screeching out its damned tune. Dragging myself out of bed, I walked through my—once again—open bedroom door and staggered, bleary-eyed, down the stairs.

Bloody hell, did Riley not know I was on holiday? Had he never heard of a bloody sleep in? Okay, so I'm not a morning person. Sue me. Opening the door and seeing Riley, I quickly hid behind it.

"Good morning, Lizzie," he said, smiling brightly. Geez, a girl could get used to seeing that smile first thing in the morning.

"Morning," I grouched as he walked past me into the hallway. He looked particularly fine this morning, I noted. Just the usual jeans and T-shirt, but the temperature in here had definitely risen.

"Are you going to close the door?" he asked, turning to look at me.

"Not until you're in the kitchen." He looked puzzled but walked past me into the kitchen anyway. Racing back upstairs, I locked myself in the bathroom. Thankfully I didn't own a full-length mirror, but what greeted me in the small mirror above the sink was nothing short of scary. I had big black circles under my eyes from yesterday's make-up, the hair on one side of my head was standing up in a big knotted mess and the other side was plastered to my face with what looked like dried drool.

Great. When Scott and I had sleepovers, I usually snuck out of bed early to get in the shower before he woke up. He had never seen me like this, which was probably one of the reasons we've been together so long.

I hurriedly jumped in the shower and washed my hair before carefully putting on some make-up. If Riley had seen what I looked like as I hid behind the door, then I had some damage control to do.

The smell of coffee was wafting up the stairs when I opened the bathroom door, so after a quick dash to my bedroom for clothes, I made my way downstairs to the kitchen.

"I brewed a pot. I hope you don't mind." Riley was leaning against the sink with a big cup of coffee in his hand.

"Not at all," I replied cheerily. A god-like man with freshly brewed coffee in my own kitchen is as close to Heaven as I'll ever get.

"Scott seems like a real nice guy." Riley seemed to have the sarcasm thing down pat. He was going to get along great with Danny and Molly.

"I'm sorry he was rude to you. He had absolutely no reason to be." I finished pouring my coffee and turned to look at him. "I think he feels threatened by men who know how to use their hands." Okay, that sounded different in my head.

Riley smiled wickedly. "I know how to use my hands alright."

Feeling the heat turn up a few notches, I looked at the floor. When I was finally able to look him in the eye, I could see he was laughing at me.

"I'll take your word for that." Like bloody likely. Given half a chance, I don't think I could trust myself not to find out how well he could use those hands. I'd been kept awake half the night thinking about them and what exactly they could do.

"I have to go into town today," I continued, moving the conversation in a safer direction. "I have an appointment at the beauty salon. Scott has an important dinner we have to go to tonight so I need to get ready. I'll get a key cut for you while I'm there, so if you need to get in when I'm not home, you can."

"You trust me with a spare key? I might sneak in during the night and attack you." He laughed.

If only.

AFTER A LONG AND painful trip to the beauty therapist, I made my way home. I was now hairless in all the right places, and had amazing eyebrows. In fact, as I pulled my car into my driveway and killed the engine, I was admiring them in the rear vision mirror, when I noticed the black sedan parked across the road. I made a mental note to talk to my neighbor. Maybe when the previous owner lived here, parking directly opposite wasn't a problem. I, however, had a tendency to not notice things when I was reversing and was afraid I was going to hit it.

As I got out of the car and walked to the house, I could see Riley had been busy. The huge builder's waste bin I'd hired was filling quickly.

"Hello," I called out, feeling quite exhausted.

"Lizzie, Lizzie, Liz, Liz, Liz! How are you?" I was engulfed in a huge hug by my brother Danny. Stepping back, he grabbed my shoulders and gave me a small shake. "You sneaky girl. You didn't tell us about your new friend in the attic. I came over here expecting to see *you* and *who* greets me at the door? Some god-like hunk-of-spunk, that's who!"

Danny has a partner and should not be looking at my hunk-of-spunk. What was I saying? I shouldn't be looking either.

Oh well…like brother, like sister.

Danny's natural hair color was light brown, but being a hair-dresser meant his hair color changed daily. Today it was jet black and spiked up into a messy kind of style. He was wearing black skinny jeans and a skin tight T-shirt. Did he and Molly know how much they dressed alike?

I smiled. "He's pretty cute, isn't he?"

"Cute is not the word I would use, and I know why you didn't tell us about him. Talk about greedy." Danny almost looked sulky.

"Remember Andrew? Your lovely partner who looks after you and puts up with all your crap?"

"Of course I do, but there's no harm in looking," he said matter-of-factly. That's exactly what Molly had said.

"I hope there's not, cause I've been doing plenty of that." I laughed. "Yesterday, I followed him up the stairs and *my God*, it was the best orgasm I've had in ages."

"Probably the only one you've had in ages," said Danny, smirking.

"Hi Lizzie, I thought I heard you come home," I heard a deep voice say from behind me. Turning, I saw Riley trying hard to hide his smile. Could the ground open up and swallow me whole…please?

"Oh, um…hi," I whispered, quickly turning my back to him and glaring at Danny. The least he could have done was warn me Riley was there.

"I've got all the old carpet out of the attic but there are a few loose boards, so I need to make a trip to the hardware store," he explained.

"Oh, okay. I…um…got you a key cut while I was out."

I dug his key out of my bag and handed it to him, keeping my eyes firmly on the floor. As I placed the key in his palm, his fingers curled around mine, just for a second. In that second, however, volts of electricity ran up my arm and down to my nether regions. The power of it actually made me feel a bit dizzy.

Was that a deliberate move on his part?

Finally plucking up the courage, I looked up into his eyes but there was no indication he'd even noticed anything had happened. I really needed to keep a check on my imagination.

After he left, I rounded on my brother.

"Why didn't you tell me he was standing there?" I almost yelled.

Danny burst out laughing. "You should have seen your face. My God, I didn't think you could go so red!"

"Shut up!" I snapped. I stormed out of the room and up the stairs, Danny following me. "What are you doing here anyway? It's the middle of the day. Shouldn't you be at work?" Danny and Andrew owned their own hairdressing salon and Danny was always busy.

"You asked me to come over and do your hair for tonight, remember?"

"Oh. I forgot. Sorry," I grumbled.

Danny was an absolute miracle worker when it came to my hair. In no time at all he had my curls behaving and had put it in a half-up-do with long curls falling down my back. If only I could control my life half as well as he could control my hair.

CHAPTER 5

*a*fter Danny left, I was bored. I couldn't do anything that required getting dirty, which pretty much ruled out doing anything around here, so I decided to go and see how Riley was getting on. I'd heard him return from the hardware store but he'd been pretty quiet for the last half hour. Wandering up to the attic to check out what was happening, I found Riley sitting on the floor with a couple of floorboards lying loose around him.

"What ya doing?" I asked.

He jumped.

Ha! Good to see I can sneak up on him as well.

"I was fixing this loose board and found this," he said, handing me a small black velvet box.

Taking a seat on the floor beside him, I opened the box and was surprised to find the most exquisite white gold, diamond engagement ring I'd ever seen. The diamond must have been at least a carat, but what made it unique was the band—lots of scrollwork and encrusted with diamonds.

"Wow," I said, breathlessly. "Is that all that's under there?" I asked, hoping it would be accompanied by a note explaining how it got there. Riley pulled up another board and looked through the years of dust and dirt. Pulling out a pile of letters tied together with a ribbon, he handed it all to me while he took another look.

"Oh, good." I sighed. I hated mysteries. I'm one of those people who liked everything to be written in black and white, in clear uncomplicated instructions. For example, I was hoping the first of these letters would tell me who they belonged to and why they were hidden. Of course, that's not how this story went, though. Nothing in life was ever that easy.

"That's it. That's all there was," said Riley, sitting back and looking at me. I already had the ribbon untied and was carefully extracting the first letter from its envelope. It was addressed to someone named Avis.

"I think Avis was the name of the lady who previously owned this house." As Riley leaned over my shoulder to look at the letter, I felt my pulse kick up a notch.

"Maybe they're from her lover." He smiled. I looked at him and once again felt my brain cells frying. Riley had the most amazing smile I've ever seen. It's like the sun—outshining anything in its orbit. I would have to work on my immunity to it or I could see I would be brain dead before the two weeks were up.

Shaking myself back to the reality in front of me, I thought back to the sale of this house. I had bought it at auction and from memory, the contract was with a solicitor somewhere in the city.

"Maybe. I'm pretty sure a trustee sold the house. I was under the impression the previous owner had no family to leave it to," I said, ignoring the palpitations I was getting as Riley reached over and took the rest of the letters from me.

Looking down at the paper in my hands, I noticed how the pages had yellowed with age and saw the lovely scrolled hand-writing on the envelope.

"This one contains a photo," he said, handing me an old black and white image of two people standing outside the front door.

The door hadn't changed in all these years; it just had less dry rot and a better paint job then.

Both people in the photo were on the small side. The lady, who I assumed to be the previous owner, Avis, was wearing a knee-length dark colored skirt and pale, long-sleeved jacket pulled in around a small waist. The man was in a dark suit, a tie and a trilby hat. They looked like the perfect couple.

"They look so happy." I smiled, taking the photo as Riley opened the pages wrapped around it. I forgot all about the paper in my hands as I watched him silently read the contents of a letter. His eyes moved from side to side as he read, amusement dancing in his eyes at the words. When he finished, he looked up at me and caught me staring at him.

Oops.

Quickly looking at the photo in an attempt to hide my glowing cheeks, I thought about the couple smiling back at me. Something about them made me want to know their story and, as much as I hated mysteries, I did love a good story. Excitedly, I opened the pages and started to read.

My Darling Avis,

Why? Why do they not accept us? Why do they hate us so? These are the questions that keep me awake at night. I live them, I breathe them, I even dream of them. The only time I'm not thinking of them is when I'm thinking of you. I pray that the answers will come to me, because if I can answer these questions, then maybe we can be together. That's the only time that I am truly happy.

Have strength my love, I won't give up.
Will.

. . .

"Wow. I wonder why they weren't accepted." I studied the photo once again.

"I wonder how long these have been hidden under here," said Riley, wiping the dust off the rest of the envelopes. I watched as he counted them. Twelve. There were twelve letters in total. One by one, we carefully opened them, pulled the yellowed paper from its hiding place and read the contents. By the time we'd finished, I sat back, rested my back against the wall and let out a deep breath as we were still none the wiser as to how or why this had all been hidden.

"We probably should try to find out who the ring belonged to and return it to them." I looked at the ring as it stared back at me from its black velvet bed. This ring had a story to tell. One I'm sure didn't end happily.

"Maybe we could talk to your neighbors. They probably knew Avis and might be able to give us some pointers on where to start looking."

Sitting here with Riley was quite fun, and I was starting to get used to the room feeling much smaller whenever he was in it. We'd sat there for about an hour, and even though I had absolutely no make-up on, I didn't feel self-conscious at all. Let me tell you, that's quite unusual for me. Most of the time when I'm around good-looking men, I act like a mute idiot.

However, the screeching of the doorbell rudely interrupted my afternoon of history and fantasy. Wondering who the heck it was, I looked at my watch and realized it was already five o'clock.

Damn.

Running down the stairs, I opened the door to a confused Scott. In his defense, he'd been expecting to find me completely made up and wearing a red dress. Instead, here I stood in my old flannel shirt and jeans, hair perfectly styled in a half-up-do and completely devoid of make-up.

"You're *not* ready?" he asked incredulously.

"Um…not quite," I answered, moving aside as he stepped in.

"But it won't take me long." I gave him my biggest smile hoping that would put him in a better mood. I should have known better.

"But I told them I'd meet them at the restaurant at six. It's already quarter past five and we have at least a half an hour drive ahead of us!" He rubbed the back of his neck, his eyes wide.

Judging by the storm brewing in those gray depths I may be in trouble.

Crap.

This was not the start to the evening I had hoped for.

Leaving Scott in the lounge room, I headed back up to the bathroom and applied the required amount of make-up in record time.

I had the dress he'd given me hanging in my temporary wardrobe—aka a packing box—and pulling it out, the first thing I noticed was the price tag. Scott had given me this dress a few weeks ago, but with everything going on, I hadn't even looked at it. I knew it was red and strapless, and that was about it.

I will admit to being shocked by the price. I guess it proved how important the meeting was to Scott that he would spend almost a month's wages on a dress for me. He wasn't usually big on gifts.

Now red isn't a color I would normally wear, and strapless was a risk when you have a bust the size of mine. But, I guess I'd just trust his judgment and enjoy the gift for what it was.

Slipping out of my clothes, I pulled the dress on feeling a little breathless. It was absolutely stunning...until I tried to do the zipper up.

Did I mention my breasts are a D cup? This dress was made for a skinny ass, B cup.

What was Scott thinking? The last time I was a B cup was when I was twelve and wearing a training bra.

Not one to give up too easily though, I managed to breathe in and flatten my boobs as much as humanly possible, and with the help of a very amused Riley, I even got the zipper up.

I can't say the reflection I saw in the mirror was a good one though. I had flesh popping out under my arms and over the top of the tight bodice, and the split up the thigh was a little bit higher than I would have liked. Actually, it was a *lot* higher than I would have liked.

Riley didn't seem to mind it though. "I guarantee if you go to a business meeting in that dress, Scott will get anything he wants," he said, laughing.

He really was enjoying this. "*Oh my God*. What am I going to do?" I asked, completely bewildered by the predicament I found myself in.

"You'd better go and show him," Riley said, his grin still firmly in place.

I thought about this for a second. Looking down at my breasts, I weighed up my options. They were limited.

Oh well…time to face the music.

I felt slightly light-headed as I walked down the stairs—probably from the lack of oxygen. Breathing was not something I had room to do. Scott stood in the hallway watching me walk down toward him, and I could see his face get paler the closer I got.

"Well, what do you think?" I asked, holding my arms out and forcing a smile on my face. I really didn't need to ask the question. What he thought was written all over his face.

"You look like a high-priced call girl!" he growled through gritted teeth. "You do know how important tonight is for me, don't you?" I could see the color returning to his cheeks, which were now starting to match the dress. I thought he might be a tad angry.

"Of course I do. But I didn't buy the dress, Scott. I mean since when have I *ever* been small breasted?" I asked haughtily.

"If you'd tried it on when I gave it to you, you might have bothered to lose some weight!"

"It wouldn't matter how much weight I lost, I would never fit this dress!" I yelled, feeling a need to defend myself. His comment actually hurt. Even though I'm not fat in any way, I've always been curvy. That didn't prevent Scott from constantly trying to change me, though. Blinking back tears, I turned and walked back to the bedroom.

I mean, I know on the right woman this dress would be stunning. I just wasn't that woman. But the right woman was the one Scott deserved, wasn't it? All he'd asked me to do today was wear a beautiful dress and look my best. Any normal woman could do that, couldn't she?

Determined not to mess tonight up completely, I opened my boxes and quickly ran through my options. I knew somewhere I had a jacket that could maybe cover up some of this cleavage. As it was, I would probably give the poor businessmen a heart attack before dinner was over.

After ripping into box after box, I decided I needed to clear out some of my clothes. Eventually I came up with the jacket I was looking for. Molly had passed it to me in one of her closet clean-outs. Along with quite a few other items, this one was too good to throw away but too *last year* for Molly. The label read 'Zac Posen' and it was black with feathers stuck to the bottom edge of it. It probably wasn't the best accessory to wear with this dress but it would have to be good enough.

Slipping it on, I realized I still couldn't quite do up all the buttons and had a moment of thinking Scott was right. I should go on a diet. I'll start that tomorrow.

Grabbing my purse, I held my head high and walked downstairs to meet him, quickly checking the clock as I did so. Hmm... five forty-five...well if Scott drove fast, we would only be about fifteen minutes late.

Riley was leaving as I walked into the kitchen but he turned and looked as I entered the room. I thought I saw a look of approval in his eyes, but then again I didn't know him well, so who knew? Scott on the other hand looked like he had gas. He had a pinched look around his mouth and a deep frown between his eyes.

"I'm sorry, it's the best I could do," I said apologetically.

"Fine."

This was the only conversation we had all the way to the restaurant.

SCOTT HAD CHOSEN a beautiful restaurant in the heart of the city. It was high-end and served only the best food and wine money could buy. The only problem was they wanted to keep their patrons comfortable and as this evening was cool, they had turned the heating up a bit too high for someone wearing a wool blend jacket. By the time dessert was served, I was sweating quite profusely.

"Are you okay, Elizabeth?" asked Donald Shepherd, the lovely elderly gentleman of our group. His manners were impeccable and several times this evening he had inquired as to how comfortable I was. His grandson Rodney, was not so gentlemanly though. If I'd caught him looking at my cleavage once, I'd caught him a dozen times. Like I said, the jacket didn't quite close, which gave everyone a small view of my generous assets.

"Yes thank you, Mister Shepherd. I'm fine." I smiled, discreetly fanning myself.

"You'd be more comfortable if you removed your jacket," said Rodney. "Let me help you." He pushed his chair backward, ready to stand up and help remove my clothing.

"*No!*"

Scott glared at me as Rodney looked a bit taken aback by my abruptness.

"Elizabeth feels the cold very easily," Scott hurriedly added, in way of explanation.

All eyes turned to me. I felt the sweat run down my neck and between my breasts. Rodney's eyes followed it.

"Yes. That's right. I feel the cold very easily." I picked up my glass of water and downed it, hoping it would extinguish the internal inferno I was experiencing. "Maybe you will all excuse me for a moment," I said, standing to make a fast escape to the ladies' room.

Inside, I stripped off the jacket and used the paper towel to mop my armpits and cleavage. It was quite a bit cooler in here and I wondered how long I could stay before Scott noticed I was missing. Sitting down on the chair provided, I slipped off my shoes and rubbed my heels. What I really wanted to do was rip this dress off and never have to wear it again. Grabbing the bodice around the bust line, I wiggled and tugged until it was up where it should be, exposing only slightly less flesh than before. I thought about going into the toilet cubicle and undoing the zipper for five minutes to allow myself to breathe, but I was afraid if I undid it, I would never get it back up. Instead, I sat back and rested my head against the chair. Taking a few breaths, I enjoyed a few moments of relaxation, knowing only too soon I would have to put the jacket on and walk out to leering Rodney, where I would have to smile and pretend I was enjoying it. I let out a small sigh. My moments of peace and quiet were over all too soon though. Just as I was contemplating slipping on my shoes, the door opened and in walked three ladies, obviously all friends.

"Did you see the way he was leering at you?" one of them said to the group.

"Yes. What a creep," replied the woman who'd been looked at. I wondered if they were talking about Rodney.

"He was trying to look in here when we walked in. Should we report him to management?" asked the third friend.

"Yeah, well he was standing outside the door to the ladies' toilets. Maybe he was waiting for someone." They all turned to me. I watched as they scanned me up and down, taking in my ample chest and the amount of thigh I was showing from the long split up the dress. Judging by the looks I was getting, they probably thought Scott was right. I looked like a hooker. I let out another sigh and leaned forward to put my shoes on. Grabbing my jacket, I flung it on as I stomped toward the door, listening to the whispers that followed.

Taking as deep a breath as possible I opened the door and prepared the speech I was going to give Rodney about how I have a lovely boyfriend and wasn't interested in him.

However, once outside the door, the only person I could see was a middle aged, tall, bald-headed man. Before I could see his face, he turned away from me and lowered his head; obviously embarrassed he was caught hanging around outside the ladies'. Maybe the women should report him to management.

CHAPTER 6

*B*y the time dinner was over and we were saying our goodbyes, I'd consumed quite a lot of wine. It had felt like the best way to get through the rest of the evening. I should probably let you know I'm not much of a drinker, so it didn't take much for me to be intoxicated. Add to that my lack of oxygen and I was holding onto Scott's arm in an attempt to stay focused and upright. Lucky for me the evening was a success and Scott was in a good mood. He even seemed supportive when Rodney slid his hand across my bottom while leaning in for a friendly goodbye kiss on the cheek.

I chose to ignore the irritability I felt at this and focused on staying happy. I was hoping later this evening I might even get lucky—if you know what I mean. I have to admit that with all the pheromones Riley put out, I was feeling amorous. So, as you can see, I needed Scott to remain in his good mood.

Allowing the valet to open the door to Scott's beautiful black Mercedes C63 AMG, I slid onto the leather seat, enjoying the cool sensation seeping through the thin fabric of my dress. I loved everything about this car but I especially loved driving it. Not that I got the opportunity very often. It was fast, and Scott complained I drove like a madman when I had my one and only drive.

His mood had improved dramatically from earlier in the evening. Obviously, all the stress of trying to win a new client had him pretty wound up. And much to my relief, he hadn't mentioned the dress.

"Where are we going?" I asked in my most seductive voice, reaching over and running my fingers through his short, dark hair.

"My place," he said as he turned to me and smiled.

Yes. I knew that look. Lucky, here I come.

SCOTT LIVED in a new penthouse apartment with a spectacular view out over the city. It was modern with lots of glass and stainless steel. It helped that he had a house cleaner. Personally, the thought of cleaning all that glass and stainless had me coming out in hives. The master bedroom was dark, with lots of black wood, and he had the largest bed I'd ever had the pleasure of sleeping in. I could understand why he didn't like sleeping over at my place. Even before I moved, he always preferred we stay here. The strange thing was this place didn't feel like a home. There were no books left lying around, no dirty dishes in the sink, even his toothbrush had a home safely out of sight in the cupboard. It was a lot like Scott, I suppose. Very pristine and never gave away any secrets.

Loosening his tie, he walked toward me and pulled me into his arms.

"I'm sorry I was such a jerk earlier. I was wound up about the meeting. It was a success though, don't you think?"

"Well, they did say they were phoning Mr. Bradley tomorrow to sign a client contract." I smiled.

"Yes, they did. They seemed quite impressed with you actually." Yeah, particularly Rodney.

"Well, I do my best!" I laughed.

"You do look very beautiful," Scott whispered in my ear. "You were lucky though." I heard the warning tone in his voice.

Looking into his eyes, I quickly realized I was about to lose him here and I really needed an evening of romance.

"Anyway, it doesn't matter now. What matters is you were truly amazing and made up for my inabilities." I smiled, undoing his tie and throwing it on the floor. I noticed a look pass through Scott's eyes and I had a suspicion it was annoyance. "I love this suit on you. The color brings out the gray in your eyes," I said, quickly diverting his attention away from the tie.

I stood on my tiptoes and lightly kissed his lips as I slipped off his jacket. He still felt a little wound up, but with a bit of coaxing his lips softened. Pulling up for air, he turned away from me and quickly hung the jacket and tie I had thrown on the floor. He then grabbed me around the waist and pulled me in close as his hand moved to the back of my dress. I felt him pull the zipper down—thank goodness—and my dress fell to the floor as he pushed me back on the bed.

"It's okay, you can make it up to me," he whispered.

Well…you can guess what happened next.

I MUST SAY my night of passion turned out to be disappointing. Not that Scott had noticed. He'd promptly fallen asleep. When I tried to wake him, asking him to take me home, he mumbled something about an early start and he would drop me home then. Anyway, it turned out *early* was seven bloody thirty. This meant that as we pulled up outside my house, all my neighbors were out picking up the morning paper, waving the kids off to school or getting in their cars to drive to work. And what was I wearing? Last night's dress, that's what.

Scott leaned over and gave me a kiss on my burning cheek. "I don't mean to be rude but you need to get out. I have to be at the office by eight. I can't be late for my meeting."

Sighing, I picked up my shoes and started my walk of shame. I noticed the black sedan parked in the street again, this time with the driver in it, but I was too embarrassed to go over and actually ask them if they could please park in a more appropriate spot. Next time.

Allowing my hair to fall forward over my face, I almost ran to my front door.

"Good morning!" called out my neighbor, giving me a smile and a small wave. Great. She was a bit nosy and I could see her mentally picking up the phone and telling all her friends what a slut the lady next door was.

Opening my front door, I almost launched myself inside. If I thought that was where my humiliation would end, I was wrong. Sitting at the kitchen table was Riley.

Geez, you have one night of what can't even be described as passion and every man and his dog had to know about it. All I needed now was my mother to turn up and then the whole bloody world would know. Even Cat was giving me the look.

"Morning," I mumbled, dropping my bag on a chair.

"Obviously you had a good night," remarked Riley with a frown.

"Yes, thanks. Scott was very successful." I tried to smile and act casual.

"Looks like it," he snapped. Getting up from the table, he walked to the sink and put his cup in it. "If you want me, I'll be in the attic stripping wallpaper," he scowled.

Well, someone got out of the wrong side of the bed this morning.

I decided I should stay out of his way for a while, so after showering and putting on jeans and a T-shirt I headed over to introduce myself to the neighbors.

It turned out my neighbors, Hazel and Adrian, have been here for fifteen years and knew pretty much everything about everybody. The people on the other side of me, Dianne and Roger, were a retired couple who visited their daughter down south once a year. The family opposite had four children, two of whom were teenagers who sneaked out through their bedroom windows so Mum and Dad won't find out, and Edward, from down the end of the street was a pastor, in case I needed him.

"Well, that's good to know," I said through slightly gritted teeth. "I was actually wondering if you knew the lady who used to live in my house," I asked trying to get the subject off me.

"Oh yes, of course we did!" She laughed, as if my having to ask was the most ridiculous thing she'd heard in a long time. "We knew Avis very well. Adrian used to mow her lawn for her. Of course, after she fell down the stairs the doctors moved her into a nursing home. We didn't get to visit her very often. We're very busy you know. Did I mention I'm a primary school teacher and Adrian is the principal?" She pushed her thick spectacles further up her beaky nose. "Well, now our children have grown up and left home, we spend most of our spare time helping children who don't get the opportunity of a good education. We do a lot of volunteer work you know and there's always something to do in the gardens here. That's what keeps Adrian busy most of the time he's home." I was thinking Adrian probably hid out in the garden for peace and quiet. "That's why our house is the best looking in the street," she beamed. "Of course, being right next to yours doesn't help the street appeal that much. But I'm sure now you own it, it will sparkle in no time." Finally, she stopped for a breath and smiled. She was quite a harsh-looking lady, with short, dyed black hair and bucked teeth. I could imagine what the school kids called her behind her back. Her husband walked toward us and I must say he was not at all what I'd expected. He wasn't bad looking with bright red hair and he actually looked very fit.

"Hi Lizzie, I'm Adrian," he said, extending his hand to shake mine. I could picture him as a principal; he spoke gently. He had a kind smile and I decided instantly I liked him. Pitied him was probably a more accurate verb, I couldn't imagine Hazel would be easy to live with.

"Hazel was just telling me you used to mow the lawn for Avis," I said pointing toward my house.

"Yes, I kept mowing it right up until it sold. Then I thought I should probably mind my own business. I didn't want to upset my new neighbors." He grinned as his eyes twinkled.

"Really, you wouldn't have upset me at all." I laughed. "In fact, mowing it would have put you on the favorite neighbor list." The sour look on Hazel's face told me she obviously didn't like my sense of humor. "I was wondering if you could tell me a bit about Avis." I continued, undeterred by her attitude.

"Well, there's not much to tell," said Hazel. "She turned eighty-seven on her last birthday. I, of course, made her a cake and took it over for her. I mean, she never had any visitors and it must have been lonely having a birthday with no one around. We're very fortunate, aren't we Ade, that our children visit us on a regular basis," she said smugly.

"Did she have any children?" I asked, looking at Adrian, secretly wishing Hazel would shut up.

"No, she actually never married. She once told me that when she was younger, she looked after her elderly mother. As far as I knew she was an only child and by the time her mother passed away, she felt she was too old to find someone special. She was a sweet lady, if a little lonely," Adrian finished.

"She did have a cat," Hazel added with distaste. "It was quite a large ginger cat. I haven't seen it in a while, which is a blessing as it always used my garden as a toilet. Didn't it, Ade?"

The cat she was talking about was at present sleeping on the window seat in my lounge room.

"Oh, you don't by any chance know the name of the Nursing Home Avis went into, do you?" I asked, standing, ready to make a fast retreat.

"Yes, we did visit her once when she first moved there. I'll write it all down for you," Adrian said with a smile.

With the new information I had about Avis, I headed back toward my house taking a shortcut across the lawn. I really did need to mow this grass. It was past my knees already and I was getting green seeds sticking to my jeans.

Damn, those things are hard to get rid of.

By the time I got to my front door, I was green from the knees down. Every time I tried to wipe them off, they just stuck to my hands. Flicking my fingers to try to get rid of the bloody things, I thought maybe throwing these jeans away would be a good idea. I didn't think I'd ever get all those grass seeds off. Now, I know the inside of my house is a mess but I didn't want grass seeds everywhere, so I decided I would take my jeans off outside and quickly run upstairs to my bedroom for a clean pair. Riley was safely in the attic so I didn't need to worry about running into him, so checking all the neighbors were safely in their houses, I slipped out of my jeans. I stepped through the open front door and was heading for the stairs when my phone rang.

Damn, I hated leaving a ringing phone. Thinking I could quickly grab it and run upstairs while I spoke, I went searching for it. Now where did I leave it?

I could hear it ringing louder as I moved into the kitchen, and that's when I remembered I had left it in my purse from last night. Picking it up, I saw it was my mother.

"Hello," I answered.

"Hel...are...there...Liz..." Damn signal. I moved out to the hallway to try to get a better reception.

"Hello. Can you hear me now?" I asked. If I stood near the front door the signal improved.

"Oh yes. Now I can hear you. Where are you, love?" asked Mum. My mum called everybody *Love*. She really is the sweetest lady. She's all of 4'7" tall, a tad plump and has short brown, curly hair she styles in an Afro. However, don't always be fooled by her exterior—she has a seriously bad temper if you push the right buttons.

"Hi Mum. What's up?"

"Well, I was thinking, seeing how we haven't seen your new house since you've moved in, I would bring Grandma Mabel over for a visit."

"That would be great." I actually loved Grandma Mabel. As I mentioned earlier, she is a bit of a wild card but you were never bored when she was around. My Grandpop passed away when I was young and she'd lived alone up until last year when she moved in with Mum and Dad.

I listened as Mum started to tell me about how she and Auntie M were redecorating her lounge room, but I lost concentration when I spotted something under the bottom stair. Kneeling down, I bent over to have a closer look.

What the hell was that? Squinting into the darkness, trying to get a grasp on what I was looking at, I quickly realized it was a rat. A very large rat—and, as I was on my hands and knees, it was now only inches from my face. So close in fact, I could see its beady little eyes and twitchy little whiskers.

"Ahhhhhh!" I screamed, jumping up at record speed.

"What? What is it, love? Are you okay?" Those were the last words I heard from Mum because I think I lost signal when I threw my phone at the rodent hunkered down under the stair.

"Ahh! Get out, Get out!" I screamed, running in circles, looking for something to stand on. I did *not* want that furry little thing running over my feet and up my legs, thank you very much. Seconds later, Riley came running down the stairs.

"What is it? What's wrong?"

"There's a rat! Under there!" I yelled, pointing to the stair, hopping from one foot to the other. Riley bent down, reached under the stair and pulled out the rat by its tail. It squeaked and squealed but he casually opened the front door and put it outside. Just like that.

I was hyperventilating at this point and had started to shake. I hate rodents. And where the bloody hell was that cat? I was obviously feeding him too well.

"Are you okay?" Riley smiled, looking down at me. "And why are your pants outside?"

Damn. In my panic about the rat, I had forgotten all I was wearing were my underpants and a singlet top. Luckily for me though, I had put on my good Victoria Secret panties and not my big old period panties. I'm not sure whether it was seeing me in my underwear or seeing me dance around like a mad woman, but Riley seemed to be in a better mood. Probably it was the latter.

"I'm fine, thank you." With that I turned and walked upstairs toward my bedroom with as much dignity as I could muster.

CHAPTER 7

*M*um and Grandma Mabel arrived within the hour. I watched from the door as Mum helped Grandma from the car and she shuffled her way toward me. When she was younger, Grandma Mabel was beautiful. I've seen old family photos of her and she stood tall with dark eyes, curly black hair right down her back, and an absolutely killer of a figure. Age had not been kind to Grandma, though. She'd gotten shorter as she got older and she now stood with a hunch. Her dark eyes had lost their shine and become watery. Her once long black hair was gray and short, permed into tight curls and given a purple rinse once a week at Danny's salon. Her spirit never changed though. She still had fire in those watery eyes.

Standing in the kitchen, looking at Riley, swishing her false teeth backward and forwards in her mouth, it wasn't hard to guess what she was thinking.

"You're lucky I'm not twenty years younger, young man. I'd be chasing after you, I can tell you that," she said with a serious look.

Twenty years? Really? Someone needs to remind her she's eighty-two. Riley seemed to take this all in his stride though.

"You're lucky I'm not twenty years older," he replied, giving her the killer grin. He actually seemed to be enjoying her. Funny, Scott never liked Mabel that much. He always thought she was a danger to herself and everyone around her.

"I should take you down to the Bingo hall. My, how the girls would like you." She grinned.

"I should warn you I'm a shark at Bingo. I used to take my Gran once a week to St Pat's," he told Grandma.

"St Pat's? You got to watch those girls over there. They cheat!" she stated, crossing her arms over her chest in a movement that obviously said *do not mess with me, I know what I'm talking about.*

"Mum! You can't say that!" My mum looked up from petting Cat. They had made an instant bond the second she walked in the door.

"I can if it's true," glared Grandma. "And you should know Nelle, because you were there." Grandma always called Mum Nelle—she pronounced it Nelly. When I was younger, I never understood why until Mum explained it was her name, Ellen, spelled backward.

"Mum, Riley just told you his gran plays there. That's like saying she's a cheat," scolded my Mum.

"Oh….well. Maybe I should rephrase that. All the girls except Riley's gran are cheats. There, that better?" Grandma asked, looking around at us for confirmation.

We all turned to look at Riley. He was smiling, so we took this as a yes.

"Well, as much as I'm enjoying this, I really should get back to work. You're not paying me to sit on my backside." This was true. I would much rather see him standing where I could see his backside. Riley stood and put his cup in the sink.

"I'll see you at St Joey's tomorrow night then, will I?" asked Grandma with a cheeky grin.

"You just might, Mabel. Should I ask for you at the door?"

"Dear God, don't encourage her," I said as he walked past,

giving me a wink. Once he was clearly out of earshot, Grandma turned to me and gave me a wicked smile.

"You kept very quiet about him, girly."

"There's nothing to be quiet about. He's doing some work for me. I will admit though, I am enjoying his company." No matter how hard I tried, I couldn't keep the smile off my face.

"It's not his company you're enjoying," she said, grinning back at me.

"Well, he seems like a nice man, but let's not forget you do have a wonderful boyfriend. Even if he is a little slow in asking you to marry him," added Mum. She was always hoping Scott would propose as she's on a mission to get one of her children married. As Danny is gay and Molly is currently single, all the attention was on me.

"Mum, I keep telling you Scott and I are happy with the way things are. Anyway, you only want me married for the grand-children."

"That's not true. I think Scott is a lovely man with a wonderful job. He could provide for you nicely. You could do a lot worse you know, Love."

"Yes, I'm well aware of that, Mum," I huffed. Scott told me at every opportunity he had that I was lucky to have him. I mean, of course I know that, but did I have to be reminded all the bloody time?

AFTER THEY LEFT, I decided to do some research on Avis. I now had Internet thanks to a lovely man who had come yesterday afternoon and connected me. It was amazing. Just like magic, contractors arrived and fixed things. Like the man who was on my roof fixing the broken tiles, and the plumber who had arrived and fixed my disgusting water. I somehow think I needed to thank Riley for this. He really was amazing.

Pulling my laptop out of its bag, I put the name of the nursing home Adrian had given me into the online search page. It turned out it wasn't too far from here, so I gave them a ring and set up an appointment for tomorrow to talk to the facility manager about Avis. While I had the search page open, I decided to type in Riley's name and see what I could find.

To my surprise I found one match. It was a photo taken at a society wedding, and he was mentioned as the best man and brother of the groom. Wow, he looked good in this photo. I should save it and use it as a screen saver. No, that's probably a bit creepy, I mean, what would happen if Riley saw it one day?

Thinking about him made me realize I really didn't know much about him. I knew he lived in a converted church, not far from here and I knew he loved his gran. I had also found out he was ex-military and had decided to become a builder when he left the army. He was now running a successful, if not overly profitable, business.

"Hey Lizzie, I'm finishing early today," Riley said from behind me. I nearly jumped out of my skin.

What's with him sneaking up on me all the time? I think I'll have to put a bell on him or something. I quickly shut the lid on my laptop and hoped he hadn't seen I was searching for him online.

"I have an appointment this afternoon so I need to go home early."

"Oh, okay," I said, a bit flustered. "I've been meaning to thank you for organizing all the contractors and getting things fixed around here. I know I was supposed to do that and I haven't been very organized. Sorry." I gave him my best apologetic grin.

"That's fine. I know all these guys anyway, so they're going to give you a good rate. It's no problem." He smiled. Would I ever get immune to that smile? I didn't think so.

"I've set up an appointment to meet the facility manager at Allora Lodge Nursing Home tomorrow morning at ten to see what I can find out about Avis," I said, trying to encourage conversation. I may not be immune to his smile but at least now I could put thoughts together after seeing it.

"Really? Would you mind if I tagged along?"

Would I mind? Now let me think about that for a moment...

"Sure, that would be great." Stupid question. Of course, I didn't mind. "You might think of some questions I wouldn't have thought of asking."

"Okay, it's a date."

Not a real date of course, as I was currently attached to Scott and let's face it, Riley would never be interested in someone like me, but I was happy to take what I could get, and just looking at his gorgeous face made me happy.

AFTER RILEY LEFT, I had a quick tidy up. Walking into the kitchen, I opened the broom cupboard to put the broom away and as I turned toward the window, I noticed a shadow pass across it.

That was strange. I wasn't expecting anyone.

Crossing the room, I pulled the old blinds and looked out to the street. Car still in the driveway, black sedan still parked across the street. No one was walking around though. I must be imagining things.

Turning to the kitchen cupboard, I finished putting the cleaning products away but my eyes kept darting back to the front window. A strange prickly feeling ran up my spine and, when I saw a face looking at me through the slats in the blinds, I nearly wet my pants. Strangling a scream, I jumped up and ran to the window. By the time I got there, whoever it was...was gone. I wasn't sure if I wanted to open the front door and check to see who was there or not. It was the middle of the afternoon, but it felt creepy. I did check the lock was firmly in place though.

Why would someone be looking in my windows? Maybe it was my neighbor Hazel checking to see what I was up to. It didn't look like Hazel though. The person looking in the window was too tall. Rubbing the goose-bumps off my arms, I walked into the kitchen and checked the lock on the back door as well. Just to be sure.

With all the cleaning done, I could sit back and wait. Friday night was my night to catch up with Molly, Danny and his partner, Andrew. We had been making Friday nights a bit of a ritual and I loved the nights we went to Danny and Andrew's. They lived above the salon and we would get all the treatments out and spoil ourselves. But tonight, they were all coming to my place.

I liked Andrew. A lot. He's a lot older than Danny—about seventeen years I think—but he's a good, grounding influence on my brother, who tended to be a bit flighty. Tonight also gave me the opportunity to show off all the work that had been done to the house. Riley worked really fast. He'd stripped all the wallpaper off the walls in the attic and had already started to build the new walls of my storeroom and bathroom we were putting in up there. The panic I had previously felt about not getting the office finished in time, subsided. I wouldn't have to explain to Scott why I wasn't ready for his client files. Riley was more than worth every cent I was paying him.

Checking the alcohol level in my pantry, I soon realized a trip to the local bottle shop was needed. Somehow, I didn't think the half bottle of cooking wine was going to be sufficient for my siblings. Getting into my car, I reversed out of my drive and screamed off in the direction of the shops. I think you already got the idea I don't drive slowly. I don't go over the speed limit very often, but I'm more than happy to reach that limit as quickly as possible.

Slowing down as I looked for a place to park, I managed to swerve out of the way of the car reversing out of its bay. The car behind me was not so fortunate, though. I heard the smash of metal and plastic as the two collided.

Thinking I should probably make sure everybody was okay, I pulled into the next available car park and ran back the twenty meters or so to the scene of the accident. By the time I got there, the at fault driver was out of his car and shaking his fist at the driver of the vehicle that had been following me. Really looking at the car for the first time, I realized the guy that had been hit was my neighbor, the one who always parked in stupid places.

I approached the two men, who were now arguing and asked if everyone was okay. My neighbor looked at me and paled slightly.

"Maybe you should sit down," I offered. The last thing I wanted was for a large man like him to pass out in the middle of the street. He looked to be in his forties, was wearing a cap over a shaved head and a gold sleeper in one ear. As I noted the scar running from his lip to his chin, I shivered against the memory that it stirred. Had I met this man before? He sure seemed familiar. He scowled back at me and I started to think maybe he could park wherever he wanted to.

"No, I'm fine," he replied, turning away from me, and pulling his wallet out of his pocket. Handing over several hundred-dollar notes to the other driver, he got back in his car and drove away.

Okay, from where I was standing it looked like the other driver should be the one paying, but who was I to argue? As he too got into his car and drove away, I was left standing alone in the middle of the street, wondering why the hell I'd bothered. Surely the bald-headed guy had to have realized we were neighbors? You would think manners alone would have stated he at least thank me for caring enough to enquire if he was okay. Huffing, I spun on my heel and headed to the bottle shop.

I PROBABLY SHOULD HAVE PHONED Danny and asked him to bring the wine, as I wasn't really the most qualified to buy alcohol. Danny always teased me about how half a glass of wine would get me drunk. I mean, as if! I was not that light weight a drinker—a full glass maybe, but definitely not half a glass.

I wandered around the store until I found the wines. There were bloody hundreds of them. Whenever I went out with Scott, he always picked the wine because all I really know is some are red and some are white. I also know you probably shouldn't pick it by the price, as I've tasted some of the cheap ones and the vinegar I have in the pantry at home tastes better. As I was looking at all the labels and thinking how I needed to find an assistant, I noticed a man with his back to me. He was tall with blond hair curling very sexily at the collar of his shirt. I was surprised to see he wore a tuxedo. It was only four o'clock, so I thought it was a bit early to be this dressed up. I did love a man in a tux though. A man in uniform is number one on my list of hottest men, but a man in a tux followed closely. This man seemed familiar though. I wondered how I knew him.

Casually walking around to the other side of the stack of bottles, I looked up and saw the man was Riley. All the air in my lungs vanished. This man was drop dead gorgeous in jeans and an old T-shirt. In a tux, he was earth shattering.

As I stood there with my mouth hanging open—very unattractively if I may say so—he looked up and saw me. A look of surprise and then embarrassment crossed his face, but he quickly covered it with a smile.

"Lizzie, I didn't expect to see you here."

Was my speech ever going to return? My heart was racing and my breath was coming out in short, sharp spurts. My God, this man was gorgeous.

"No, I didn't either. Um…that is—expect to see you here," I stammered. "I'm here to buy some wine, which I know nothing about, but if Danny and Andrew came over and there's no wine, they'll complain all bloody night long." Great, now I was babbling. He gave me a self-conscious smile.

"You're probably wondering why I'm in a tux?"

"No, no, not at all. What you wear is none of my business. In fact, you could wear nothing at all and I wouldn't mind!" I cringed. I really needed a filter between my brain and my mouth. I saw him blush.

"I have a date." He smiled shyly.

For some reason my stomach had started to do this churning thing. That was an emotion I would have to address later…when I was alone.

"Well, that's great." I said, aware my voice was overbright.

"Actually, she's out in the car, if you'd like to meet her."

No. Crap No. I did *not* want to meet her.

Here I was standing in my old denim jeans and thin jumper with my hair just a mass of uncontrollable curls. I did *not* want to meet some stunningly beautiful woman, with sleek hair; all dressed up to the nines and looking like the perfect partner for Riley.

"That's okay, I really should just grab any old bottle and get home. Molly will be there waiting for me." I started to slink toward the exit.

"No, it will only take a second and you'll love her, I'm sure of it." Riley was smiling and looked quite intent on me meeting his date. Oh well, better to suck it up and get it over with quickly. After picking up the first bottle I could get my hands on, we headed to the registers. Riley stood behind me, and as he leaned forward to put his wine on the counter, all I could smell was his aftershave—rich, elegant and woody. Geez, he smelled good. I wanted to turn around and bury my nose in his neck, and stay there forever. I'm sure he already thought I'm strange so maybe I could get away with just a quick smell. Turning toward him, I gave what I thought was a discreet sniff. He was looking down at me, smiling. He smiled a lot, that's why he had those totally sexy crinkles around his eyes. He leaned in close and whispered in my ear.

"Did you just smell me?"

The feeling of his breath on my neck was totally orgasmic and along with his aftershave, the slight minty smell of his breath and his mouth so close to mine, I wasn't sure if my brain would ever start functioning again. The burning of my cheeks brought me back to my senses. My eyes left his mouth and moved to catch his. The five o'clock shadow on his jaw and around his mouth seemed to make his eyes look bluer than ever. Damn, he was sexy.

"Yes. You smell very nice," I stated breathlessly. With that I turned my back on him, paid for my wine and walked to the door quickly, hoping the fresh air would clear my head.

Catching up with me, he walked outside by my side. Feeling self-conscious, I took a deep breath, smoothed my top down and followed him over to his truck.

Crap, crap and triple crap. I hated meeting beautiful women. I felt inferior as it was without being presented to a totally gorgeous, sophisticated and, I'm sure, intelligent woman. But as he opened the passenger door, I looked inside and strangled a gasp.

Sitting on the seat was the most elegant lady I had ever seen. She sat with her hands neatly folded in her lap, holding her purse and was wearing a pretty blue dress with pearls strung around her neck and her white hair pulled back in an elegant bun. When I looked at her face, I was surprised to see the most beautiful blue eyes looking back at me. Riley's eyes.

"Gran, I'd like you to meet Lizzie Fuller. Lizzie, this is my gran, Ruby Thomas. This is the lady I'm doing some work for on the old Victorian over on May Street, Gran," he explained.

So, his date was with his Gran?

"Oh, how lovely to meet you, Lizzie. I've heard so much about you and your house. Riley's been telling me about the renovations you're doing over there." She had his killer smile as well.

"Lovely to meet you too, Mrs. Thomas," I said, extending my hand to her. She took it in both hers, holding on as if her life depended on it.

"Oh, please, call me Ruby. Oh my, you really are quite beautiful, aren't you? Riley wasn't exaggerating when he told me that." My stomach flipped as I turned and saw Riley going pink on the tips of his ears.

So, he thought I'm beautiful? Well, that was interesting.

"I'd like to take credit for the renovation but Riley's doing all the work." I smiled. She was still holding my hand, so I moved a step closer to make the stretch a bit less uncomfortable. "So, where are you two going then? Somewhere nice judging by the way you're both dressed."

"Yes, Riley takes me dancing every Friday evening over at the dance hall on Elm. My George and I used to go there every week, but now Riley takes me." I noticed her eyes got a bit watery at the mention of George who I assumed was her husband. "I can't complain though. I'm the envy of every woman there with Riley on my arm. He's a pretty good dancer too, if I may say so." She smiled, her eyes twinkling. She was obviously very proud of her grandson.

"Well, we probably should get going, Gran. You don't want to be late." I noticed Riley's ears were still pink as he stepped away from the truck to allow me to pass.

"It was lovely talking to you, Ruby. I hope you have a fantastic evening." She gave my hand a squeeze as I attempted to move back.

"Thank you, dear. I hope to meet you again soon," she said, finally letting go. As I walked past Riley, I looked up and grinned. What a sweetheart.

"See you tomorrow, Lizzie."

"See you, Riley."

CHAPTER 8

*M*ost mornings I tried to get out for a walk before I started work. Even though I hadn't officially started work yet, I felt it was time to get back into some sort of routine.

If you followed the river along toward town, it got more commercial with a boardwalk and lots of restaurants and coffee shops. I had my usual walk mapped out and followed the same path every day, finishing at my favorite coffee hangout. I figured after walking for nearly an hour any calories I consumed with my regular Frappuccino and muffin would be void. It's funny how you see the same regulars every day, both at the coffee shop and on my walk. There's the man with the glasses who wore his pants too tight and way too high, who always sat with his laptop. He gave me the giggles. He would be sitting there all alone, typing away and suddenly start talking to himself. The first time I saw this, I'd slowly backed away from him thinking he was crazy, but soon realized he was talking on his phone. The elderly are the friendliest as they always smiled and said hello. Others use the track to get fit—like the man with tanned skin. Honestly, the leather on my couch looked softer than his skin. And of course, I can't forget the person who's gender neutral. They always dress in shorts and a blue T-shirt, have short hair and is a bit on the plump side. Their smile is always on the large side and I guessed they loved life.

Since buying the house I hadn't had the chance to get down here, but this morning I got up early—Riley opened the door at 6.30 am anyway—and put my walking clothes on. It felt good to be out and away from all the mess at home. Riley was making good progress in the attic but the rest of the house was still a mess. Even though I couldn't wait for it to be finished, I knew that when it was, Riley would be out of my life. I was enjoying having him around even though I knew I shouldn't be enjoying his company quite as much as I was. But still… what harm was a tiny little crush?

After finishing my walk and dark mocha Frappuccino, I headed home to get ready for our meeting at Allora Lodge. Riley was waiting for me when I walked in the door.

"You're running a bit late," he said with a smile. I took a moment to enjoy the glow, before hearing what he actually said. Looking at my watch, I realized he was right. Crap. Time gets away from you when you're on holidays.

After such a relaxing morning I did not need to hear another lecture on how I was always tardy. But Riley was looking at me, leaning backward against the counter, long legs stretched out in front of him with that casual relaxed stance he has.

"Sorry, it was so beautiful down there this morning, I lost track of time." I started telling Riley about the man in the tight pants. "He must have been hot today because he was in his summer outfit. Usually, it's his black jeans and black turtleneck top with his belt pulled two or three notches too tight so it gives him a big muffin top. The summer outfit is pretty much the same but its black shorts and black T-shirt with the belt pulled two or three notches too tight." I smiled. Riley laughed. I was really going to miss his company when he finished working here.

AFTER A SUPER-FAST SHOWER, I put on a clean skirt, little camisole top and a lightweight sweater, and headed downstairs.

"We can take my car if you like," I suggested, pulling my keys out from the bottom of my handbag.

Riley shrugged in a *yeah whatever* movement and we headed outside.

Now if I haven't mentioned it previously, I drive a Mini Cooper S. It's adorable. It's red and has two black racing stripes running up the bonnet, across the roof and down the back hatch. It's also turbo-charged so it goes like the clappers.

Getting in, I started the engine and waited for Riley. I watched as he folded himself into the passenger seat, narrowly missing his head on the roof, his knee hanging over the gear lever. As tight a fit as it was for him, I was enjoying every second of it, changing gear more often than necessary as it meant I would have to touch his knee.

It took about twenty minutes to get from my house to the Allora Lodge Nursing Facility, and I will admit by the time we got to our destination, I was one very happy girl.

As I parked in the visitors parking, I took a good look around. The building was utilitarian-looking, with pale bricks, a green tiled roof, and sparse gardens surrounding it. Inside it, was just as depressing. When the time came for me to have children, I was going to be very nice to them in the hope I don't end up in a place like this.

Stepping up to the unattended reception desk, I rang the bell and we waited until a nurse appeared. I asked for Lorraine Spencer, the lady whom our meeting was with and it didn't take long for her to arrive. She was a small lady, about fifty, wearing a dark blue uniform with the Allora Lodge logo on the left breast pocket.

"Come into my office," she said, using her arm to steer us

toward the room on our left. It was pretty small considering the size of her desk and all the paperwork she had in piles around the room. "I apologize for the mess. I never seem to have enough space for everything. I keep hoping one day we'll get a large donation and I might be able to get a bigger office." She smiled. "Now, you mentioned on the phone yesterday you had some questions about a previous resident here," she said, sitting down behind her desk and clasping her hands in front of her.

"Yes, her name was Avis Miller. I bought her house recently and we found something that would have belonged to her. I was hoping you could tell me if she has any living relatives so I could return the item to them," I explained.

"Well, as you know all information about Avis is protected by the privacy act so I can't tell you too much, but I can tell you she had no living relatives. She came to us after a rather nasty fall. She was only with us for four months before she passed, but she was a sweet lady. She was friendly to the other residents but didn't really connect with anyone. It was quite sad that she never had many visitors during her time with us," she said, shaking her head. "It's not uncommon though. Do you have any idea how many family members put their relatives in here and basically forget about them?" she sighed, looking at Riley.

"Could you tell us who her visitors were?" he asked, trying to keep her on track. He gave her the killer smile, so anything he requested was pretty much going to be done. I saw the dazed expression enter her eyes.

"Well…I…umm…ummm…I'm not supposed to give out that information," she stammered, "but how about I go and see what I can find out." I could actually see her brain stop working there for a moment. I guess it proved any age bracket could be sucked right into Riley's orbit.

"Seriously, with that smile you can get whatever you want, can't you?" I asked once she'd left the room. He smiled back at me. He knew the power of his talent.

Lorraine was back in no time with a large black book in her arms.

"Now, let's see what we can find. Our computer records show what day she had visitors and I was right when I said she didn't have many. Only two in fact. The first one was a couple, Hazel and Adrian Maxwell, and the second one is a John Smith." I knew about Hazel and Adrian as they had told me about their visit, but John Smith? Seriously, could he not have had a more common name?

"Do you keep a record of addresses of visitors?" I asked, hoping this would give us some more information. She shook her head.

"No...sorry. We don't have a need for that kind of information."

"What about on Avis's records?" asked Riley. "You must have someone listed as a contact for her. Who was notified of her death?"

Lorraine stopped for a second, looking at Riley before clicking a few keys on her keyboard.

"I'm sorry, but that information is protected. I can't tell you even if I wanted to. Can I ask what it is you found?"

I looked at Riley. There was no harm in telling her.

"Riley was renovating the attic and found a pile of love letters and an engagement ring. The ring looks valuable, so I thought it should be given either to a relative or back to the person who gave it to her."

"An engagement ring?" Now we had her attention. "Well, isn't that interesting. Do you think it belonged to Avis?"

"Yes, the letters were addressed to her," said Riley.

"Well, who would have thought," she said, more as a comment than a question. "I know Avis liked one of the nurses here named Susan. How about I give her a call and see if she's free for a chat." Lorraine picked up the phone and pressed a few buttons. Within a minute Susan knocked on the door. Lorraine introduced us all as Susan took a seat opposite us.

"Do you remember Avis Miller?" Lorraine asked. Susan nodded. "Well, this lovely lady and her friend have bought her old house and are renovating it. They found an engagement ring that belonged to Avis—with some old letters—and are trying to track down the original owner," Lorraine explained, grinning. I think our story was the highlight of her day.

"Avis was such a lovely lady." Susan smiled. "I got quite attached to her while she was here, but she never mentioned anything about ever being married or engaged." Susan stopped and looked thoughtful.

"Did you ever hear her talk about a William?" I asked.

"No sorry, but I'll give it some thought. Sometimes conversations will come back to me when I'm least trying to remember them."

"Thanks anyway," I said. This was turning out to be a waste of time.

"You know Susan, while you're here I should get you to look at Mrs. Turner, she was feeling a bit under the weather this morning." Susan and Lorraine got up to leave the room.

Well, that's strange. Is this the end of the meeting? As she walked out of the room, I noticed she glanced at Riley. Once they were gone, he got up and walked around the desk.

"What are you doing?" I whispered in panic. I hated the anxiety I feel when sneaking around, already my palms were sweating and my pulse had picked up. Flashbacks of getting caught while sneaking a look at Christmas presents at the age of seven were coming back to me.

"She was signaling to me to look at the computer once she was gone."

Seriously? He got that from the look she gave him?

"She said she couldn't tell us who Avis's emergency contact

was because of privacy laws. Well, this way she's not telling us, is she?"

He looked quite happy with himself. I have to admit that's pretty clever really. Grabbing a piece of paper, Riley took down some information. He'd just sat down in his seat when Lorraine came back into the room.

"Well, I'm sorry I couldn't have been more help," she said with a smile. "But I hope you found your visit to us useful. Susan will let me know if she remembers anything else and I have your number, Lizzie, so I will contact you as soon as I find anything out," she said as she shepherded us to the door.

"You've been a big help," said Riley, giving her his killer smile again. I think that was payment for her deception.

THE NAME RILEY had written on the paper was that of a solicitor in the city. I can't be certain because I no longer have the contract, but I'm pretty sure it was the solicitor who sold me my house. I thought it was interesting he was also her final contact. No friends or family–just a solicitor. But then what did I know? He could have been her friend after all.

I gave the number a ring once we were back in the car and set up an appointment to see a Mr. Patrick Johns on Wednesday. Hopefully he could shed some light on this. I was wondering who John Smith was when my phone started to ring.

"Hello, baby!" It was Mum. I was about to turn thirty-two and she still called me baby.

"Hi Mum. What's up?"

"Well, I was thinking that, seeing how your birthday is on Tuesday, we would make Sunday dinner for you. Would that be okay, love? It's just...your father and I have a tournament at the bridge club on Tuesday night and we wouldn't be able to have it then."

"That's fine, Mum. Scott has actually organized a night out for my birthday. I think we're having dinner in the city and going to a show afterwards. I'm hoping it's *Wicked* but he won't tell me." I smiled, thinking about it. I hadn't seen Wicked yet but from what I'd heard, it's spectacular.

"Oh, that'll be lovely," said Mum. "Maybe he might have a special something for you." I know she was hinting at a ring, but I hoped he didn't. Yes, about seven months ago I was hoping for commitment, but now I was starting to feel a bit uneasy with our relationship. I know I'm lucky to have a boyfriend like Scott, but lately I was feeling like I didn't want to be lucky. I wanted to be wanted. I wanted a relationship that was equal, where he felt just as lucky to have me.

After talking to Mum for another few minutes about Grandma Mabel—apparently, she hadn't stopped talking about Riley since she came over yesterday—I hung up.

"Grandma says hello." I smiled. "I think she has a crush on you."

"Old ladies love me." He smiled back.

"Yeah, not just the old ones, I bet."

CHAPTER 9

It was sort of a tradition that every Sunday night the family would get together and Mum would cook a big roast. I must say Mum cooked the best roast. Grandma Mabel was always there to help her, but after she set the oven on fire last year, she was told to stay out of the kitchen. When I walked in, I found Molly in the kitchen with Mum. Danny, Andrew and Dad were watching Antiques Roadshow in the lounge. Grandma Mabel was in her usual high-backed chair, head back, eyes closed, mouth open and sound asleep.

"How can you hear the television over her snoring?" I asked as I gave Dad a kiss on the cheek. She sounded like an old chainsaw he once owned.

"You get used it," he said looking around me, obviously more interested in the antiques on TV.

Mum and Dad had lived in this house my entire life, but every time I came here, it looked different. Mum got bored very quickly with the décor, and when Auntie M and she put their heads together, it sometimes became a bit overpowering. Like now for instance. She's lucky to have Dad and that he's an extremely patient man because this week she'd changed the curtains and all the cushions on the couch. They all matched beautifully with a lovely floral print in scarlet. This of course didn't match the floral carpet which was an awful mix of brown, mustard and orange. Nor did it match the purple couch.

"You've put new curtains up," I said to Mum as I walked into the kitchen.

"Yes, aren't they lovely?" Mum was so cute when she was excited. Her whole face glowed and she kind of had this scrunched-up look around her eyes.

"Gorgeous, Mum. Do you think there's anything on the color wheel you might have forgotten to add?" asked Molly sarcastically.

A lot of people say Molly and I are a lot alike, but I think this is only in looks. Molly is far more outgoing than I am, far more confident and much better dressed. She's the oldest of the three of us, and even though she sits here in her four-inch Jimmy Choo's, skintight, pink-sequined halter-top and skintight jeans, don't be fooled. When she gets her teeth into something, she's like a bulldog, never letting go.

"Well, just because your house is very sterile-looking, Molly, it does not mean you have to be sarcastic about mine," said Mum, rather irritated. I have to agree, though. I thought Molly was right.

Mum and Dad's house wasn't particularly big, so when I left home they converted the bedroom Molly and I had shared growing up, into the dining room they never had. This of course had the added advantage of neither me nor Molly ever being able to return home to live. After Danny moved out, Grandma Mabel moved into the only other spare room.

As Mum called dinner, we all piled into the dining room and sat down to eat. Dinner was always a noisy affair in our family, everyone spoke at once and never waited his or her turn, but somehow we all managed to follow the conversation, even Grandma Mabel. After her nap, she was bright and chirpy once more. I looked at her thinking how sweet she looked in her purple calf-length polyester dress, complete with matching purple hair. Just as my heart was melting, she lifted her left bottom cheek and a distinctive noise coming from her rear end was followed by a seriously bad odor. Grandma continued to eat, a completely innocent look on her face as if nothing happened. A second later the odor hit and I saw her wrinkle her nose.

"Who let Polly out of prison?" she asked, looking around the table, her eyes stopping on me.

"Don't look at me. Everyone knows it was you," I quickly stated, making sure everyone knew it wasn't me.

"Oh, Mum! We're at the dinner table!"

Grandma shrugged and feigned innocence. Waving my hand around to clear the air, I looked up to see Danny leaning in toward me.

"Hey Lizzie," Danny whispered. "I was thinking about Molly's birthday next week and what we should get her." Molly's birthday is exactly one week after mine even though she is two years older.

"That's good, because I don't have a clue," I replied.

"I think we should go out to the animal refuge and rescue a dog for her."

"Do you think that's a good idea?" asked Andrew, who was sitting between Danny and me.

Actually, I thought it was a great idea. Molly had been down since she'd broken up with her last boyfriend and something that would give her unconditional love was exactly what she needed to get her mind off men.

"Have you been out there for a look at what they've got?" I asked.

"No, but I have looked on the Internet. There's this one dog, his name is Harper. He's a cross between a Maltese and who-the-hell-even-knows. After dinner I'll show you," said Danny, taking a second helping of the potatoes.

Dinner continued on as usual but I was having a hard time concentrating on the conversation. I just couldn't wait to see Harper. Molly had been heart broken when she split with her boyfriend Adam. So much so that I was actually worried she would never be the same again. Like I said before, Molly is very outgoing and loves nothing more than male attention, but after Adam, she hasn't been interested. She'd thrown herself into her work. As a photographer she was highly talented, but this new hurt had made her talent shine even more. Maybe there was always an upside to everything.

After dessert, (Mum's famous homemade chocolate cake), we left Molly and Andrew with the dishes—I got out of it because it was my birthday dinner—and got onto Mum and Dad's computer.

It didn't take Danny long to find the website we were looking for and suddenly, there in front of me was a full-size image of the saddest dog I'd ever seen.

Harper was listed under the oldies and was described as a pure white Maltese terrier. In the picture, he didn't look pure white but he did look old. He was so old, he only had two teeth, and so as I looked at his photo, his tongue was hanging out of the side of his mouth. But none of that mattered, he'd already grabbed my heartstrings. He was exactly what Molly needed—something to love and take care of.

"Danny, you're a genius." I turned and gave him a big hug. He really was the most thoughtful brother a girl could ever ask for.

"By the way, for your birthday, I'm giving you a makeover," he said. Like I said, always thoughtful.

"I can meet you there tomorrow and we can have a look at him, if you like?" I said.

"Sure, tomorrow works for me but it'll have to be in the morning. I have a big day planned."

TRYING to find the animal refuge was a feat in itself. When I did finally find it, I realized it was not a track that liked little Mini Coopers. It was muddy, bumpy and full of potholes big enough to actually lose my car in. But I could hear the dogs barking as I drove closer, so even though my car complained every inch of the way, I forced it to negotiate its way around the holes and over the bumps until I reached the gates. Sitting in the car, waiting for Danny to arrive nearly broke my heart.

When Danny did finally arrive, we made our way to the reception area and asked to have a look around. Now, you would think the amount of noise coming from behind these gates would have been a good indicator to me as to how many dogs were actually here. But no, I was shocked by the sheer number of abandoned animals. There were big ones, small ones, medium-sized ones, black ones, brown ones...the list went on. They were all so beautiful I didn't understand how anybody could leave them.

We found Harper pretty quickly, which was good as I was starting to get a bit upset. He was standing in a pen with two other dogs, both of which were jumping up and trying to get our attention. Harper, however, was just standing back checking us out, his tongue hanging out of his mouth, just as it had in the photo. The attendant told us he was about ten years old and needed to go to a home without a cat. He hated cats apparently. Luckily, he wasn't coming to live with me.

"What do you think?" Danny asked.

"I think I want to take him and run. This place is really starting to get to me."

Danny bent down near the fence and called Harper over. It took some coaxing but Harper eventually succumbed to the pressure. As Danny managed to put his hand through the wire and give him a pat, the other two dogs seemed to back off. I wondered if they had some sort of gentleman's agreement concerning visiting humans where, once a dog was selected by a human, the other dogs backed off and respected the chosen one.

Probably not. I'd say it was more likely they had grown bored with the lack of attention.

I could tell Harper probably was white but at the moment he was almost a yellow color, and looked to be a few pounds underweight. He had the darkest brown eyes, making me fall in love with him even more.

"He has the biggest wanger I've ever seen," said Danny incredulously. I rolled my eyes. Trust Danny to notice the dog's manhood. Bending down next to Danny, I took a look.

My goodness, he was right.

"Maybe he used to be a stud dog," I suggested.

"I think the other dogs might be a bit jealous of that, little man," Danny said, talking to Harper.

"Do you think Molly would like him?"

"I think she'll love him, but we should probably bring her here before we buy him," said Danny thoughtfully.

He was right. Molly needed to bond before she took a dog home. "We'll bring her out here on Thursday. It's the only day I've got any free time this week."

Saying our goodbyes to Harper, we headed back to the reception. They were happy to take a deposit, but kept checking that we were talking about Harper, the small white Maltese.

"What's wrong with him?" I asked.

"Oh, nothing. It's just people don't usually want the oldies, they usually only want the puppies. We all thought Harper would be here for the rest of his life."

"A housebroken one is definitely what our sister needs. She's had enough of un-housebroken men," said Danny with a smile.

CHAPTER 10

I was awoken Tuesday morning by my phone ringing. I knew it would be Mum.

"Happy Birthday, Love!" she yelled. She thought as she was the one who had to endure the pain and suffering of my birth, then it was her right to be the first to wish me happy birthday.

"Thanks, Mum," I mumbled. A sleep-in would've been good.

"Now, I know you're heading over to Danny today for your makeover, so I've left your present there. Dad and I are going to be busy so I thought that would be best." She sounded worried about this, so I quickly reassured her it was fine.

"Thanks, Mum, that's great." I listened to her story about the bridge tournament before hearing my call waiting. A quick look at my phone told me it was Molly.

"Mum, Molly is trying to call me on the other line, so I'll have to go."

After saying our goodbyes, I spent the next half an hour lying in bed talking to Molly. Danny had asked her to leave some time free on Thursday for a surprise and she was bugging me for clues. While chatting to her, I heard Riley arrive and let himself in. He closed my bedroom door on his way past. I had to remember to talk to him about that door again. Even though he'd changed the lock, I still woke up every morning to it wide open.

I'd had a particularly restless night thinking about all those poor dogs left at the refuge and about Avis, but mostly about Scott. I was feeling uneasy about tonight, actually. Yes, I was excited about seeing a show and a night out in the city, but Mum wouldn't be right, would she? I really hoped he wouldn't propose. I wasn't ready to answer. A year ago, I would have jumped all over him if he'd popped the question, but a lot had changed in the last few months.

After hanging up from Molly, I took the box containing Avis's engagement ring out of the drawer next to my bed. It was extraordinary. I wondered why Avis hadn't married Will. Was he still alive? Had he married someone else? Who the hell was he?

So many questions, so few answers.

I didn't have to be at Danny's until lunchtime so I decided to stay in bed and re-read the letters looking for any clues we might have missed the first time round.

None of the letters were dated, so there was no chronological order. Reading them made me sad. They were full of pain, heartache and strength. The first ones at least, were full of hope. Whatever the obstacle, they were determined to jump it. The last letter was different though.

MY DARLING AVIS

I'm sorry. I cannot do this anymore. I love you too much to see the pain I cause you. Of course, my heart wishes things were different. That life had given us a different path. But I realize now this was not to be. I see the pain our choices have caused you and it breaks my heart. I have to end this, before it destroys us both.

I love you enough to let you go.

I pray life will be kind to you and you get all you deserve.

With all the love in my heart, I'm saying goodbye.

Will

THE TEARS WERE RUNNING FREELY DOWN my face. I couldn't imagine what all-consuming love felt like. I'd never experienced it—especially not with Scott. Does everybody get a chance at that kind of love? And if so, why did fate not allow them to be together? It broke my heart to think the universe showed them their soul-mates only to take the chance away again. Fate really did play cruel jokes on us at times.

With my puffy eyes and soggy tissues, I crept to the bedroom door and sneaked into the bathroom. That way I wouldn't accidently run into Riley and be humiliated once again when he saw what I looked like in the morning.

I could not shake the sorrow I felt after reading the letters. Putting my head under the hot water, I tried to drown my mood. It was my birthday. I should be happy.

After I'd completed the usual morning routine of shower, hair and make-up, I headed down to the kitchen, my mood only slightly brighter than before. I stopped in the doorway as a bouquet of flowers sitting in a vase on the table, caught me by surprise. The card had my name on it. Opening it I read:

YOU BRIGHTEN MY DAY, *happy birthday Lizzie.*
Riley x

WOW, this man really knew how to take my breath away. Hugging the card to me I took a closer look. It wasn't a huge bouquet but it contained the brightest pink flowers I'd ever seen. It was so happy looking I couldn't get the smile off my face.

"I thought I heard you walking around." I turned and saw

Riley standing at the door looking sheepish. His eyes smiled even when his lips didn't.

"Oh my, these are lovely. Thank you."

"It's not much. I saw them at the shop this morning when I got the paper and I thought of you." He shrugged like it wasn't a big deal.

Funny, it didn't feel like a big deal. It felt like a *huge* deal. There were so many butterflies in my stomach, I thought they must be having a party.

"What's happening with you today?" I asked, looking away from him and trying to neutralize the electricity that seemed to be floating in the air all of a sudden.

"Busy day fitting a toilet. Then it's on to the painting," he said. "The new carpet is being laid Thursday so you'll be able to have your office furniture delivered by Friday."

"Really? That's good."

Even though I'm one year older, and the day had started on a bit of a downer, right now, hugging my card, the world seemed like a really amazing place.

I SPENT the next few hours in the salon with Danny and Andrew, and I have to admit they were true miracle workers. By the time they'd finished, I looked like a completely different person. My unmanageable curls were now sleek, soft and sexy. For all of you out there with curly hair, if you've ever had it straightened you will understand the feeling of the swish. If you swish your head from side to side your hair moves strand by strand, not in a solid mass. For those lucky members of society who already have this hair, please, count your blessings. Swishing my head from side to side, I walked to my car and headed home noticing a storm had started to build.

Of course, it had. I had straight hair and couldn't get it wet or

—like Cinderella—I would turn into a pumpkin. Let's hope the storm blows away. Pulling into my drive, I noticed my neighbor had had their car fixed as the black sedan was now parked back in the same awkward spot. I couldn't go and speak to them about it today though. I was worried my hair would get rained on.

Once inside, I ran to the bathroom and decided to do the smoldering sexy eye thing to match my now straight, sexy hair. So, it was after about an hour of primping and preening that I put on my new dress. I'd bought myself an off-white, calf-length gown with shoestring straps that draped across my body to my hip and then fell on the bias toward the floor. It hugged me where it was supposed to hug me and fell loose where I needed it. With a quick spray of my favorite perfume, Dior J'adore, I grabbed the matching wrap and felt like a million dollars as I headed downstairs to wait for Scott. I'd noticed over the last hour or so the storm was now quite black and menacing. Riley was standing in the kitchen when I walked in. He turned and stared for a few moments before clearing his throat.

"Wow…you look… um… stunning," he whispered.

"Thank you." The air thickened and I could feel the electricity bouncing around, but that could be from the storm. I'm not really sure what was going through his mind, but I could see his breathing get more rapid. He hadn't taken his eyes off me since I had walked in. The silence seemed endless as I waited to hear what he was going to say next.

"I hope Scott appreciates what he's got." His voice was low and his gaze felt intimate.

All indication of a smile had vanished as the energy in the room intensified. My pulse quickened and the butterflies were at it again. Could he really like me? No, of course not, I was imagining things. Before I could respond though, my phone started ringing.

Feeling all fluttery and grateful for the distraction, I quickly turned and picked it up. It was Scott's office.

"Hello Lizzie, this is Belinda speaking." Belinda was Scott's assistant-slash-secretary. With her short blonde hair, silicone implants and regular trips to the Botox clinic, she kept herself pretty well maintained for a woman of her age. Personally, I always thought she resembled a puffer fish after those treatments, but whatever floats your boat really. Each to their own.

"Hi Belinda, what's up?" I asked, a bit irritated and uneasy. I could feel Riley's gaze on my back as I walked into the hallway to get a better phone signal.

"Sorry Lizzie, Scott's been tied up in a meeting. He's going to be late and wondered if it was possible for you to meet him at the restaurant?"

I felt Riley brush past me as he headed out to his car, never once looking back. The back of my throat had started to close and my eyes were stinging with tears. I really had to try and figure out what my emotions were all about.

"Sure Belinda, whatever suits," I said quietly. The storm outside had started to blow as lightning flashed across the sky and thunder shook the house. Now I had to drive in this…great.

BY THE TIME I got to the restaurant, I was exhausted. The storm had raged the whole way, with lightning striking around me, thunder crashing and rain pelting my little car. I felt relieved to hand the keys to the attendant in the valet parking at the restaurant, and was looking forward to sitting down with Scott.

This was the *In* place to be seen at the moment and I have to admit it was nice, if a bit flashy. Personally, I preferred somewhere a lot quieter and more intimate, but I appreciated the effort he put into tonight. Walking up to the front desk, I announced who I was and was told that Scott had not arrived yet but I was welcome to wait in the bar. Crap, I hated waiting in the bar on my own. You always got approached by single men on the prowl looking for easy prey. Never mind, nothing I could do about it now, so I walked in and found a quiet table in the corner.

The crowd was mostly young professionals networking. The accounting firm I worked for was upmarket, with high profile clients, so I should feel at home here and be networking myself, but it just wasn't my scene.

The waiter approached and I ordered a diet coke. A drink would have been quite nice. I was feeling a bit worked up and anxious after my drive in, and the five minutes I'd spent in the kitchen with Riley had me confused, but that was something I'd have to analyze when I had more time. I sent Scott a text letting him know I was waiting and then sat back and crowd-watched until he arrived. Thankfully, only one sad soul approached me, eyes locked on my cleavage and offered to buy me a drink. When I politely refused, he actually asked me if I was only into women. I mean, he obviously thought the only way a girl would turn him down was if she was a lesbian. I told him, that no, I just wasn't into him. With this, he left me alone. Thank goodness Scott arrived not long after.

"Sorry I'm late, Elizabeth," he said, placing a kiss on my cheek. "I'm sure you can appreciate I had to finish my meeting. I couldn't keep a client waiting." No, only his girlfriend. On her birthday.

"That's okay. I understand." Of course I didn't bloody understand but what was I supposed to say?

"What are you drinking?" he asked as he signaled the waiter. Telling him it was a soft drink, he responded, "Of course, you're driving aren't you? You had better stick with the coke so you'll be okay to drive home tonight. I know you're not much of a drinker." He laughed.

Well, I guess I wasn't staying at his place then.

Scott had me pretty much up-to-date on the comings and goings at the office in no time. It didn't sound like I was missing much. He always told me the boring stuff about which client was doing what and never the interesting stuff like who was doing who. Hey, bookkeeping was really boring. I at least needed the office gossip to keep me going. After receiving a very dirty look from Scott for asking this very question, we moved to the dining room and ordered our meal. I ordered the chicken salad as I remembered I was supposed to lose weight, and Scott ordered the steak. I figured I could sneak in a dessert seeing how it was my birthday and had my eye on the tiramisu when the waitress came to take our order. I watched as Scott looked at her, his eyes starting on her face and then slowly working their way down the length of her body, then all the way back up again, lingering longingly on her legs. He did this quite quickly and if I hadn't been watching his face, I would have missed it altogether. I didn't, however, miss the look of admiration in his eyes.

Wow, my boyfriend was checking out another woman on my birthday. Classy. "Like what you saw, Scott?" I asked. I know I should have ignored it but I couldn't help myself.

"Whatever are you talking about?"

"I saw you check her out," I said.

"You're being ridiculous. I would not check out a waitress," he scoffed.

"Really? It certainly looked like you checked her out. You even took your time studying her legs," I snarled.

"Elizabeth, is that jealousy? You know how I feel about that."

"Scott, you've spent more time looking at her legs than you have at me all evening. You haven't even commented on how I look and I put a lot of effort in for you tonight," I sulked. I mean, I didn't have much high ground to stand on here as I'd been perving on Riley all week, but at least I didn't do it in front of Scott.

"Yes, I'm sorry. Your hair does look lovely, not its usual unruly mess," he stated. With this he reached into his pocket and pulled out a small square box all wrapped up in pretty pink paper with a silver bow.

"Happy birthday, Elizabeth." He smiled, handing me the box. I gasped.

Oh. My. God. Is that what I think it is? What am I going to do? Okay, I have to calm myself down and do the only thing I can do—sit here and stare and hope it goes away.

"Well, are you going to take it?" he asked with a little laugh to cover his embarrassment. The people at the table next to us were watching, obviously intrigued with what was in the box and expecting to hear a proposal.

"Um...thank you?" I said as I reached to accept the gift. I looked up and saw a look of relief cross Scott's face. With shaking hands, I gently undid the bow. I was smiling like a demented idiot as a nervous giggle escaped my throat. A large dose of panic lurked beneath, but I bravely continued on my mission. Pulling back the wrapping, I saw a tiny black box. Dread sat heavily in my stomach. Did I really want to open this?

The lady at the table next to us was looking excited, her hands tucked under her chin and a huge grin on her face. Pulling all my courage together, I opened the box. A giggle of relief escaped from my lips and I quickly covered it with my hand. Inside were the sweetest diamond earrings I had ever seen.

"Oh, these are really lovely. Thank you." My voice was shaking from a combination of relief and adrenaline.

"You look relieved. What did you think was in there?" Scott asked curiously.

"It doesn't matter, these are perfect." The lady at the next table looked away, obviously disappointed.

"Please don't lie to me, Elizabeth. Something was clearly bothering you before you opened the box," Scott asked, sounding a bit annoyed.

"I thought it might have been a ring," I replied, embarrassment now clearly burning on my cheeks. Damn my mother for putting stupid ideas into my head.

"A ring? Like an engagement ring?" Scott asked, incredulously. He looked like it was the most ridiculous thing he had ever heard.

"Well, it's a small black jewelry box and we have been together for quite a long time now. Most girls would jump to that conclusion, you know," I said a bit indignantly.

Scott started to laugh. I huffed as I watched him sit back in his chair and laughed the hardest I'd seen him laugh in a long time, which to be honest, wasn't really that hard at all. Scott wasn't known for being jovial.

"Well, that is ridiculous."

Humph.

"Why are you laughing?" I asked. "Why is it ridiculous?"

"Oh, Elizabeth," Scott said. "As if I would marry you."

"What's that supposed to mean?" I asked, his words stinging. I know I didn't want a ring to be in the box, but it doesn't mean I want to hear I'm not marriage material.

Realizing his blunder, Scott sobered up quickly. "It's your birthday, Elizabeth, let's not ruin it," he said placing his hand over mine.

Too late for that.

CHAPTER 11

*W*hen was this house ever going to be quiet in the morning?

I really felt like a sleep in, but with all the banging and clattering going on upstairs, my chances were nil. My alarm hadn't even gone off yet. What the hell had Riley up so early? My head was pounding and my stomach churned as I made my way to the bathroom. I felt like I had a hangover.

Oh, that's right, I probably do. I remember getting home around eleven last night, and being uptight and irritable. Finding the left-over wine, I'd gone into the lounge room and listened to classic Lionel Ritchie on my iPod singing about how he was *stuck on you* and cried for hours. I wanted someone to be stuck on me, and yet there I was on my birthday, alone and drinking straight from the bottle. As I'm not much of a drinker, it didn't take long until I was at the bottom of the pit of self-pity. Geez, I really needed to get a grip. It's not like I have a bad life, you know. Feeling marginally better after my shower, I headed downstairs to get some coffee, hoping it would cure me.

"I didn't expect to see you here this morning. I thought you would have stayed in the city last night." Riley gave me the killer smile, looking particularly happy about something.

"Change of plans. Could you pour me a coffee too, please?" I asked, sitting down at the table and putting my head in my hands. Riley poured me a cup and handed it to me.

"Did you get to see *Wicked*?"

"No, Scott gave me two tickets to see it on Saturday. I might take Molly with me."

"It looks like you had a bit of a party when you got home. I found the empty bottles in the lounge this morning."

Bottles? There was more than one? Geez, no wonder my head hurt.

"I had a bit of a pity party," I said, half embarrassed.

"Yeah, I thought something like that must have happened. Lionel Ritchie was stuck on repeat when I walked in." Riley's smile really did light up the room. It just couldn't cure a hangover.

"How come you're here so early?"

"I had a few things I needed to finish in the attic before the carpet gets laid tomorrow, and seeing how we have the solicitor at ten, I thought I'd get a head start on them."

That's right, I'd forgotten about the solicitor.

"I think I'm going back to bed for a while. Would you wake me up in a couple of hours, please?"

Shuffling back upstairs, I fell on the bed and immediately fell back to sleep.

BY THE TIME I'd had a couple more hours sleep and some aspirin, I was almost human again and ready for another trip into the city. We were in Riley's truck this time, which was a bit of a pity as I wasn't able to touch him every time a gear needed to be changed. Oh well, probably for the best as I still hadn't analyzed what had happened in the kitchen last night.

Riley appeared to be deep in thought, so our trip was a quiet one. It's funny how I feel comfortable even when we're not talking. I actually never feel like I have to prove myself to Riley. Probably because he has no romantic interest in me.

Patrick Johns' office was in the heart of the city, and walking in I had a good look around. It didn't take long as his office wasn't very big. The reception was unpretentious in its decoration with a mahogany desk for his secretary and a small two-seater lounge pushed against one wall for visitors. The beige walls were decorated with the many certificates and awards Mr. Johns had received over the years. One of these was a plaque presented to him by the Global Ministry. I knew of this ministry, as I passed it on my way to my parents. It wasn't like the church I'd attended Sunday school at, which was very traditional. The Global Ministry held its service in what used to be the basketball stadium, and they sang a lot. Loudly. I knew it had a large, growing congregation, so they'd knocked down the stadium and built a big new building—supposedly big enough to hold all 1200 of its followers. Looking at the plaque, I was distracted as the door to another office opened and a man I presumed was Mr. Johns stepped out. He looked about sixty with salt and pepper-colored hair and glasses perched on his hawk-like nose. His suit was a bit too big for him, but he seemed friendly enough as he introduced himself and invited us in.

"What can I do for you lovely folk?" he asked with a smile, closing the door behind us. Sitting down, Riley quickly filled him in on our mission and asked if he could give us any information that might be useful to us.

"I'm sure you are aware I can't divulge any personal information about Ms. Miller, but what I can tell you is her estate was sold and the proceeds given to a local charity. It was the local cat shelter, if I'm not mistaken. I personally oversaw the clearing of the house. Any furniture and personal belongings were also donated, all except her photos. Because of the age of some of them, we felt it would be beneficial for those to go to the local library for their archives," he mused.

"Did Avis ever mention anyone named Will to you, Mr. Johns?" I asked. I watched as he started to fidget in his chair.

"Not that I remember. If you don't mind me asking, why does this interest you so much?"

"We found some letters and a ring hidden under the floor and wanted to return them to their original owner," Riley said.

"I see. Unfortunately, my connection with Ms. Miller was purely professional and even then our meetings were brief. What information did the letters contain?" he asked. His eyes had got brighter, and all of a sudden, I could visualize him in a courtroom. Looking around his inner office, I don't think he got that opportunity often though.

"Not much really. We felt they were personal and should be returned to the writer. Destroying them doesn't feel right," I added.

"The writer may no longer be alive. Maybe you should bring them to me and I'll take a look at them. See if I can do some digging for you," suggested Mr. Johns with a smile.

This sounded like a nice offer, but I didn't think we'd be taking it up anytime soon. I had a weird feeling Mr. Johns was holding out on us.

"Also, I know legally the ring belongs to you now," he said, turning to me, "but maybe you'd like to hand it to me to be sold and given to the charity as well. After all, I'm sure that's what Ms. Miller would have wanted," he said, giving me a sweet, almost sickly smile.

"Thank you Mr. Johns, we'll keep that in mind if we can't find who it belongs to." Riley stood.

Time to go by the looks of things. And not a moment too soon as my scalp prickled and the feeling of uneasiness grew.

WALKING BACK out into the street, we decided to grab some lunch and worked our way to a sandwich shop not far from my old office. This particular shop was a favorite of mine and was very retro, stuck between a sushi bar and a bookshop. After ordering my usual turkey and cranberry Panini, Riley and I found a booth and sat down to wait for our order.

"Next stop the library," said Riley. We'd decided we should take a look at Avis's old photos to see if they held any clues.

"Yes, I'm actually excited to see the photos. I wonder if any of them were of the house." I thought for a moment. "Did you feel Mr. Johns knew more than he was letting on?" I asked, quietly shredding my napkin as I spoke.

"Funny you should say that, but that's exactly what I felt."

"But what? Do you think he knew who Will was?"

"No idea, but whatever it was, he wasn't about to tell us."

Thinking about this, I nearly missed Belinda walking in with Scott. They walked straight to the back of the shop and sat in a booth in the far corner. Riley noticed them too and he looked at me, eyebrows arched. Belinda had obviously visited her cosmetic surgeon recently as her lips were looking awfully swollen, but apart from that she was looking very nice with her designer suit and four-inch heels, towering over Scott. Something about the way they looked at each other seemed a bit more intimate than a business lunch.

"That's weird. Scott told me he had a meeting on the other side of the city today. That's why we left the restaurant early last night. He needed his rest to be ready for it," I said, twisting the remnants of my napkin between my fingers. The feeling of unease that had been creeping around in my stomach ever since we'd visited the solicitor was now on its way to full-blown anxiety attack. Then again, it could just be the hangover causing the sick feeling in my stomach.

"Why don't you go over and say hello?" suggested Riley.

I looked at him, deciding what to do. "Okay, I'll just be a minute." I got up and headed over to their booth.

"Hi, Scott, Belinda." I smiled tightly. Both of them jumped so high they physically lifted off their seats.

"Elizabeth. What are you doing here?" asked Scott, obviously annoyed I had interrupted...whatever I was interrupting.

"I was visiting a solicitor here in the city. I told you about it last night, remember? I thought you had a big meeting today on the other side of the city?"

"What?" A look of confusion crossed his face but he quickly recovered. "Oh yes, that's right. It was cancelled," he said, looking flustered, a small bead of sweat sitting on his top lip.

"Is everything alright?" I asked looking from him to Belinda and back again, my stomach clenching.

"Yes, of course, why wouldn't it be?" he asked, avoiding eye contact altogether.

"You just seem a bit uptight, that's all."

"I'm not uptight. I just don't like all the questions," he snapped. "I haven't questioned you as to why you are here, have I?"

"Well no, but I told you last night I would be here." I could feel my blood pressure rising, but decided a deep breath would be much more beneficial. "Riley and I are just getting lunch if you'd like to sit with us," I suggested.

"Oh no, I don't think so. Belinda and I are running late for another meeting. We should probably go, Belinda." They both stood and almost ran out of the shop, without waiting for their order.

"What was that about?" asked Riley when I returned to the table. "I hope they didn't leave on account of me being here."

"No, some unforgotten meeting they suddenly remembered they were late for," I shrugged. It was all very strange. If Scott had been with anybody other than Belinda, I would think he was having an affair. But Belinda? She was the same age as my mother.

I TRIED to push all thoughts of them aside as we made our way to the library. I think it was the hangover making me restless, as even after two strong coffees I still couldn't think straight and had a dull throbbing in the front of my head.

The Westport library was in an old, small, two-story municipal building that was extremely bland and boring. For such a small library, it was surprisingly busy and it was hard to find a place to sit. This afternoon they were holding a workshop on how to manage stress and anxiety. I was thinking I should probably stay and join in as my stress and anxiety levels were pretty high. Riley however, dragged me away and over to the counter where a particularly pretty lady sat.

He had to pick the pretty one, didn't he? I mean, sitting right next to her was a large, frumpy looking woman with a frown on the face. Why didn't he go to her instead? Okay, after my run-in with Scott my imagination was working overtime. It didn't help that Riley had been so close all freaking day, and looked and smelled like heaven on a stick, just tempting me to lick him. In fact, running my tongue up his neck might improve my mood and help with the hangover. It would actually be doing both of us a favor, really.

I scowled as Miss Pretty Library Lady fluttered her eyelashes at Riley and directed us upstairs to where the old photos were kept. It turned out there weren't very many of them we were interested in, only five in fact, all black and white.

Struggling to concentrate on the photos and not on Riley, I turned the photo over and read the writing on the back. The first one was taken in 1949 and was of an older woman standing with a younger woman in front of my house. Wow, my old house was in such good condition then. If only they'd kept it up. I could only assume it was a photo of a young Avis with her mother. The next few photos were similar. One of them was of Avis with a lady—maybe a friend or neighbor—and something about her was familiar. I just couldn't put my finger on what.

But there was nothing to give us any clues to who Will might be.

Damn.

CHAPTER 12

Waking up to a bright and sunny day with all signs of the hangover gone, told me today was going to be a good one. The carpet was being laid in my newly painted office and it was going to look great. Riley had done an amazing job ripping the old bathroom out and remodeling so I now had a small toilet and basin area, and storeroom for all the files that were on their way. I wasn't sure where Riley was. Earlier in the morning, he was hammering something or other upstairs but he'd gone pretty quiet in the last hour or so. Never mind, he's a big boy, he would sort himself out.

With my iPod blaring the latest Lady Gaga album, I spent a good hour or so in the bathroom applying make-up and trying to get my hair to behave. By some miracle it actually looked okay. With just the right length, just the right amount of humidity, and just the right amount of hair product, it can be tamed. Of course, all planets must also be in the correct alignment for this to happen.

Today, Danny and I were taking Molly to the animal shelter to—hopefully—bring Harper home. Molly still had no idea what we were doing as I had done a good job keeping my mouth shut.

Right on time Danny picked me up and we headed over to Molly's. Danny looked pretty cute today with his straightened black hair slicked back to emphasize the large amethyst earring he wore in one ear. He'd obviously dressed for the occasion, as he was in casual three quarter cut off pants and a purple over-shirt open at the front showing us all his black *I heart Dogs* T-shirt. Reaching Molly's, Danny beeped his horn to let her know we were waiting. Molly came running toward us, obviously thinking her surprise involved more shopping than anything else. She'd dressed in white jeans and a tight black knitted top, hair tumbling down her back in beautiful ringlets. Looking down at myself, in my plain denim jeans, white T-shirt and hoodie, I felt like the ugly duckling of the family.

Once we reached the animal shelter, it took Molly a minute to get her bearings and figure out what we were doing.

"Happy birthday!" yelled Danny. "We thought we'd give you a new roommate."

"We've already picked one out for you but wanted you to see him before we bought him," I explained.

She looked a bit shell-shocked, but followed us silently through to the reception area. I was feeling a bit concerned as silence was unusual for Molly.

We were greeted by a lovely lady and when we asked to see Harper we were directed to the paddocks out the back. Today, he was accompanied by another dog and an attendant. Because of the storm we'd had on Tuesday, the ground was muddy and the once little, sort of white Harper was now little, brown, muddy Harper. Unlike the first time Danny and I had seen him—when he'd sat back and quietly checked us out—as soon as Molly entered the gate he ran straight to her and jumped up against her leg. It was as if he'd been waiting for her.

Molly immediately sat down in the mud and God knows what else and put her arms around him. Danny and I, mouths agape, turned and looked at each other. Molly was usually very concerned with her appearance and always particular about her clothing. To sit down in the mud was unheard of. When she looked up at us, tears were running down her face. Of course, by this time Danny and I were also in tears. The attendant just looked at us and smiled, obviously used to this kind of reaction.

"Do you like him?" I asked, digging in my bag for a tissue.

"He's gorgeous. Is he really mine?" she asked quietly.

"If you want him to be, yes," answered Danny discreetly wiping his face with the back of his hand.

I think the answer to that was obvious. We were directed back to reception to pay for him and fill out all the necessary paperwork while the attendant gave Harper a bath. With all this done, we headed back to the car with our newest family member. I wondered if Harper knew how lucky he was. He was going to be the most spoilt dog ever to have walked the earth.

"I have to take these forms down to the council office to register him within the next fourteen days," said Molly, reading from the forms she had been given. She'd finally stopped crying and was now looking lovingly at Harper, who had his head sticking out the car window, tongue flapping.

"I wonder if you have to register a cat. Can I come with you when you go, Molly? I have a few questions for them."

"Let's go now on our way home then," she suggested.

THE COUNCIL OFFICE wasn't far from the animal refuge, and Danny waited in the car with Harper while Molly and I went inside. We watched as Harper stood, paws on the window, nose pressed to the glass, obviously wondering if he was being abandoned all over again.

Inside Molly filed all the necessary paperwork for Harper, while I joined another queue to ask about Cat. I was served by a woman who looked a little younger than me, with cropped, bright red hair and matching lips.

"Can I help you?" she asked.

"Yes, I was hoping you could tell me if I need to register my cat."

"Yes, you do," she said, handing me some forms to fill out.

"The thing is," I said with a small embarrassed smile, "I don't know his real name. I've just been calling him Cat." She paused, giving me a strange look, so I quickly explained the situation.

"Oh, you're the lady who bought that house. I heard you've got Riley Thomas working for you. Is that right?" she asked, her eyes twinkling, leaning forward, and preparing herself for any gossip that might come her way.

I hate the way gossip spreads around small communities. "Yes, do you know him?"

She started nodding her head, reminding me of a bobble-head doll. "My sister used to date him for a while in high school. Phew, he's a hot one, is Riley." I think that was a roll of jealousy that ran through my stomach but before I had a chance to examine it, she continued. "As far as I know he's not dating anyone at the moment. Lucky you." Turning her attention back to her computer, she asked, "Is it a ginger male?"

It took me a second to catch up with the conversation but when I nodded, she continued. "That cat is already registered with us," she said. "He used to belong to Avis Miller. His name is Mister."

"Mister? Really?" That was only slightly better than Cat. Obviously, Avis's imagination was no better than mine.

Once all the necessary paperwork was completed Danny dropped me home, and getting out of the car, we waited while Harper made a quick pit stop at Hazel and Adrian's fence, promptly lifting his leg. I think he's going to fit in well with our family.

I watched Danny reverse out of my drive, and then walked up

to the front door noticing it was open. That was strange because Riley's truck wasn't in the drive. Maybe it was around the back. Pushing the door all the way open, I called out to Riley.

Silence. A prickly feeling ran up my spine and the hair on my arms stood up. Telling myself not to be stupid, it was broad daylight, I ventured in. I left the front door open in case I needed to make a fast getaway and looked around. Everything seemed to be the way I left it. The TV was still in the lounge, the coffee-maker was still on the kitchen bench and the leftovers of Mum's homemade chocolate cake were still in the fridge. Obviously, I hadn't been robbed. Maybe Riley hadn't pulled the door closed properly behind him when he left. Still feeling a bit freaked out, I turned toward the front door. And screamed.

A hand reached out and grabbed my arm as another hand was placed over my mouth to stop me from screaming. At the same time I was being pulled backward against a large, hard body.

Fight or Flight? Fight or Flight? Fight obviously...someone was between me and the front door.

As disgusting as it was, I opened my mouth and bit down hard. The hand instantly dropped and I heard a sharp intake of breath. His grip on me loosened enough so that I spun around, leg pulled back and kicked the poor man's groin—smack bang on target—as hard as I could. It was as he dropped to the floor onto his knees, hand held tightly against his manhood, that I realized...it was Riley.

Now, I know my first thought should be *Oh My God, what have I done* but actually, it was more like *Oh My God, my foot touched his man business*. I was about to yell at him for scaring me, when he put his finger to his lips in the shush position and pointed upstairs. Someone was up there.

I quietly opened the freezer door, pulled out the frozen peas and handed them to Riley. I know someone was robbing my house, but I needed to make sure a certain godlike man's godlike parts were going to be okay. Riley's face had turned a slight greenish color, so I sat on the floor next to him and waited for his breathing to return to normal.

"I'm so sorry. I thought you were a burglar attacking me," I whispered. He didn't respond. That's probably a good thing as I think the response may not have been printable. We sat there quietly for what felt like hours but was only a couple of minutes. Feeling a bit better, Riley stood and limped over to the cupboard drawers. I felt a moment of panic when he pulled out a large knife. Was he *that* upset with me? Thankfully he turned toward the hallway and motioned for me to stay.

Was he kidding? What if whoever it was in the house had crept downstairs while my attention had been somewhere around Riley's nether regions? What if they were waiting to murder me once Riley was out of the room? No, far better to stay close to him. He gave me a feeling of safety. Even though, after I had kicked him in the groin, he was probably more of a danger to me than any maniac lurking upstairs.

Creeping up the stairs, right behind Riley—yes, I am trying to focus on the job at hand and not his backside, okay?—I listened intently for noises. I heard a car door close and an engine turn over, a dog barked in the far distance and the neighbor's phone was ringing. But no noises that told us someone was in the house. Quietly checking all the rooms, it didn't take a genius to realize someone had been here. All the boxes in my bedroom were upended and the contents thrown around the room. Whoever it was; was looking for something. It was the same in the bathroom. Even the laundry basket had been searched. The attic was pretty much untouched. There was nowhere up there to hide anything. Thankfully, no damage was done.

"What do you think they were looking for?" I asked, when we were certain we were now alone.

"I don't know. When I arrived, I saw you entering the house. Then I saw the curtains in the upstairs bedroom move. Someone was definitely there. I came in behind you hoping to get you out safely. Next time I think I'll leave you to defend yourself," he said, looking at my right foot.

"But how did they get out?" I continued, ignoring the dirty look he was giving me. "You have to go through the kitchen to get out the back door and we could see the front door from where we were."

"He must have jumped out of the window in the bathroom. It was open when we went in."

"Should we call the police?" I asked. When I first moved in here, I was scared of the boogey man, now I was scared of something much more real. "Do you think he'll come back?" I couldn't tell what Riley was thinking. His expression was guarded.

"I'll call the police. You look to see if anything's missing," he said, pulling his phone from his pocket.

AS FAR AS I could tell the only thing missing was a particularly expensive pair of pink Victoria's Secrets panties, but then they could just be lost in the wash. The police thought it was a robbery interrupted and that there was no danger of the perpetrator coming back.

They obviously wanted something smaller than the television and hadn't found it. Riley made a trip to the hardware store and replaced every door and window lock in the house before he headed home. I attempted to clean up the mess in my bedroom but felt a bit empty about it all. I wasn't in the house at the time of the break-in, but what if I had been? What would I have done?

Getting out the largest can of hairspray I owned, I put it next to the bed. Mace would be better, but a woman has to be resourceful, right? Making sure the bedroom door was locked and that Cat—aka Mister—was on the inside with me, I pushed a chair under the door handle and climbed into bed. My mind was on full alert, listening to every creak and bump the house made.

And let me tell you, with a house this old, there were a lot. I heard a car pull up outside a few times but when I peeked out of the window I couldn't see anything. By the time my bedroom clock read 1 am, I was fed up with tossing, turning and being freaked out of my mind, so I sat up and decided to read a book. I didn't think sleep would arrive anytime soon. I didn't have to turn the light on as I'd never turned it off. Sleeping in the dark tonight was definitely not on my To Do list.

I got up and grabbed my bag and rummaged through it looking for my mobile phone. eReader really is a fantastic invention, isn't it? I found Avis's ring first though, so I pulled it out of my bag, lifted the lid and removed it from its black velvet bed. Placing it on my finger, I looked at the diamonds sparkling in the light. Even after years of being hidden, it still sparkled. It felt strange having a ring on my finger and I allowed myself to think about someone giving me such a gift. I knew for certain it wouldn't be Scott.

What about Riley? Would I like him to give me a ring? Sure he's amazing to look at, but would I want to spend the rest of my life with him?

When sleep finally came I spent the next few hours tossing and turning as strange dreams filled my mind, but thankfully no dreams of strange men standing over my bed.

THE FOLLOWING morning I woke with an imprint of the ring on my cheek. Looking at my alarm clock I saw it was already 8.15 am. The day had begun without me. I'm surprised Riley clattering about upstairs didn't wake me, but all was quiet. Taking the ring off and putting it safely back in my bag, I rubbed my cheek as I headed to the bathroom for my usual morning routine. This done, I wandered down to look for coffee.

I wasn't sure what was happening with the house today. The

carpet was laid in the attic yesterday and I must say it looked amazing. I'd chosen an off-white shade of paint for the walls to contrast with the new latte-carpet. With a new blind on the window, it was all ready for the new office furniture.

The coffee sitting in the pot was still hot, so obviously Riley had been here this morning. After pouring a cup, I decided to have one more look at the attic before all the furniture arrived, so I walked up the two flights of stairs to my new office. What greeted me was a room that was complete, furniture and all.

My desk was over near the window, the new bookcase against the new walls with my new printer ready to go and gorgeous flowers on my desk.

Riley was a true miracle. He'd done all this while I was asleep this morning. I sat in my new chair—top of the range leather—and smiled. This was fantastic. Everything smelled new and I couldn't wipe the smile off my face. Doing a full 360 in the chair, I spun around to find Riley leaning against the doorframe of the little storeroom, smiling at me.

"Do you like it?" he asked. I stopped spinning to look at him and my heart did a little flip.

"You are truly awesome, Riley. I can't thank you enough." I smiled, yet I knew my happiness was about to end. My agreed two weeks was up. The house hadn't felt lonely since Riley'd been in it.

"What happens now?" I asked quietly. Riley still hadn't broken eye contact with me, which was causing my heart rate to go into the cardiac arrest zone.

"That's up to you. Do you want me to stay?" he asked quietly. This felt like such a loaded question.

"Of course I do." I actually never want him to leave.

"Then how about Monday morning I start work on the bathroom?" he asked giving me the megawatt smile.

I SPENT the rest of the day sorting the files Scott had couriered over and organizing my new office for Monday. A few times I thought I heard a car pull up outside, but every time I checked there was no one there. My imagination was going wild again. By the time I had everything filed and stored, it was starting to get dark and, as it was Friday night, I had a night out to get ready for.

Tonight, we were all meeting at Danny and Andrew's, so I decided to take the letters and let the others read them. See what they could make of them. I also wanted to talk to someone about Riley.

"The house feels so alive when he's in it," I was explaining to Andrew and Danny, later that night. "But what about Scott?" I whined.

"What about him?" asked Danny "He's a cow's ass. Dump him, I say."

"I agree," said Molly. "Even though I've never set eyes on Riley. You did promise I could come and perv on your handyman, if I remember rightly."

Yeah, there was a reason she'd never seen Riley. If he got one look at Molly, he'd be hooked.

"Besides, Riley is far nicer to look at," continued Danny. We were sitting in his salon with treatments in our hair, facemasks on our faces and glasses of wine in our hands. Andrew gave me a refill.

"Oh no, thanks Andrew," I said attempting to cover my glass. "I have to drive home tonight."

"No you don't. Why don't you stay here? You and Molly can crash on the couch and go home in the morning," suggested Danny. "Harper has already made himself at home." We all looked at Harper who was laying on the couch, on his back, legs in the air, snoring.

"Okay, fill me up!" Not hard to talk me into that, I hear you say? Well, you're right. The thought of another restless night, alone and lonely did not appeal to me right now. A night of company was exactly what I needed. "The thing is," I continued, getting the conversation back to where I wanted it, "Riley is out of my league. He could have any woman he wanted and there is no way I could compete with any of them. I know I'm lucky to have Scott, so I think I should just be grateful. It's just with all this stuff about the ring and the letters, I seem to be spending a lot of time with Riley and he's so wonderful. Do you know he holds open the car door for me?" I was now leaning forward, very intent on what I was saying, the wine already having an effect. "I mean what man does that these days? And you should see my office. While I was sleeping in this morning, he carted all the furniture up two flights of stairs and set the whole room up for me. It was actually very romantic." I sat back and smiled.

"Can I read the letters?" asked Andrew, ignoring my monologue about Riley.

"Yeah, let me have a look at that ring again," said Molly. While Molly and Danny admired the ring, Andrew sat reading the letters. When he'd finished he looked thoughtful.

"Why do you think they were kept apart?" asked Molly.

"You know, not all families are as understanding as yours is. You're very lucky to have them," Andrew smiled. "I've met quite a few parents in my time who couldn't accept their sons for the choices they made."

"But love isn't a choice," I said.

"No, you're right, it's not. But what you do with it—is. You believe in the fairytale of love, you're caught up in the romance of it. But what happens when the honeymoon period is over and you have to live with your choices. Not everyone can do that."

"That's pretty deep, Andrew," said Molly.

"Yes, well I've been around a bit longer than you," he said, smiling.

"Look at this photo. This one is Avis, right?" asked Danny, pointing to Avis in the photo. I nodded. "She was wearing this ring then." Danny was right. Avis had the ring on her wedding finger.

"Maybe you should get the ring valued and see if it's worth anything," suggested Molly.

That's actually a good idea. "Hey Molly, do you want to come and see *Wicked* with me tomorrow? Scott gave me two tickets to see it and I thought of you," I said.

"What happened to Scott taking you?"

"Not his thing apparently."

We spent the rest of the evening discussing Scott and Riley and what I should do. If only the choice was mine.

CHAPTER 13

*S*unday night dinner with the family came around quickly and this was Harper's first time with us all together. It would be interesting to see how he fared. Grandma Mabel was on fine form tonight, telling us all about her outing with the seniors club at church. Apparently, all the seniors' clubs at the different churches took it in turns to host a group day. This month's turn was at the Global Ministry.

"I had a blast!" chuckled Grandma. "Those girls there didn't stand a chance against me in the knobbly knee contest." She lifted her skirt so we could all take a look at her knees. "Now this here's a good set of knees, done me proud, they did." Grandma's knees resembled those of a chicken's. Only I think a chicken's had more fat on them. "That Ben Willett couldn't keep his eyes off them." I'm not surprised, he was probably wondering the same thing we were—how did they hold her up? "I think I might ask him to sit with me at next week's gathering." She smiled.

"Mum, how old are you? You shouldn't be looking at men!" My mother looked horrified.

"Why not? I'm old, not dead." She was back to swishing her

106

false teeth around again. It was a habit she had when she was thinking. What she was thinking about, I didn't want to know.

"What's it like at the church?" asked Molly. "That building is absolutely massive."

"I remember when it was a tiny thing. Not too many people attended. We were all a bit more traditional I suppose back then, but I guess if you like singing then it's the place to be," said Grandma. "I went to school with the son, you know. We all thought he was a bit weird. He had an older sister but you never saw too much of her. Kept pretty much to herself. The father was very strict. I remember Charles being afraid to do the wrong thing or he got a belting. So much for being a man of God."

"I heard it's the same family who still runs it. I read somewhere David Thornton is the pastor there now," said Danny.

"Yes, he's Charles' son. I think he followed in his Granddad's footsteps," explained Mum.

"Molly, what's wrong with Harper?" asked Andrew. Harper had been sitting on Grandma Mabel's knee and she'd been rubbing his belly but at the moment he seemed to be squirming in pain. Molly immediately rushed over to him to see what was wrong.

"He was gettin' a bit excited with me rubbing his belly if you know what I mean. It's been a long time since I've had a response like that," said Grandma.

Molly lifted Harper's front legs up and we all got a look at what Grandma meant. Harper had got himself in a bit of a predicament. His man business had popped out with all the attention from Grandma and got stuck. It appeared to be hurting him because he'd started to yelp.

Molly panicked. *Oh my God*...what do I do?" she yelled.

"Calm down, for a start," said Danny, even though I could tell he was feeling on edge as well. It was probably a man thing.

"Try to push it back in," suggested Mum.

"How do I do that?" asked Molly.

"If you have to ask that, my girl, you need to get out more," said Grandma. Molly looked at Grandma.

"I've actually never had the opportunity of putting one back in, Grandma," she said, glaring at Mabel.

"Try rubbing it," said Mum helpfully.

"Won't that make it pop out more," I asked.

"Oh, for goodness' sake," said Andrew walking over and picking up Harper, who was yelping quite loudly by now. Handing him to Molly he put his hand on Harper's man business and started to rub. Up and down, up and down. Is that how you get it back in, I wondered.

"I think it needs some lubrication," said Danny.

"Put some spit on it," suggested Grandma. We all stopped and looked at her.

"Maybe some Vaseline would be better," suggested Andrew.

Mum ran to the bathroom and came back with the Vaseline. Opening the bottle, Andrew put some on his fingers and worked his magic on Harper. It did the trick. Harper stopped yelping and Molly instantly started crying. Andrew just walked to the bathroom to wash his hands.

"It looks like he's had some practice at that," said Grandma.

We all looked at Danny, who was now bright red.

———

MONDAY MORNING ARRIVED before I knew it. My holidays were officially over. The weather seemed to feel the same way as I did —overcast and dull. Today was my official first day back at work and I decided I should dress for the occasion. If I was working in the city, I would have had to wear a business suit to work every day, which consisted of straight fitting knee-length skirt, business blouse and short, fitted jacket—all very professional-like. I had put a lot of thought into what I was going to be wearing now I was working from home. The right outfit might make me feel more motivated to actually do some work. With this in mind, I decided my very best sweat pants and sparkly pink T-shirt were the right garments for the occasion. Start as you mean to proceed is my motto.

Sitting at my new desk, I looked around the room and gave a deep, contented sigh. Even though I had to work in here, this office was my favorite room in the house. Not just because it's finished, but I loved the little dormer window that looked out over the yard and down the street, and I loved the slanted ceiling. It had a really safe, cozy feel. It was so lovely sitting here in my comfy chair, with the breeze blowing in through the window, Cat —sorry Mister—curled up asleep on the window seat and my beautiful lavender candle burning. It was all very relaxing. I could almost have a nap.

After about an hour of thinking about everything but work— and maybe a five-minute cat nap—I decided that working from home might not be a good idea. Maybe I should pop downstairs and grab a cup of coffee. That would get me going.

Walking down the first flight of stairs, I saw Riley in the bath- room. He'd started pulling the old toilet and vanity out. Looks like I'd be doing the midnight dash upstairs for a while.

"Do you want a cup of coffee?" I asked. He looked up from what he was doing and smiled.

"Sounds great. I'll be down in a minute."

Pouring two cups of coffee, I sat at the kitchen table and waited for Riley to join me.

"I've been thinking maybe we should pay a visit to the ceme- tery and put some flowers on Avis's grave," I said when he walked in. He sat opposite me and picked his cup.

"Okay, sounds like a good idea. Do you want to go today or are you too busy working?" He grinned. He knew not much had been happening up there.

"Smart Ass." I smiled. "Whenever you're free. I assume you want to come as well."

"I just want to fit off all the plumbing and then I can take a break. How about after lunch?"

AFTER LUNCH we made the fifteen-minute drive to the only cemetery in town. It was very old and was divided into two sections—the old gravesites and the new. The old graves had lots of big stone headstones and monuments, a lot of which were crumbling with age. Some of the richer people even had crypts, which even though I respect each to their own, I found a bit creepy. Actually I found them a lot creepy. Riley was close and it was broad daylight, so I figured I would be safe from any ghosts today.

The new section of the cemetery was more like a garden, with lots of grass. Many of the gravesites had small stones, about the size of a house brick, stating who they belonged to, and all were numbered. We'd been given the site number from administration, so we walked over to where Avis lay, being very careful where we walked. She had no headstone, no flowers, nothing to mark she was there. Just a number.

It was so quiet. Even though a major road ran right past, it was almost as if the entrance gates protected everyone in here from the noise of the outside world. A few people walked around, heads bowed in respect. One family stood together with their arms around each other for support. An elderly lady and a woman I assumed was her daughter placed flowers on another grave. I noticed a lone man walking closer, his head tucked low under his hat, the collar on his jacket lifted up against the wind. I was overwhelmed by sadness. Bending down, I placed the flowers we had brought on the grass.

"Hi Avis. I know you don't know me, but I bought your house." I looked at Riley. He probably thought I was crazy talking to the ground, but then he thinks I'm crazy anyway. "Riley and I found some old letters of yours and a ring. We've been trying to find out who the ring belonged to before you. We thought it was important someone who cared about you should have it." I stood up. The lone man had stopped at a grave two down from us and knelt down, seemingly praying. I looked at Riley.

"Maybe we should say a prayer for Avis," I suggested. He shrugged, but stepped up beside me.

"Dear Lord, please look after Avis in Heaven and make sure she has a lovely place to sit. I hope one day she'll be with Will. I don't know if he's there yet, we're trying to find out, but if he is then I hope they are together. Amen." I could see Riley smile next to me.

"Oh, and Avis," I said, trying my hardest to sniff discreetly, "Mister has moved in with me. Well, I suppose technically, I moved in with him, but either way, he seems happy."

Wiping the tears from my cheeks with the back of my hand, I felt Riley put his arm around my waist and pull me closer. This place was so sad. I couldn't help it. Turning, I put my face to his chest and allowed the tears to flow freely. I don't know who I was crying for. Maybe some tears were for Avis, dying alone, without the one person who truly loved her, and maybe some were for me. I was lucky to have a wonderful family, but I still felt a loneliness that could only be filled by true love.

If anything, our journey to find Will had made me realize what I was missing in my life. Riley held me tight against him, both arms around me and I felt so protected, I never wanted to move. In fact, I would melt into his skin if I could. But nevertheless, it was time to pull myself together and grow up.

Be grateful for what you have, Lizzie.

Pulling myself away, I looked in my handbag and found some tissues.

"I'm sorry I lost it there," I sniffed.

"That's okay. I understand. Have you lost someone you loved?" he asked.

"Only my Grandpa, but he died 30 years ago." I saw the amusement in Riley's eyes.

"Do you mind if we make another stop before we leave? I want to visit my Grandpop," Riley asked, all amusement disappearing.

"Really? Why didn't you say earlier? I would have bought some more flowers."

Following Riley, I walked to the opposite side of the grassed area. The weather seemed to be getting worse, with the wind picking up even more and the clouds looking like they were about to burst. Riley didn't need to look for numbers here. He knew exactly where he was going. Stopping in front of a grave with many flowers on it and a small granite headstone, I read:

George Joseph Thomas
5ᵗʰ January 1925 – 13ᵗʰ April 2010
Loved and missed by everyone

"HEART ATTACK." Riley looked at me. "I miss him every day, but it's been especially hard on Gran. She was devastated. They were married for sixty-four years," Riley said quietly. I saw the cloud darken his eyes. He obviously loved his grandfather as much as he did his gran. I reached over and squeezed his hand.

"What was he like, your grandfather?" I asked. "I never knew either of mine." Riley's grip on my hand tightened as he smiled at the memories.

"He was amazing. Totally devoted to Gran. I remember, when I was about fifteen, I had this big fight with Mum and Dad and I ran away to live with Gran and Pop. I only stayed there a week and then Gran talked me into realizing I had a pretty good Mum and that I should go home," he said fondly. "But I remember my

Pop used to leave Gran these messages. Every day, he would leave them somewhere for her to find. They were always little love notes. As a fifteen-year-old, I thought this was a bit gross. I mean they were really old, you know?" He laughed that wonderful throaty laugh I'd heard a lot of since knowing Riley. "He left them in the strangest places. Sometimes in steam on the bathroom mirror, sometimes in the ashes of the fire. This particular day he had written it in the butter. It just said *I Love You*. Gran looked so happy when she found it. She told me how lucky she was she had someone in her life who loved her that much, and how much it meant to her that—even after years of marriage—he still took the time to find new ways to tell her." Riley smiled. "I decided there and then *that* was the kind of love I wanted in my life one day. When I find it, I will never let it go," he said so quietly it was almost a whisper. He looked down to me through those beautiful lashes. I could see the vulnerability in his eyes and felt my heart squeeze. The stillness surrounded us and it felt like we were the only people left in the world. He still held my hand and squeezing it tighter, he looked straight into my eyes. I'm sure he could see right into my soul.

After what felt like an eternity, he whispered, "Do you love him, Lizzie?"

I felt my heart miss a beat. I didn't know what to say. Of course I didn't love Scott. I thought I did, but the last few weeks had proved me wrong. What I wanted to say was *No, I think I'm falling in love with you,* but I knew I would never have the courage to say that. Before the right words could form in my brain, the Heavens opened and rain poured down. Now I don't mean just a shower, I mean large, pelting drops that soaked us in a matter of seconds. Squealing, I started to run back toward the car, Riley close behind me. It was then I noticed the lone man, his face still hidden under his hat, standing in the rain near Riley's truck, watching us run toward him. As we got closer, he turned his back and disappeared into a black sedan.

ON THE DRIVE HOME, neither Riley nor I spoke. I thought if he asked again about Scott, I would tell him the truth. At least, the part about me not loving Scott. But maybe he meant nothing personal by it. It was probably just a simple question about love, not the mammoth event I'd made it out to be. There weren't any signs of anything special happening between us. In fact, he was just being his normal self. Maybe it was my imagination back there, listening to him tell the story of his Gran and Grandpop and how they loved each other. With the way I'd been feeling at Avis's grave, it was likely I'd projected the feelings onto Riley I wanted to hear.

"Did you notice the man standing alone at the cemetery?" I asked to break the silence. "The one wearing the long black coat?"

"Do you mean the one who was praying when we were at Avis's grave?"

"Yes. He was watching us when we were over at your Pop's site."

Riley stopped at a red light and looked over at me.

"Did you happen to see where he went?"

"Yes, I saw him get into a black sedan. No idea what type of car it was though, but it looked similar to one my neighbor has. You know, the one who always parks in really inappropriate places?"

"Would that be anything like the black sedan that's been following us since we left the cemetery?" Riley asked.

"What? Are you kidding?" I looked at him surprised, but as I went to turn to look over my shoulder, Riley reached out and touched my arm.

"Don't look back, I don't want him to know we know he's there."

"Why would anyone be following us?"

"I don't know, maybe it's just a coincidence, but I think I'll head into town for a while and see if he follows us there." Driving through town, Riley pulled in at the local Kmart.

"Let's go in and see what happens," Riley suggested, finding a parking spot. "Apart from that it's afternoon tea time and I'm hungry, so we can get something to eat."

How could he be hungry at a time like this? Someone was following us.

As we parked the car, I had a discreet look to see where the black sedan went. It had followed us into the shopping center car park, but I tried to calm my nerves by telling myself that could just be coincidental. I noticed Riley was a lot more relaxed about this than I was. I'd never been followed before and didn't know the correct protocol or anything.

"What should I do?" I asked, feeling a bit panicky.

"Just act normal." Riley looked at me and smiled.

Okay…normal. I could do that.

"I need to pee," I said, looking at Riley. Alright, normal wasn't going to be as easy as I at first thought it would be. Working our way through the shops, I found the toilets but hesitated before I went in.

"What?" asked Riley.

"Will you be okay out here on your own?"

"Yes, I'll be fine." I could see him struggling to cover his smile.

"But what if he sneaks up behind you and hits you with something?" I asked, my eyes darting around everywhere. Personally, I'd had lost sight of the man in the car park. Shows how good I was at this.

"I'll be alright. I think we may have lost him in the crowd."

I breathed a sigh of relief and walked into the loo.

CHAPTER 14

*W*e decided to grab some lunch and take the ring to the jeweler for a valuation. The jeweler we chose had been around for a long time and was well respected in the community. Mum and Dad had used him for years. I have memories of being here as a child, looking at all the sparkly diamonds, totally awe struck. Not much had changed apparently. I was still mesmerized by the diamonds.

As we walked in I saw an older man, who I remembered to be the jeweler, Brian Hogan, behind the counter serving a young couple, obviously looking for an engagement ring. Sighing, I took the time to have a good look around. Riley wandered over to the watches, talking to someone on his phone, but I found myself drawn to the rings. Within seconds I was hypnotized.

"Can I help you?" asked a lady who appeared from a back room. She looked about my mum's age and was dressed fairly formally with a black skirt and a white blouse buttoned all the way to the neck.

"Oh, I was just admiring these," I said with a smile.

"They are lovely, aren't they?" She pulled out a tray of rings from the cabinet and placed them in front of me. "Which one appeals to you the most?"

That was easy. "That one," I said pointing to the floating two-carat diamond in a solitaire setting.

Taking it out of its case, she lifted my hand and placed it on my finger.

Wow. The diamond was huge and the way it sparkled in the light was breathtaking. Something about the lighting in a jeweler shop made diamonds even more alluring. I know I should have said no to her and never tried it on, but hey some things are too hard to resist.

Riley, of course, picked this moment to walk over to me. "Expensive taste, I see." He smiled.

"I'm sure she's worth it." The lady smiled at Riley.

Oh...she thought we were together. Better set her straight. Taking the ring off, I placed it back on the counter as Riley put his arm around my shoulder and smiled at me.

"Yes, she is." Turning to face him, I raised my eyebrows and saw the playful glint in his eyes.

"What we're really here for," I said, turning back to the lady and elbowing Riley in the ribs, "is to get a valuation on a ring we have." Digging into my bag, I pulled out the ring and handed it to her.

"Oh my, that is beautiful, isn't it," she said, picking up her little eyeglass and looking at it through the magnifying lens. "It has our markings on it," she muttered. Removing the eyeglass, she looked at me. "It was made by us. All the jewelry we make, we mark," she said showing us some tiny markings on the inside of the band. "This is quite old. I personally have never seen it before." The jeweler behind the counter had finished serving the lovebirds, so she called him over to us. "Brian, these lovely young people would like to get a valuation on this ring."

"Yes. Hello, Elizabeth," he greeted. I was quite surprised he remembered my name. It had been many years since I'd been in this shop. "How is your mum? It's been quite a long time since I've seen her."

"Oh, she's good, thank you, Mr. Hogan. I'm actually quite shocked you remember me."

"Well, your mother and grandmother are quite memorable, if you don't mind me saying." He chuckled.

"Not at all. That's actually a very polite way of saying it." I grinned back.

"Now, what do you have here?" He took the ring and looked at it through the jeweler's glass. "It was more than likely made by my father, but then again it could have been my grandfather. It does look quite old. If you give me about an hour I can give it a good clean and have a valuation certificate made up for you," he said, placing the ring back on the bench.

"Do you think your father would remember who it was made for?" I asked excitedly.

"I could ask him, but I'm not sure if he will remember as he has made so many pieces over the years. He's quite elderly now and his memory isn't what it used to be. But I have to photograph it for the valuation certificate, so if you like, I can show him the photo and see if he recalls anything," he offered with a smile.

"If it's not too much trouble, that would be fantastic." I smiled back at him. He reminded me a lot of my dad with his kind eyes and gentle smile. "But don't worry about a valuation certificate, we only needed an idea of the value. There's a bit of a story attached to the ring and we're trying to track down the original owner." I quickly filled him in on the story so far, hoping that when he spoke to his father someone may recall something useful.

"Oh, what a sweet couple you two are," said the assistant. "Most people would sell the ring and keep the money." Brian looked at the ring.

"Well, the clarity of the diamond is exceptional and it's made from platinum, not white gold, so I would give you a rough estimate of about $10,000. Of course, I would need to weigh and measure it to give you an exact value." Brian looked up. "It has quite a unique band, so there's a chance Dad may remember it."

I knew Brian was still talking but my mind was stuck on the $10,000 bit. Maybe returning it wasn't that important after all. I mean, I did buy the house and that meant everything in it became mine, right? I looked at Riley to find him smiling at me. I think he can read my mind sometimes.

After Brian photographed the ring to show his father, I gave him my number and thanked him for his time. Walking outside, Riley turned to me.

"I rang my brother about the man who was following us. If we see him again we need to get a license plate number and he'll run a check on it for us. He thinks it was probably a coincidence though."

"Yeah, I've been wondering why anyone would want to follow us. I think the break-in has made me a bit paranoid."

Working our way back through the shopping plaza to the car, we passed a florist, so I made a quick detour and bought a small bunch of flowers.

"Do you think on the way home we could stop by the cemetery again? I didn't feel right not leaving anything for your Grandpop."

AFTER AN UNEVENTFUL TRIP HOME, via the cemetery, I spent the rest of the day trying to get some work done. I had a meeting in the city tomorrow with Scott and the client to talk about how their financials were looking so far this year. I was supposed to have had the figures sent to him yesterday, but hey, shit happens.

By sunset, I had everything pretty much up-to-date. So, I backed everything up, emailed the figures to Scott and closed my laptop for the night. Riley had left a few hours earlier, so it was just me and Cat. I really needed to stop calling him that and use his proper name, but habits are hard to break. Turning the TV on in the lounge, I went into the kitchen to find what was left for dinner. A trip to the supermarket would be advantageous but who had the inclination for that?

Finding some left-over spaghetti, I zapped it in the microwave and gave Cat some biscuits.

I went back to the lounge. My oversized armchair was probably big enough for two, but it was perfect for me to spread out on. Which is exactly what I did. Ready for a bit of TV time to catch up on my favorite shows, I put my feet up and relaxed. I had to admit life wasn't too bad at the moment. Sure, the décor of the room was pretty awful, but progress was being made. If I could keep Riley around long enough to finish the whole house, I'd be set.

About half an hour and quite a bit of channel surfing later, I came across a local current affairs show doing a story on the Global Ministry. I thought of Grandma Mabel and how she'd enjoyed her day there, so I turned up the volume and listened. It was just a human-interest piece about the family who ran the church but it proved to be interesting.

Apparently, Grandma was right when she said the grandfather of the present minister had started it. He'd had two children —a girl named Mina and a boy Charles. The grandson, David Thornton was the present minister. Even though it was his father, Charles, who had made the church what it was today, David had continued to help the congregation grow. Not much was said about Charles' sister, only that she'd married and had a child, and that she kept pretty much to herself, never in the public eye like her brother. Not everyone was cut out for that kind of attention, I suppose.

The story continued to show footage of the Sunday Services they held and there was a lot of singing and arm waving. I think my Sunday school training had made me a bit more of a traditional girl, even though I rarely stepped foot inside a church anymore. I know I should go more often than once a year at Christmas, but Mum always told me you could pray behind a bus stop so that was more my kind of scene, speaking to God in a more relaxed setting. When it was over, I did a bit more channel surfing and found a rerun of Big Bang Theory, so I sat back for a few hours of laughter.

It was midnight when I found myself asleep in the chair, now covered with a blanket and the television off.

RILEY WAS WAITING for me when I got out the shower the following morning.

"I wondered if you would mind if I gave my brother Jared a look at the ring and the letters. I thought with him being a detective he might be able to track a few things for us," he said.

"Yeah, sure. They're still in my bag from yesterday," I said walking down the stairs. Reaching the kitchen, I grabbed my bag and pulled out everything Riley needed. I decided to keep the photo, though. I didn't think it would be much use to him.

"Are you still going into the city for your meeting today?" Riley asked, once we'd both had a cup of coffee.

"Yeah, my meeting's at eleven thirty, but I should be there a bit earlier so I can go over some notes with Scott." This was always the plan but rarely did I ever get there early.

"Did you want to get a lift in with me? I'm meeting Jared at twelve so I could drop you first and then meet him at the station after that," Riley asked.

Now that's a hard one, I thought. I could make the boring trip into the city by myself or spend half an hour or so with Riley.

"Sounds good. What time are we leaving?"

WITH RILEY DRIVING I should have been at my meeting with plenty of time to spare, but today we kept being stopped by road-works. By the time Riley dropped me off, I was running late. Damn and double damn. Scott of course, was waiting.

"You're late, Elizabeth," he said, stating what I already knew. He walked over to me and kissed me on the cheek. Lucky for me, the client was also running late, so I was let off without a lecture.

"You only just made it. I believe Mr. Thompson is in the lobby waiting," said Scott, frowning.

"Where's Belinda?" I asked, ignoring his disapproving look. "I didn't see her at her desk."

"She went home sick," he said walking to the other side of his desk and sitting down. "I thought after this meeting, maybe I would take the rest of the day off and we could spend some time together."

"That would be nice. I haven't seen much of you lately." I couldn't say anymore as there was a knock at the door, and Mr. Thompson was escorted in by the office junior.

The meeting took a bit over an hour and the client seemed happy with how things were progressing, so Scott was in a particularly good mood when we headed out to lunch. As we walked toward the restaurant I filled him in on all that had been happening with the *Will Hunt* as I was calling it.

"I think you are making too much out of this, Elizabeth. I mean really, it all sounds like a coincidence to me," said Scott, as we walked side by side. Saying it all out loud in broad daylight had me questioning it as well. It all sounded a bit far-fetched. Things like this just didn't happen in everyday life.

After lunch I talked Scott into a walk around the park. As he still thought I should lose a bit of weight and I had consumed a whole piece of mud cake with lunch—yes, it was delicious and worth every calorie—he didn't hesitate in agreeing.

After a few minutes in the park itself, it was easy to forget you were actually in the city. It was so beautiful here. It was pretty busy though, as many people tried to enjoy their lunch break away from their offices. Scott seemed relaxed as we walked, so I decided to bring up our last meeting in the sandwich shop.

"Anything new happening at the office?" I asked, not wanting to be too direct. "Any new gossip?"

"Really, you just can't let that one go, can you?" I could feel the tension in Scott start to return.

"I was only interested. It's a bit lonely out in the suburbs." I smiled, trying to get him to relax again.

"Nobody new is sleeping with each other, the last I heard. Not that I actually listen to that rubbish."

"It's not rubbish, Scott. Office affairs actually do happen." I looked at him to see if there was any indication of guilt. None. I must have been imagining it. My imagination had been really busy lately.

"You know, Elizabeth, there are a few things we need to talk about."

Uh-oh. That didn't sound promising. I turned to face him, preparing myself for the worst. What I didn't prepare myself for though, was to be pushed to the ground. I'd noticed a young guy in a hoodie walking behind us for the last few minutes, but as this is the city, I didn't think too much of it. However, I thought a lot more of it when he grabbed my bag from my shoulder, pushed me and ran in the opposite direction as fast as he could. Trying to keep hold of my bag meant I didn't get my hands out in front of me as fast as I should, and I fell hard on the concrete, banging my head as I landed. I could hear Scott yelling for someone to stop the bag thief but he didn't heroically chase the baddie down and save my bag. Shit, shit and double shit.

Do you have any idea how inconvenient it is to lose your bag? I did. This wasn't the first time I'd lost one. Admittedly, the last time it wasn't actually lost. I had just misplaced it but only found out after I had cancelled every debit and credit card I owned, replaced my license and had the huge expense of a new bag, wallet and phone. Doing a quick check, I realized I wasn't bleeding, so taking Scott's offer to help me up, I got back on my feet.

"Well, that was a good way to ruin a perfectly good afternoon," said Scott, not bothering to check if I was okay. I'd actually gathered a bit of a crowd, which I admit was embarrassing, as I had worn a skirt. It had flipped its way up to my waist, showing all and sundry my underwear when I fell. Quickly tugging it back into place, I looked up to see Riley standing in front of me. Of course he was. It seemed that whenever fate had an opportunity for me to embarrass myself, it made sure Riley was there to see it.

With him was another man who, I assumed must be his brother. Groaning inwardly, I smoothed my skirt down and prayed he had actually missed the sight of my backside in the air.

"What happened? Are you okay?" Riley asked, concern flashing in his eyes.

"Someone just snatched her bag!" said Scott with a frustrated sigh.

What the hell was he frustrated about? I was the one kissing the concrete. I looked at Riley and gave a half smile, trying to cover my embarrassment.

"Someone ran up behind me and grabbed my bag. No biggie," I said. I was feeling a bit sick in the stomach, and for a brief second, thought I was going to throw up but managed to take a few deep breaths and steady myself. "What are you doing here?" I asked Riley.

"We just had some lunch on the other side of the park and were walking back to the station," said Riley, looking at me concerned. Remembering the man next to him, he turned. "Lizzie, this is my brother Jared. Jared, this is Lizzie." Jared held out his hand to me. "And this is Scott. Her boyfriend," Riley added, almost as an afterthought.

Without looking at Scott, Jared took my hand and held it for a second longer than necessary. I think he was assessing me. I had already taken in every bit of him and must say, these Thomas boys come from exceedingly good stock. Jared was slightly shorter than Riley but not by much. He also had blond hair and a toned body, but his lovely blue eyes were just a shade or two less brilliant. All-in-all he was gorgeous, just not as gorgeous as Riley.

"You should come down to the station with us and report what just happened," he offered.

"Yes, that sounds like a good idea to me," said Scott.

"Why?" I asked. "There's nothing they'll do about it." I swayed on the spot. Riley reached out and grabbed me around the waist and helped me to a nearby bench.

"Why is the ground moving?" I whispered. Anything louder than that was starting to hurt my head. I closed my eyes but it seemed to make the dizziness worse. Riley reached out and gently lifted my hair back from my face to take a look at the bump forming on my forehead.

"Why don't you come back to the office with me?" asked Scott. "You can get your car and I'll follow you home." I'd forgotten to tell Scott I'd got a lift in with Riley.

"I think she should see a doctor first," suggested Riley.

"I think so too," agreed Jared, who was now kneeling down in front of me and looking concerned. "That's quite a bump you've got there. It's more than possible you've got a concussion."

"No, I'm fine. I just want to go home." I stood up quickly, ready to go. Uh-oh, shouldn't have done that. Quickly turning toward the bin next to me and holding on with two hands, I threw up. I could hear Scott groan as Riley reached over and pulled back my hair. Normally throwing up in public would be particularly embarrassing, but right now, I didn't care.

"I'll call an ambulance," said Jared pulling his phone from his pocket. I was feeling too sick to argue. All I wanted to do was close my eyes, go to sleep and wake up when I was feeling better again.

CHAPTER 15

I hate hospitals. I hate the sound of them, I hate the smell of them, I hate the way you have to wait for hours before anybody sees you, but most of all, I hate the anxiety I feel when I'm in them. I wanted everybody to be better and no longer sick or dying. If a magic genie appeared and granted me three wishes, my first wish would be that hospitals were unnecessary because nobody got sick or injured. I know that's an unrealistic wish, but there you have it. That's my wish. My other two wishes involved Riley and a private beach in the Caribbean, but I didn't think I had any more chance of that coming true than my first wish.

I was at present lying on a bed in emergency, with Riley and Scott sitting beside me, waiting anxiously. I'd had a scan and a doctor had seen me a while ago, had looked in my eyes, taken my blood pressure—I'm not sure now is the best time to find out the result of that one—had scribbled on a chart and left, all without telling me a thing. The tension in the cubicle was building. I'd informed Scott I'd driven in with Riley this morning and he didn't seem too happy about it. I'd tried to explain car-pooling was great for the environment but since I was slurring my words a bit, he didn't seem to be taking me seriously. Riley glared at Scott and gave the distinct impression there was no love lost there. Ignoring them both, I turned my back and tried to have a nap.

"Hey…Sleepyhead…wake up." Riley gently rubbed my shoulder to encourage me to wake up. If he had any idea, he would be around the other side of the bed facing me, and he'd strip naked. That would be about the only reason I would want to wake up about now.

Not to be outdone, Scott came around to the other side of the bed and rubbed my forehead, attempting to push my hair out of my face.

"Ouch, that hurts," I said, pushing his hand away. The nurse had given me something for my headache but with the noise coming from the cubicle next to mine, it didn't seem to be helping. "What the hell is going on over there?" I snapped, rolling away from Scott.

"Keep your voice down, Elizabeth," he scolded.

"Why? They can't hear me over all that racket." My mood wasn't improving. "And when the hell is the doctor coming back. I just want to get out of here."

"There are other people here that need attending to," said Scott, attempting to soothe me. If the pounding in my head subsided a bit, I might have had some sympathy for the poor woman next to me.

"I think she's in labor," commented Riley.

Humph. Well okay. Maybe she has a reason then. But they really needed to give her some drugs that would stop her screeching, though.

"I'm sorry, she's just really loud."

"At least she's keeping you awake." Riley smiled.

"I can think of better ways to stay awake," I said, smiling back at him. Oops, did I just say that out loud? Lucky for me, they have no way of knowing what I'm thinking, which is good because

Scott would be quite shocked. I heard a curtain pull back and looked up in the hope it would be the doctor coming back to tell me to go home, but I was disappointed when I realized it was the curtain belonging to the lady next to me.

"Pastor Thornton!" she yelled. "Thank goodness you're here. I don't know what to do! It hurts sooo much!"

"There, there. Why don't you calm down, Angela, and then I'll see what I can do," I heard him say. His voice was soothing and if I listened to it for long, it would lull me to sleep.

She started to cry. "I have no idea what is happening. No one will help me," she sniffed.

"You're having a baby, Angela," he said matter-of-factly. I have no idea what her response was as it was a mixed-up noise of her wailing and speaking.

Oh please, someone shut her up.

"God is watching over you, Angela, so let us pray."

It went silent for a few minutes and I could visualize them, heads bowed, praying. Gee, praying shut her up fast. I know I should have more sympathy, but if you had been laying here for the past hour listening to her constant wailing—with a pounding headache I might add—you wouldn't have much sympathy either, I'm sure.

Hearing the curtain pull back, I assumed the doctor had returned for her but as much as I was straining to listen, all I could hear was her moaning. Well, at least she'd turned it down a notch from the screaming. After a minute or two the doctor pulled back her curtain, left her cubicle and entered mine.

"We've had a good look at your scan, Ms. Fuller, and there doesn't appear to be any major trauma," he said, standing at the end of my bed and looking over my chart. "The injuries to your hand are superficial and will heal nicely if you apply antiseptic ointment on it. You do have concussion and will need to be monitored for the next twelve hours." He looked at both Scott and Riley. "Other than that, you are free to go. If anything changes or if you have no improvement in the next twelve hours, you will need to come back for another assessment. Here's a prescription for some pain medication, which will help with the headache. Don't take anything for another 8 hours though. What we've already given you is quite strong." Giving me a final smile, he turned and left, closing the curtain behind him.

"Thank goodness for that," I muttered, standing up so I could get dressed. Turning to look at Riley and Scott, I raised my eyebrows. "Well, are you going to let me get dressed in private?"

"Is that wise?" asked Scott. "You're not exactly steady on your feet. I'll stay and help you."

He turned and glared at Riley who, understanding he wasn't being welcome, walked out from behind the curtain. Not that it mattered if Riley stayed or not. He'd seen my knickers more times in the last week than Scott had in months.

I'd just finished putting my clothes back on when my curtain was pulled back with a flourish. Even though my back was turned, there was only one person I knew who could open a curtain with such drama. Turning, I saw Danny standing there in all his glory.

Today his hair was fire engine red, he was wearing a skintight black T-shirt—with a huge *I love my husband* logo on the front—skinny jeans and painted red finger nails to match.

"*Oh. My. God.* There you are! Do you have any idea how worried I've been?" he yelled, rushing at me and pulling me into a big hug.

"Danny, keep it down, my head is killing me," I said. "How did you know I was here anyway?" I asked, confused.

"Molly told me."

"How did Molly know?"

"Dad told her."

"How did *Dad* know?" I was getting a bit impatient now.

"Well, Mum told him of course."

He looked at me, hand-on-hip as if I was stupid. Did I really care how he found out?

"I phoned your mother when you were brought in," Scott explained.

"Why did you do that? It's not like I've been admitted," I said, irritated.

"Well, we didn't know what was happening, did we? So I thought it best for your family to be here. I can't stay all night and someone should stay with you."

"I was here," stated Riley, who'd walked back in behind Danny.

"Yes, but you're not family, are you? It would be inappropriate for you to stay here all night," said Scott, giving Riley a disgusted look.

"Now, now boys. No fighting," said Danny, turning his gaze on them, his face quite animated. There was nothing he loved more than watching two grown men fighting over someone. Preferably it would be over him but Danny wasn't really fussy. "I'm taking her home and Andrew and I are going to get her better again. First though, I think that totally cute doctor over there should check me out. I may have caught something just being here," said Danny wrinkling his brow and looking toward the ER doctor.

"I'm not sick, Danny. I've just got a concussion and need to sleep, and you haven't been here long enough to catch anything."

"Well, alright," said Danny with a wistful sigh.

As we walked out, the curtain next to us pulled back and out stepped who I assumed to be Pastor Thornton. He was quite commanding in appearance, dressed in an expensive cashmere sweater over neatly pressed wool slacks. As he walked past Danny, he turned and stared. I watched as he looked Danny up and down and saw what could only be described as disgust in his eyes. Danny's overtly gay appearance obviously offended him.

His features went hard and cold, and if looks could kill, Danny would be toast. Gee, what about *loving thy neighbor* and all that.

"You're just lucky I found you. We've been here for ages trying to find out where you were," said Danny, thankfully unaware of the looks he was getting from the good pastor. Just then, Andrew appeared.

"Sorry, we had a bit of trouble getting past the nurse," he said, passing Pastor Thornton on his way. As Andrew tended to dress a bit more conservatively than Danny, he didn't so much as get a peek. What I wasn't expecting was Mum, Dad, Grandma Mabel and Molly all following him. Mum came rushing toward me, crying.

"Oh, *Love*. I've been so worried about you."

She pulled me into a hug so tight I thought she might break a rib. I really wish my family were less enthusiastic with the hugging as my head was still pounding.

"She's right about that. Do you know how many toilet stops we've made getting here? I always forget how sensitive her bowel is to stress," said Grandma Mabel.

"It is not! I just had too much to drink before we left home, that's all," replied Mum, indignant.

"Yes, well, we're here now," said Andrew, trying to distract the conversation away from Mum's bowel habits.

"Yes, and you're all about to leave," I said. Everyone looked at me. "I'm fine, just concussion, no big deal," I sighed. With that I led the very noisy parade outside into the cool night air.

"I'll run and get the car," said Andrew, racing off in the direction of the car park. I looked over at Riley and smiled. Bless him. With all the chaos that surrounds my family, he hadn't run away screaming. He was smiling back at me as I noticed Molly step into his line of vision.

"We haven't met yet," she said, holding out her hand. "I'm Molly," she said, quietly assessing him.

"Pleased to meet you, Molly." He took her hand and gave it a small squeeze, giving her the megawatt smile.

Suddenly I felt nauseous. I'm hoping it was the concussion but I actually think it had more to do with Molly and Riley. I get told all the time I'm quite pretty but next to Molly, I'm really beige.

Scott stepped over to me, took my hand and smiled.

"Well, I can see you're in good hands now, so I'll say good-night, Elizabeth." Seriously not even my mother calls me Elizabeth.

"Yeah, thanks for staying, Scott." I really needed to appreciate him more but next to Riley he also seems very beige. With that he kissed me on the cheek and turned to leave for his car.

"Wait a minute, Scott," Molly called. "My car is parked over there and I don't want to walk alone. I'll walk with you. I'm sure you'll protect me from any bad guys lurking around in the dark," she said with a small smile. Personally, I thought Scott would probably hand her to the bad guys.

As I watched them walk away, I saw Andrew driving slowly toward us and pull up at the curb. Mum, Dad and Grandma Mabel all piled into the back. Danny got in the front. I'm left standing on the footpath. They really didn't think ahead, did they?

"Oh Love, I'm sorry. We were panicking a bit when we left and didn't really think it through." Mum looked concerned.

"It's okay, Mrs. Fuller, I can drive Lizzie home," offered Riley.

"Well, if you're sure. But we don't want to put you out," said Mum.

"Really, it's no problem. Lizzie got a lift in with me, so it's no trouble," he smiled.

Danny, ever the matchmaker, was quick to pipe up. "Mum, get back in the car, it's fine. Lizzie is in good hands." He looked at me and smiled. Even in this light, I could see the glint in his eye.

CHAPTER 16

I slept soundly that night. Whatever the hospital had given me for painkillers, was finally starting to work. My headache was easing to a dull thud. I don't remember a lot about what happened after I got home, but I woke this morning and nearly stepped on Riley. He'd camped all night on my bedroom floor.

Looking at my clock I was shocked to see it was already nine thirty. It's a wonder Cat hadn't been in here by now demanding breakfast. Riley woke as I was trying to step over him.

"Hey, are you okay?" he asked, his voice husky from sleep. His hair was all messed and he had a serious five o'clock shadow happening. He looked totally edible. I sighed. Life could be so unfair.

"Yep, just need the little girls' room." I quickly turned my back on him and hurried from the room. He may look edible but I'm almost positive I look anything but. Reaching the bathroom, I looked in the mirror and stifled a scream. I looked horrific. Apart from the usual bad hair and smudged make-up, this morning I had a huge green and black lump on my forehead, not far above my left eye. Looking down I also noticed I was in my nightclothes of pajama pants and camisole—no bra. I don't remember getting undressed and whether or not I had any help with it. Geez, I hope I didn't embarrass myself.

After having a quick shower, I attempted to cover my bruise with make-up but I think I just made it look worse, so I gave up and worked my way to the kitchen for a much-needed cup of caffeine. Riley was already there waiting for me, cup in hand. He looked a bit dark around the eyes this morning, like he hadn't gotten much sleep.

"Why did you sleep on the floor?" I asked, taking the cup from him.

"The doctor said you should be monitored for twelve hours so I didn't think I should leave you alone. You've been getting phone calls since about five this morning from your family. I ended up turning the ringer down so it didn't wake you." He looked at me, concern in his eyes. "I hope you don't mind that I answered it, but I thought they would probably be worried."

"No, not at all." I looked down into my coffee. I didn't know how to respond. I was so touched that he cared enough to do that for me.

"I hope I didn't overstep any boundaries?" He sounded worried, bending to look into my eyes.

"No, no. I'm just touched you stayed with me all night and slept on the floor," I said, looking back up at him. "You could have slept on the bed next to me, I wouldn't have minded. I know the floor must have been bloody uncomfortable." For some reason, I was feeling really shy.

"Are you kidding me? The way you thrash around in your sleep, there was no way I was getting anywhere near you," he said, giving me the megawatt smile. I think he was kidding. Just then the phone rang.

Riley picked it up off the bench and looked at the display. "It's Danny...again. He's already rung three times this morning. It's a toss-up between him and your mum as to who worries about you the most," he said, handing me the phone.

"Yeah, he's a pretty sweet brother when he wants to be." I took the phone and pressed answer. "Hi, Danny."

"Oh…finally! You're awake. Do you know how many times I've rung to see how your night went only to find you were still asleep? I just hope you were in bed with Adonis," Danny yelled. I blushed. I looked up to see if Riley could hear Danny from where he was standing and judging by the smile he had plastered on his face, I was thinking, yes, he could hear quite adequately. Quickly walking into the hallway, I lowered my voice and spoke back into the phone.

"Danny! I was just telling Riley what a sweet brother you are being so worried about me, but you're just ringing for some juicy gossip! Well, I'm sorry to disappoint. Nothing happened…not that I can remember anyway," I added.

"Yeah, but he stayed with you, didn't he? That means something you know."

"Yeah, it just means he's a really sweet guy."

"Are you kidding me? No guy is that sweet unless he wants something. Where did he sleep then?"

"On the floor."

"See. Only a man with lust in his heart would sleep on your crappy hard floor to make sure you were okay."

I sighed. There was no point arguing with Danny once he had his mind set. "Whatever. Are you interested in how I am feeling?"

"Not really. You're obviously okay or you wouldn't have answered your phone." My headache was returning. "But you'd better ring Mum. She's been worried about you all night."

"Okay, I'll do that now. Bye Danny."

"Bye, big sis. And remember to phone me when you do have some gossip. I want to be the first to know." With that, he hung up.

I dialed Mum's number and Grandma Mabel answered.

"Hello, Fuller residence. How may I help you?" Wow, Grandma was being formal this morning.

"Hi, Grandma. It's me, Lizzie."

"Well, well, well. How are you this morning, my girl?" she asked.

"Not too bad. What's with you, answering the phone all posh?"

"I've been having etiquette lessons at the seniors club. I figured if I want Ben Willett to ask me out, I'd better get up to scratch. It's been a while since I dated you know. In fact, I think the last date I had was in 1947."

I could hear her swishing her teeth around, obviously remembering her last date. That was enough information for me. I did not want or need to know any more.

"Can you let Mum know I'm alive and well and there's no need to keep ringing?"

"Okey dokey. Over and out."

I think she needed more lessons.

THE REST of Thursday passed in a blur but on Friday, I woke up bouncy and as good as new. Well, when I say I woke up bouncy, what I really mean is after I'd had my shower and two cups of coffee, I felt bouncy. Work on the house was progressing nicely with Riley working on my bathroom, so I thought I should catch up on some work. By six o'clock that evening though, I'd had enough. I'd spent the last two hours searching for two cents in a damn bank reconciliation and when I finally found it, I realized it had been there in front of me all along. I was frustrated with myself so much at times.

Closing my laptop, I walked down the stairs to see how Riley had got on today. The sight that greeted me as I stopped at my bathroom door created a fear in me I cannot describe. As I bravely stood there, frozen to the spot, I looked at where my—admittedly crappy—bath-slash-shower had sat…and all I saw was floorboards and plumbing.

Riley was walking up the stairs as I turned on my heel to stare at him.

"WTF!" I yelled, hysteria bubbling just below the surface. "Where the hell is my bath?" I asked, fairly close to hyperventilating.

"It's gone to the restorers. But don't worry, I've sorted out the shower problem," he said with a smile. "Come with me."

He turned and walked down the stairs. I was dumbfounded. I had no idea how he was so calm. All I could think of as I watched his back disappear, was that he must have some amazing shower down there waiting to be temporarily installed. *Okay, calm down and take some deep breaths, Lizzie. This may not be as bad as you imagined.*

Following him through the house, I stepped out the back door —yes, that's right—the *back door*—and saw what looked like a small tent with no floor and no roof.

"What is that?" I asked, warily. I think I knew the answer but I really hoped I was wrong.

"It's a camping shower. I've hooked up the water and a solar hot water heater so you can have a hot shower," Riley said, looking pleased with himself.

Wow. My neighbors were going to love this. "Riley, I don't get it. Why is it there?" I looked at him baffled. How could this ever be considered a good idea?

"What's not to get? You get undressed, walk inside and turn the water on, and it's there because there is nowhere else to put it."

"But what happens when it's windy? It looks like the thing will blow over. I don't want to give my neighbors a heart attack, they already don't like me much." I began to panic. Riley honestly thought this was a good idea.

"It's okay, Lizzie. It's safe. I've secured it well. Your bath should be back in a week, and I promise I'll get it fitted as quickly as possible."

"Riley, I really don't know about this." How was I going to get in this thing twice a day? Sometimes I showered late and there was no way I would come outside to do that at night.

"How about you have your shower a bit earlier and I'll stay here until you're finished," said Riley, reading my mind. "I'm usually here when you get up anyway, so the morning won't be a problem."

This all seemed so simple to him. I suppose men don't stress about this kind of thing like women do.

As I was standing there contemplating hell, I heard the front door open and Harper came running through the house looking for me, closely followed by Molly. I hoped Cat was hiding somewhere.

"What on earth is that?" asked Molly, looking at my new bathroom.

"It's my shower," I said quietly. Choosing to ignore her fit of giggles, I turned to Riley.

"Anyway, how come you're still here?" I asked, my hysteria now turning to irritability. Today was Friday and Riley usually had his date with his Gran.

"Gran has gone to stay with Jared for a couple of days. Jared's wife, Shelly, is due to have her baby any day now and she wanted Gran to be at the birth," he said with a shrug.

I thought about this for a second and thought about Grandma Mabel being at the birth of one of my children. I felt the shudder run all the way down to my toes.

Turning to Riley, Molly said, "Well, you can join us for our Friday night get-together then. Danny and Andrew will be here soon. It'll be fun."

Riley looked at me, almost asking for permission.

"Yeah, it'll be great." I wasn't actually sure if it would be great.

I had this jealous feeling when Molly was around Riley. Looking at her dressed in her low slung jeans and fitted T-shirt, with not a smudge of make-up out of place, I felt totally inadequate. Maybe fixing myself up a bit would be a good idea.

"I might take this thing for a test drive," I said, taking a deep breath and looking at the shower. I can do this, I thought as I walked upstairs to retrieve all the necessities. I'm an intelligent, modern day woman, who can do anything she puts her mind to.

By the time I had got back downstairs, I still hadn't quite convinced myself, though. It didn't help that Danny and Andrew greeted me as I walked into the kitchen, drinks in hand, ready for the show. Bloody family.

"Are you kidding me?" I asked them.

"No way am I missing this," laughed Danny, his camera phone in hand ready to do cinematography.

"You are not videoing me taking a shower!"

"Yes I am. When you fall over and the whole thing topples down on top of you, I'm sending it in to Funniest Home Videos and will win lots of money." He thought he was so funny. I looked at Riley and glared. At least he had the decency to look unamused.

Walking out to the shower, I wondered how I was going to do this. The tent was very small and stepping inside it, I felt the walls touch my shoulders. My head stuck out the top.

"Riley! It's not tall enough," I yelled. Riley came out, followed by everyone else. Danny had his videophone in hand.

"This isn't going to work," I whined.

"Sure it is. Just make sure no one walks past and peeks in over the top." He smiled.

Humph. "Well, don't all stand there watching," I huffed.

Making sure the tent flaps were closed, I started to undress and throw my clothes over the top toward the chair sitting near the door. I have to tell you, it was not easy. Every time I moved my arms, the tent would sway from side to side, causing me to nearly fall over. When I was finally naked, I turned so I was facing away from the back door—just in case someone came out —and looked up to see my neighbor, Roger, staring at me across the fence. Giving him a little two-fingered wave, I decided facing the house was probably my best option. I'm sure Danny, Molly and Andrew didn't want to see me naked...and Riley? Thinking about that had me sweating.

After having the fastest shower in history, I turned the water off and looked for my towel. Shit. I'd left it on the chair along with my clean clothes. I really hadn't thought this through.

"Molly!" She was probably the best one to call. Unfortunately, no one could hear me over the music they had playing. "Molly!" I waited for about a minute, goose-bumps breaking out all over me. Shivering, I looked around. No one was looking. Roger had gone back inside—probably to take his heart medication—so maybe I could quickly sneak over and grab my towel. This was seriously the worst idea Riley had ever come up with. Tomorrow I was showering in my swimsuit.

Opening the flap in the shower, I tiptoed over to the chair, and just as I was getting close to it, the back door opened. I screamed, grabbed at the towel and silently prayed it was Molly standing there. But no, of course it wasn't. Who do you think it was? Yep, you guessed it. It was Riley.

Now, he was a gentleman and turned his back to me quickly, but not before I saw the look of total shock register itself on his face.

"I'm so sorry, Lizzie. I thought I heard you calling out and wanted to make sure you were okay," he stammered.

Even in the fading light, I could see his ears and neck were red. Wow, I should write a book on 101 Ways to Embarrass Yourself. I'm almost an expert on the subject. By the time Riley had opened the back door and sprinted inside, I was almost in tears. My original plan had been to have a shower and make myself look good so I wouldn't feel so insignificant next to Molly.

Instead, I had embarrassed not only myself, but also Riley. Sitting down on the chair, I put my head between my knees and took some deep breaths.

Ahh! Why did this always happen to me? When the shaking had passed, I stepped back into the shower and got dressed. Now all I had to do was hold my head high, walk back into the kitchen, past Riley and hide in my bedroom for the next decade.

Okay, more deep breathing. If I walk fast, he may not even see me. That was the plan at least.

Opening the back door, I stepped inside to see Molly and Riley sitting next to each other, deep in conversation. I didn't stop to see what they were talking about and neither of them looked my way as I walked by. I couldn't tell whether Riley was telling Molly how disgusted he was, or if he was checking out her cleavage and realizing he was working for the wrong sister. Either way I wasn't stopping to find out.

When I reached the safety of my bedroom, I closed the door and burst into tears. I had absolutely no idea how I would ever face him again. Maybe I should send him a text message saying:

Thanks for all your work. I'll post you a check. Bye.

At least that way I would never have to look him in the eye again.

Finding a box of tissues among the unpacked boxes in my room, I pulled out a couple and gave my nose a very unladylike blow. As I was wiping my tears, I heard a knock at the door.

Thank goodness. Molly could help me send Riley home without me even having to look at him. But opening the door, I looked out to find a rather coy-looking Riley. Well, there goes my plan about never having to face him again.

"Hey," he said. Looking at my puffy eyes, his expression softened. "I really am sorry, Lizzie. I thought you were still in the shower and something scared you. I didn't for a second want to embarrass you." He held out a glass of wine. "Thought you may need it," he said smiling. I took the glass and downed it in one go, hoping the alcohol would kick in nice and quickly. Leaving the door open, I stepped back into the room. I could still feel the humiliation stinging the back of my throat.

"I'm the one who's sorry, Riley. I can't think how many times in the last few weeks I've embarrassed you. You seeing me naked just tops it off." Sitting on the bed, I put my head in my hands, unable to look him in the eye.

"You've never embarrassed me," he said, following me into the room and closing the door behind him. His voice had gotten soft and husky as he sat on the bed beside me. "And you have no need to be embarrassed. I didn't get that good a look, but what I did see was quite impressive."

I could hear the laughter in his voice. He was trying to make me feel better, I thought, as I turned to look at him. He was sitting close to me, so close, we were almost touching, and those beautiful blue eyes looked at me so intently I felt my breath catch in my throat. I'm not sure if it was my imagination or not, but something in the air had changed. Sitting there, holding my breath, completely paralyzed by his eyes, I watched as Riley searched my face, his gaze lingering on my mouth. As I felt him move closer, never breaking eye contact, the door suddenly flung open and Molly rushed in.

"She's gone!" she cried. "We've lost Grandma Mabel!"

$\mathscr{I}$t took a minute for my body to catch up with my brain, but when it did, I went into full panic. My heart was racing at a million beats per minute, I was sweating and I felt sick. I'd never lost anybody that I could remember. Other than my grandfathers, whom I don't remember anyway, the only thing I had loved and lost was our old dog, Digger. We'd had to have him put to sleep when I was fourteen and I cried for about a month.

"How?" was the only word I could get out of my mouth.

"She went to seniors club this afternoon and never came home," cried Molly.

"No, I mean how did she die?" I whispered. Molly looked at me with confusion.

"She's not dead, Lizzie. We've really lost her."

"What?"

"Mum just rang to say Grandma went to seniors club this afternoon and never came home," explained Molly slowly, obviously thinking she was talking to an idiot. I felt my temper rise.

"Molly, don't you dare talk to me like I'm the stupid one. You came running in here telling me we'd lost Grandma. What the hell was I supposed to think?" I yelled, walking around the room, arms waving, and adrenaline pumping.

"Don't yell at me, Lizzie! I can't think straight," she yelled then burst into tears.

I looked over at Riley who was running his fingers through his hair, looking like he wanted to pull it out. Yeah, I understood exactly how he felt. Walking past Molly, I went downstairs to find Andrew on the phone and Danny in tears. What can I say? We're good in a crisis. When Andrew hung up, I asked him to please explain what the hell was going on.

"I was talking to your mum. She went to pick Mabel up from seniors club at four o'clock but she wasn't there. She's rung around all her friends but of those she could contact, no one has seen her."

"Did she leave with anyone?" I asked. It was now seven-fifteen, so Grandma had been missing for quite a few hours.

"Not that we can find out," answered Andrew.

"Well, what should we do? We can't just sit here doing nothing!" I was starting to panic all over again.

"Your mum has called the police but she hasn't been missing long enough. Because of her age, they are concerned though."

I knew what everybody was thinking. Recently an elderly man on the news had got confused and wandered off. He was found the next day, hidden behind a dumpster, dead. Well, I for one was not letting that happen to Grandma Mabel. If she was going to die today, it was after we found her and I had my hands around her neck for scaring us so badly. Picking up my car keys, I headed for the door.

"Well, is anyone coming? I'm going looking for her," I said looking back at everyone in the room. All at once people were moving, grabbing bags and phones. Once outside, we decided mine wasn't the best car to take, as we wouldn't all fit, so we took Riley's truck and headed for St Joseph's church. It felt like the best place to start.

It DIDN'T TAKE LONG to get to the church. At this time of night the traffic was quiet. That pretty much summed up the atmosphere inside the truck. Everyone was lost in their own thoughts about Grandma. Danny, Andrew and Molly had got in the back and I'd got to ride shotgun with Riley. I could hear Danny sniff occasionally and saw Andrew reach out and hold his hand. Molly was sitting very rigid, staring out the window, looking like she was hardly daring to breathe.

We found Father John at home in his small stone cottage behind the church, really handy for visitors like us. He greeted us with warmth as he opened his door.

"Come in, come in," he said with a small smile. Father John was a sweet man, about fifty years old, and had a kind voice. Tonight, he was dressed in jeans and a blue collared shirt. The only indication he was a priest, were the little crosses pinned to his collar. I was always surprised that priests dressed normally when they weren't in church. I kind of thought they dressed in robes or at least with their dog collar on, but I suppose that was a uniform to them, just like a suit was a uniform to most business men. We walked into his living room and took a seat.

"We're looking for Mabel," explained Andrew.

"Yes, Ellen rang me and asked if I had seen if she left with anyone. To be honest, I was so busy helping one of the other members I didn't really see anyone leave. I assume you've done a ring around her friends and informed the police?"

"Yes. The only person we can't contact is her friend Eunice. She's not answering her phone. Was she at seniors club today?" asked Andrew.

"Yes, Eunice was there but she left for her daughter's as soon as we'd finished. It was her granddaughter's birthday and they were having a dinner for her tonight," he explained, looking at his watch. "You could try to see if she's home yet. Sometimes she doesn't hear her phone ringing."

That sounded like a good idea. At least it gave us something to do. We all felt useless sitting around doing nothing. Father John got up and moved over to a small antique desk on the far wall, opened a drawer and pulled out a small book. Flipping through it, he looked up.

"Eunice lives in the over 50's village, The Grange, on Pickett Street. She's number 142. Do you know where that is?" he asked.

"Yes, I do," said Riley.

Thanking him for his time, we all piled back into Riley's truck and headed over to the Grange Village. As Eunice lived toward the back of the village, it took us longer to find the correct unit than it did to actually drive there. Who would have thought a retirement village could be so big?

Winding our way around the narrow lanes, we finally stopped at number 142 and saw the lights were on. Getting out of the truck, we walked up to the door and knocked. The poor lady, you could see the anxiety in her eyes as she opened the door to us, keeping the chain firmly in place.

"Can I help you?" she asked. She looked to be about the same age as Grandma and reminded me of Mabel with her tightly permed hair and long, narrow face. Andrew, being the only one of us capable of explaining the situation properly, said Mabel was missing and asked if she'd seen or heard from her.

"Oh dear, you'd better come in." She closed the door, released the chain and let us in. Danny was the first to enter and without being offered, immediately took a seat on the couch, his concern over Mabel neutralizing his normally perfect social etiquette. Deciding this was a far better option than standing in the door-way, we followed suit. Once seated, I looked at Eunice to find her smiling at the three of us.

"Well, I can tell you are Mabel's grandchildren. You all look so much like her." She smiled.

Danny, Molly and I looked at one another, horrified by what we had just heard. Unaware of the fear her words had created, she continued. "Mabel is such a character, she's always keeping us entertained with her stories. Only the other day she was telling us how she was going to get a new bikini so she could join the swimming group." She laughed at the memory. "Oh my, you should have seen the picture of the bikini she was getting. It was some skimpy little thing with pointy breasts. Mabel thought she would look fantastic in it." That sounded like Grandma. Even though I think she has a grip on reality and knows she's in her eighties, there's a part of her that thinks she still looks like she did in her twenties.

"Have you heard from her this evening?" asked Andrew.

"No, but I haven't been home. She was spending a lot of time with Ben Willet this afternoon. I think he has a bit of a crush on her." She giggled, reminding me of a teenager.

"Do you know how we can contact him?" asked Riley. Danny, Molly and I still hadn't had the power of speech return.

"Let me make a few calls. I don't know his address but a friend of mine would. I won't be a moment." She stood and walked toward the tiny kitchen. We all waited silently, hoping we would get a lead on what happened to Grandma. Finally Eunice returned with an address.

"Now, my friend Roger says this is where Ben lives," she said, handing Andrew a piece of paper. "Please let me know if you find her. I won't be able to sleep tonight if I don't know she's safe."

———

BACK IN THE TRUCK, Riley pointed us in the right direction. Ben lived on the other side of town, so it took thirty minutes to get there. By this time, it was nearly ten o'clock at night and Grandma had been missing for a good five to six hours.

Reaching Ben's house, we took a minute to assess the situation. The house was an ordinary looking single-story affair with lots of colorful flowers in pots around the front door, all lit by the streetlight on the footpath. The bright cheerfulness of them seemed in direct opposition to the mood of our group. The lights in the front of the house were out but looking up the side we could see a light was on toward the back.

Knocking, we all stood back and waited as we heard shuffling, followed by the sounds of a door lock being opened. As light spilled out to greet us, I blinked and took stock of the man who opened the door.

He was not what I'd expected. If he was under a hundred years old, I'd be shocked. His skin was about two sizes too big for him, and he had the best tan I'd ever seen. But it was what he was wearing that shocked me the most.

Nothing. He was wearing absolutely nothing.

It was a bit like a car crash, when you know you really shouldn't look but you can't help yourself, then you regret it for the rest of your life. I heard Danny inhale very quickly and looked at Molly, who stood with her mouth hanging open. Riley and Andrew seemed to take it all in their stride and pretended not to notice. Opening the door naked was obviously a common occurrence for Mr. Willett, as he didn't seem fazed by it at all.

"Hello. We're looking for Ben Willett," explained Andrew, his eyes never straying below Ben's shoulders.

"That's me. What do you want?" he snapped.

"Hello, Mr. Willett. I'm Andrew and this is my partner Danny, his sisters Molly and Lizzie, and our friend Riley," said Andrew, introducing us all.

"Congratulations. What do you want?"

Taken aback, Andrew continued, "Well, we're looking for Mabel Phillips. Would you have seen her by any chance?"

"What if I have?"

"Well, the thing is, she's been missing since this afternoon and we're trying to find her." Even patient Andrew was starting to get a bit flustered by now.

"Doesn't mean I've seen her," snapped Ben.

I couldn't take it anymore.

"Listen. If you've seen Mabel, tell us!" It had been a long evening and I was running out of patience. Riley reached over and put his arm around my shoulders. I'm not sure if it was to soothe me or stop me from jumping across and grabbing Ben Willett by the throat.

"What's all this racket about?"

I looked behind Ben and there was Grandma Mabel, dressed in her bra, knickers and the pink slip she always wore under her dress. I was so overcome by relief, my knees gave way and I felt Riley hold me tighter to stop me from falling. Molly started to cry and Danny ran over to Mabel, pulling her into a big hug. I could see the confusion on Grandma's face that quickly turned to irritation.

"What are you all doing here?" she asked.

"We could say the same for you, Grandma. We've been looking for you for hours, running all over the place trying to find you!"

"No need to shout. I'm standing right here," Grandma said to him. "And can't a woman have a bit of privacy once in a while?" she snapped. From where I was standing it was pretty obvious what was going on here. Looking over to Ben and Mr. Droopy, I felt myself shudder.

"Of course you can, Mabel," said Andrew, being the first one to pull himself together. "It's just you need to tell people where you are. Everybody has been so worried about you. Ellen has even called the police."

Grandma started swishing her teeth. This thought had obviously never occurred to her.

"Hmm. Well you can take me home anyway. Not much happening here," she said looking at Ben.

GETTING BACK TO THE TRUCK, we realized we were one seat short, so I got in the back and scrunched up next to Molly. Luckily Mum and Dad's house wasn't too far away.

"I'm actually glad you came when you did. Ben wasn't showing me a good time, if you know what I mean. Those pink tablets aren't what they are cracked up to be," said Mabel.

"What pink tablets Grandma?" I asked.

"You know, the ones that make his bits stand to attention."

"Do you mean the blue tablets?" asked Danny.

"Oh. Maybe that's why they didn't work then," she said thoughtfully.

This was all way too much information for me.

"Grandma, doesn't the church frown upon sex outside of marriage?" asked Molly.

"Well, the rules are more like guidelines at my age. You've just got to take the opportunity when it's there. I mean, he could be dead tomorrow." There's a thought.

By the time we'd dropped Grandma home and got back to my place it was nearly midnight. As I was waving everybody goodnight, I noticed the black sedan pull away from the curb and slowly disappear into the night.

CHAPTER 18

Standing in my shower, the following morning, I looked out over the back yard and groaned. That was it, this grass had to be mowed. I could put it off no longer. Another one of the disadvantages of showering on the back deck is that I have to look at the grass. And the weeds. And the crumbling fence. It didn't make for a good start to the day.

I decided I needed to borrow Dad's mower and would ask Riley if I could borrow his truck so I could pick it up. I also decided that once this job was over, I would have to give Riley a huge bonus. He'd done so much more for me than we'd originally agreed on. Luckily for me, Riley was very easy going and agreed to pick me up at nine am.

By the time we had picked up the mower, I'd listened to a lecture from Mum about the way 'I look at Riley and please remember I have a lovely boyfriend', and made it back to the house, I was even less enthused about starting the job at hand. Plus, starting Dad's mower was always a bitch. I'm pretty sure the mower's as old as I am and only likes to be started by a male. I'd long ago realized that was because the ripcord was longer than my arm and I just couldn't pull it far enough to start the damn thing. However, not one to be beaten, I gave it my all today. Twenty minutes later, I was kicking the stupid mower and cursing when I heard my neighbor call over the fence.

"Yoo Hoo," called Hazel with a little wave. *Great.*

"Hi, Hazel, how are you?" I called back. She waved me over to where she was standing. Looking around, I could come up with no excuses not to go, so I reluctantly walked over to her.

"I was wondering if you've seen a large, ginger cat hanging around?" she asked.

"Why's that?" The large, ginger cat in question was at present sound asleep on my bed.

"Well, I happened to be looking out my back window the other night and saw him toileting in my garden again. If I catch it, I'm calling the pound," she said with a huff. Looking at my garden and then at hers, I could understand why Cat preferred hers.

"I'll keep my eye open for it." I smiled, making a mental note to keep Cat inside for a while.

"I hope you don't mind me saying," she said, leaning in toward me and lowering her voice, "but you are a busy girl on the man front, aren't you? I don't know how you have the energy."

What? Was she kidding? It's been that long since I've had a man—except for that one unmemorable night with Scott recently—that I can hardly remember what passion felt like. Dreams involving Riley do not count, okay?

"What do you mean?" I asked, a bit confused.

"Well, it's not good for the neighborhood, you know. Oh, don't look like you don't know what I'm talking about. First there's the Mercedes, then there's this one," she said, pointing to Riley's truck, "and then there's the black car that's always parked out front."

Whoa, slow down a minute. "Which black car are you talking about?" I asked.

"The one that always parks opposite your drive. I know he's

with you because we never saw him before you moved in, so please don't deny it."

"How often do you see this car?"

"Well, most nights since you moved in. I see this truck move out and the black one move in. You're not running some sort of business are you?" she asked, looking horrified.

What the ...? "No!" What sort of a person did she think I was? I mean I know she didn't like me that much, but seriously?

"Well, you don't exactly conduct yourself properly, do you? First, I see you take your pants off at the front door, and then we have to put up with you showering outside. I mean, my husband doesn't want to see you naked in the backyard. And I've seen some of the people you entertain."

"What do you mean by that? The only people who come over are Riley and my family. And if your husband doesn't want to watch me showering—in my swim suit I might add—then tell him to stay inside at seven in the morning and six in the evening." With this I turned on my heel and stomped toward the house.

"Riley!" I yelled. I could hear him banging around in the bathroom upstairs, so up I stomped. "When is my bath coming back?"

Riley sat back on his heels. He'd been tiling the bathroom floor. "They said it would be about a week. Why, what's wrong?"

"My neighbor is a pervert and his wife is a bitch!" I'm not sure Riley was taking this seriously as he had a big smile on his face. "And the black sedan has been parked outside every night since I moved in." This removed the smile. I retold the conversation I'd just had with Hazel.

"Can you believe the nerve of her? She actually asked me if I was running a business selling my body!"

"Maybe I should have a chat with her. See if she got the license plate number." He was obviously more concerned about the sedan than my reputation.

About twenty minutes later he was back. "Hazel seems like a

nice lady." He smiled. "She invited me in, gave me a coffee and cake."

"Maybe she wouldn't be so upset if it was you showering on the back deck," I snarled.

"Lizzie, Lizzie. There's no need to be jealous. She's not my type." He laughed.

"Did her snooping come to any good?" I asked, referring to the license plate.

"No. She thought it was just another of your boyfriends. She was a bit concerned that I didn't know about the others." He started to chuckle. I have to say it is a particularly sexy chuckle, all deep and throaty.

"Geez, I should be so lucky," I said, more to myself than Riley.

"What's that?"

"Nothing."

"Seriously though, this guy worries me. Too many things have been happening for all this to be coincidental. I'm going to talk with Jared again. Keep your doors and windows locked when you're alone and don't shower unless I'm here."

"Do you think this guy wants to hurt me?" I asked, suddenly scared, real fear creeping in.

"No, I think he's just watching you for some reason. As for the shower, from what your neighbor tells me, it's a pretty good show."

CHAPTER 19

The rest of the weekend went pretty quick and uneventfully, and before I knew it, Monday had arrived. Stupid me had organized with Molly to go shopping in the city for a new bag, wallet and phone to replace the ones which were stolen. Don't get me wrong, it could be fun shopping with Molly, just as long as she was the one spending the money. But it could also be a bit stressful. Sometimes I felt like her bag lady, my only purpose in life being someone to hold and carry everything she bought, while I followed her around like a lost puppy. By the time we were heading home, my feet were killing me, my back was aching and I had a serious tension headache brewing behind my eyes. The traffic was busy, but I didn't care. Sitting bumper to bumper with the bus in front of me, I let out a contented sigh. I had survived another shopping day with Molly.

"How's the hunt going for the owner of the ring?" she asked, closing her phone and turning toward me.

"Not great," I admitted. "Riley gave the ring and letters to his brother Jared to see if he could dig anything up, and I lost the only photo I had when my bag was stolen. We did take the ring to Brian Hogan for a valuation, though. Do you remember him,

Molly? Mum used to go in there when we were kids. He still remembered who I was and I haven't been in there since Billy bought me that friendship ring when I was fourteen."

"I remember that ring. It was seriously ugly," scoffed Molly. I laughed.

"Yeah, I know. At the time I thought it was so romantic and beautiful, though."

"Whatever happened to Billy?"

"He broke my heart and moved to Canada with his family about a month after giving me that ring. He was the first in a long list of men who broke my heart, but he was the only one who bought me a ring." I shrugged, tapping my fingers on the steering wheel, getting a little impatient, as I'd been stuck behind a bus for the last ten minutes. "I've still got it, you know." I laughed, indicating and changing lanes, hoping to get around the bus before he stopped at the next bus stop. Looking in my mirror, I noticed about two cars back was a black sedan that looked awfully like the one that had been stalking me. I felt my heart skip a beat.

"It's funny how we hang onto those things, isn't it? I've still got my first piece of jewelry a boy ever bought me as well," said Molly, completely unaware of my erratic heartbeat.

We were in the city, so surely it couldn't be the same black car, I thought. There must be hundreds of them driving around. And how would he have found me? Though, my car was pretty easy to spot. Driving around the bus, I pulled back into the lane and watched my rear vision mirror to see what happened. Sure enough, it followed me, all the time keeping at least one car between us, meaning I couldn't get a look at the driver.

Hmm. I could hear Molly chatting away about one of her ex-boyfriends, but I wasn't exactly listening. My mind was on full alert to see what the black car would do.

A few minutes later, he'd done nothing. He was still there. *Okay, stop being so ridiculous, Lizzie.* How the hell would the driver of that black sedan have followed me? Molly and I had been in loads of shops today, there was no way we'd been followed. Even I had trouble following Molly around and I was right next to her.

Taking the next left turn, I checked my mirror just in case. Two seconds later, I noticed the black sedan make the turn. There were no other cars between us now, but it was still too far behind me to see the driver. So I slowed up a bit to allow him to get closer. But he kept the same distance back.

Now that alone made the alarm bells in my head start to clang. Everyone, and I mean everyone, in the city was always in a hurry to get somewhere. There was no such thing as a slow driver.

Taking a deep breath, I thought, okay, let's see if it is him. I'd been living and working here for the last ten years and I knew these streets pretty well, so at the last minute, I pulled into a small one-way street on the right. Just as I was turning, I looked in my mirror and saw the black car pull across two lanes of traffic, cutting off anybody in his path. Okay, it was him. Damn. What the hell was I supposed to do now?

Molly was still chattering about some ex-boyfriend, but I had absolutely no idea who she was talking about. First of all, my mind was solely on the black car following me and second, Molly had that many ex-boyfriends I couldn't keep up.

Reaching the T section at the end of the street, I made a quick decision and turned left, earning me the blast of someone's horn as I cut them off. Once around the corner, I started darting between cars at every chance I got, hoping I would lose the car tailing me. Sure enough, the black car followed.

"What the hell are you doing?" asked Molly, holding on to the door handle on one particularly sharp turn.

"I'm being followed by that black sedan," I replied, my heart racing. "I'm trying to lose him."

"Don't be ridiculous, Lizzie. Why would anybody be following you?" Molly attempted to look over her shoulder, but I was changing lanes and turning corners so quickly it was hard for her to turn around.

"Yeah? Well watch in the side mirror and see what happens when I do *this*." I jerked the wheel to the left and jumped into another bus lane. At the first opportunity, the black car did the same. I took a few more left turns, pretty much driving in one big circle and watched as he stayed behind me the whole way.

Molly had gone quiet. I think she was just hanging on and maybe saying the odd prayer when finally, the driver of the car had enough. Stopping at a red light, the black car pulled up alongside me. I watched as the passenger window rolled down, and I looked in to see that the driver was the same bald man who had been involved in the minor car accident. The same one who I thought was my neighbor. Only this time, hanging on his rear vision mirror, was a very expensive pair of pink Victoria's Secrets panties. The same ones that had gone missing from my house at the time of the break-in.

Feeling the blood drain from my face, I looked back at the man to see him smiling. Reaching over, he unhooked them from the mirror and pulled them toward him, caressing the fabric as he did so. I felt like the world had slowed down and everything was moving in slow motion as I watched him pull the fabric toward him and inhale deeply, all the while keeping the self-satisfied smile plastered to his face. As the light turned green, he dropped them in his lap, blew me a kiss and sped away.

I took a few deep, shuddering breaths and tried to relax my fingers which were now white-knuckled on the wheel. The cars behind me honked their horns for me to move, but my brain wasn't sending the right signals to my feet. In fact, my brain wasn't really doing much. I just sat and stared after the car as he drove away, trying desperately to control my breathing. Molly, who'd been sitting very quietly, reached over and grabbed my hand.

"Lizzie, we have to move. You can't stay in the middle of the road."

Cars were pulling around me and a few people were giving me impolite hand gestures. Finally, my brain started to function once again and I managed to move my little car out of the way. Pulling over to the side of the road, I placed my head on my hands and tried to control the shaking.

"What the hell was that about?" yelled Molly.

I quickly explained the situation with the black sedan and how it had been stalking me for a while. "I don't suppose you got his license plate number?" I asked.

"No. Why didn't you tell me about this before now?" asked Molly, her voice going up a few octaves.

"Because I didn't really believe it. Why would someone break-in to my house and follow me?"

"When did all this start happening?"

"Not long after I moved in."

"Do you think this has something to do with the house, or do you just have an admirer?"

"Well, if he's an admirer he has a strange way of showing it!" I hadn't told her about the panties being mine. That was freaking me out more than anything else. Putting the car back into gear, I started the drive to Molly's house, checking for the black sedan the whole way there.

IT WAS dark by the time I dropped Molly home and drove into my street, and tonight the moon was hiding behind the clouds. It was actually one of those beautiful nights when the nearly full moon backlights the sky behind the dark black clouds so that the edge of the cloud is illuminated and casting an eerie glow. I would have liked to have sat for a while enjoying the effect, but the anxious feeling sitting in the pit of my stomach was totally ruining it for me.

It was darker in my driveway than normal, adding to my anxiety, as the streetlight was out, and as I turned off my headlights and sat looking at my house, I thought how dark and uninviting it looked. Just the idea of leaving the safety of my car didn't hold appeal but I knew I couldn't sit there forever. However, as I was contemplating the walk to my front door, the clouds miraculously parted and lit up the sky, giving me enough light to notice the black sedan pulling into the street behind me. It had no headlights on and was almost silent. If it hadn't been for the unexpected moonlight, I would never have seen it until it was too late.

Shit. What the hell was wrong with me? I'd spent so much energy trying to lose him this afternoon, I had actually forgotten he knew where I lived. Of course he was going to turn up here eventually.

Watching my rear-view mirror, I saw the car door open and the bald-headed man start his walk across the street. Okay, if I was ever going to panic, now was the time. Quickly locking my doors and using two hands to put my key back in the ignition, I started the engine and put the car in reverse. It was as my heart was drumming a beat even Led Zeppelin would be proud of, that I planted my foot on the accelerator and squealed my way out of the drive, nearly running over the rubbish bins sitting at the curb in the process. Bald man realized what was happening and ran back toward his car, but my little Mini was too quick. Rapidly changing through the gears and barely slowing for the corners, I sped away from my house as quickly as humanly possible, not stopping until I was completely sure I'd lost him.

"What am I going to do?" I asked out loud, nearly crying. I'll be honest and tell you that there was that much adrenaline pumping through me, I was barely able to slow down. My mind was racing at a million miles an hour. In the past I'd never had to choose between the fight or flight thing, but I now knew I was excellent at the flight part.

Okay, like Mum always told me, deep breaths, in through your nose and out through your mouth. I practiced this for a few minutes and tried to think clearly. If he'd been following me long enough he knew where my parents lived and would probably go there looking for me. The same with Danny and Molly's, and I didn't want anyone to get hurt in any of this, which left me really unsure of my next move.

Arghh. Where the hell will I go? I am so not good at fear. There should be some sort of Phone App a girl could use when she was being chased by some bald-headed lunatic and didn't know what to do. Taking some more deep breaths, I tried to think this through. I started to run through a list of all my relatives who may be able to put me up for the night.

There was Auntie M and Uncle Frank. Hmm, maybe not. If I turned up there pumped full of adrenaline and telling them stories of being chased, they would make a soap opera out of the story that would evolve. No, not my best option.

What about Aimie, my old roommate? Picking up my phone ready to dial her number, I looked at the date and realized she would be working and probably not even in the country as she was a flight attendant.

Damn. Now what? I know. I'll stay with Scott. I actually don't know why I didn't think of it before. Scott's place would be perfect as bald-headed Sedan Man probably didn't know where Scott lived, and even if he did, Scott lived in a secure building, so he wouldn't be able to break-in anyway.

Good thinking Lizzie. I just had to call Scott and warn him I was on my way. I know, you would think most men would enjoy an unexpected visit from their girlfriend, but not Scott. He hated surprises. Dialing his number, I waited until his message bank kicked in and left a message explaining what was happening. Putting my car back into gear, I pointed it in the direction of the city and continued to call Scott on the drive, but each time it went to message bank. By the time I got to his apartment building, he still wasn't answering, but luckily for me the doorman knew me.

"Hey there, Lizzie. How are you on this fine evening?"

"Okay, thanks Stan. I'll be better once I've had a hot shower and am snuggled up to Scott. How about you?"

Stan was a lovely guy and I felt rude not asking how he was. All the time though, I kept looking around scanning for the black sedan. I was sure I'd lost him about an hour ago, but I was edgy. Maybe Scott would have a Xanax I could pinch.

Looking at Stan, I waited the obligatory few minutes and found out how his wife Beryl's gout was, gave him my sympathies—apparently she was not the easiest to live with when her gout was playing up—and headed to the elevator. Finally, I felt like I could relax. The familiarity of the elevator and the knowledge that this was a secure building gave me a sense of protection. I was looking forward to that shower and comfy bed when the elevator stopped at the top floor and the doors pinged open. Scott kept a spare key hidden under the fire extinguisher. Finding it, I opened the door and let myself in.

The apartment was dark when I entered, so I flipped a few switches and watched as light filled the room. Everything seemed in place as I looked around, dropping my bag on the lounge as I walked past it. Nope, better go back and pick that up. As much as I wanted to relax and throw my bag and shoes wherever they fell, I knew that would get Scott upset when he got home. Picking it up, I slipped my shoes off, placed them neatly at the door and headed toward the bedroom to use the ensuite. Thinking of Scott's ensuite and the spa showerhead almost had me running up the hall.

Hmm, that was strange. There was a light coming from under the door.

My anxiety levels were pretty high tonight and I knew I just needed to relax. He'd probably forgotten to turn it off this morning. Admittedly, that wasn't like him, but I guess we all forget things sometimes. My footsteps slowed as I got closer to the door as I could hear voices coming from the other side. The voices were muffled but I could definitely hear a female giggling.

Stopping, I took a moment to process what I was hearing. It must be the anxiety, I thought, making me hear things. He'd probably left the television on as well. Slowly forcing my feet to move, I strained to listen for any other sounds that would indicate if it was the television and not what I was thinking. I felt sick standing outside the bedroom door, debating whether I wanted to open it or turn and run.

Putting my ear to the wood, I held my breath and listened. Yeah, my heartbeat was pretty loud, making all other sounds almost distant, but I definitely heard Scott's laugh.

He was in there. But did I want to open this door and see who he was with? Yes. I had to know.

Reaching out for the door handle, I felt it cool against my burning skin as I pushed the lever down and opened the door. I instantly regretted it. There was Scott, buck-naked, standing over Belinda—I'm sure you can fill in the blanks as to what they were actually doing.

It's strange how fast emotions can change in you. Ten minutes ago, I was anxious and running from a crazy man. Five minutes ago, I was feeling safe and secure, and now–I was just sick.

Everything moved in front of me in slow motion. I watched as Scott turned to look at me. I held my breath as Belinda screamed. The world stopped turning for a few seconds as I fought the urge to vomit right here on his bedroom carpet. Scott moved quickly picking up the nearest cover he could find, Belinda used her hands to cover herself, and I turned and ran to the bathroom, locked myself in and gave in to the urge to throw up.

I knew things hadn't been great between us lately, but I had no idea he was having an affair. Especially with Belinda. How could he? I knew I had the hots for Riley, but I would never act on it while Scott and I were still together. I would have the decency to end it properly.

Of course it all made sense now. The cancelled dates, how we'd only slept together once, the late nights he always had at work. With Belinda there to help him.

The prick. The bastard. The coward. I washed my face with cold water and towel-dried it as I looked in the mirror above the sink.

Was I that unattractive he had to have a woman almost twice my age?

Finally getting control over my stomach, I opened the door and prepared myself for a confrontation with Scott. But he'd made himself scarce. Belinda had been sent to do damage control.

"Lizzie, I need to explain. We love each other very much, but he didn't want to hurt you."

Just looking at her made me sick all over again. "How long, Belinda?" I asked, using all the bravery I had. I did *not* want to start crying in front of her. I would *not* show her how hurt I was.

"Six months," she whispered.

It felt like someone had hit me with a baseball bat. "Wow. Jokes on me then, I guess."

I turned and almost ran out of the apartment. Belinda didn't even try to stop me. It was only when I reached my car that I allowed myself to cry. I don't really think I was crying for the end of the relationship, I pretty much knew that was over. But I felt humiliated and betrayed by a man I thought cared about me. Instead, all the time in the last six months we'd been together, he'd actually been with her as well. Probably comparing notes. And she'd known about it.

I started to think about all the conversations I'd had with Belinda over the last few years. The times I had asked for her advice on what to get him for his birthday. The time I'd shown her the sexy nightie I'd bought, and the time she'd helped me plan a surprise weekend away with him. Then, she too betrayed me. I thought she was a friend—admittedly not a close friend, but still a friend. What kind of people were they?

Driving blindly, crying and scared, I found myself back home before I'd really thought it through. To be honest, at this point, I didn't care if some crazy man wanted to hurt me. In fact, let him try.

Stopping in the street, I scanned for the familiar black sedan. When I didn't see it, I figured he'd probably given up for the night. Making a run for the door, I ran inside, locked and bolted it, picked up my deadly can of hairspray and went from room to room checking all window locks, cupboards and hidey-holes.

When I was confident no-one was there, I picked up Cat—I had long since given up trying to use his real name—locked myself in my bedroom, placed a kitchen chair under the door handle as added security and prepared myself for a restless night.

CHAPTER 20

*A*s usual, Riley arrived bright and early the next morning, ready to do some work. I hadn't slept much and was feeling particularly tired and cranky before he arrived, but seeing him smile at me totally changed my mood for the better.

At about three-thirty this morning, I'd decided I should call the police first thing and tell them what was happening. I wasn't sure if they could do much, but at least if they found my cold, dead body one day, they'd have some idea of where to start looking for my killer.

Riley walked in as I was on the phone and I saw the look of shock on his face that I was actually up this early.

"Thank you, Officer. I'll see you soon," I said, hanging up the phone. Riley looked at me, eyebrows arched.

"I think it's time I let the police know what's going on," I said. I'd also decided to keep the details concerning Scott to myself for now. It was still too raw. "I'm not sure what they can do, but I don't feel comfortable here anymore." I shrugged my shoulders and gave Riley a small smile. "I'm going for a quick shower before they arrive."

After running back upstairs, putting on my bikini and grabbing all the necessary items, I walked back out to the deck for my shower. Luckily, it was warmer this morning. The clouds from last night had gone and left us with what promised to be a beautiful day. It's a shame my mood didn't match the weather.

Every time I thought of Scott and Belinda, I got a lump in my throat and a sick feeling in my stomach. I knew I would have to tell my family soon, but it was embarrassing. How stupid had I been, thinking all this time how lucky I was to have Scott as my boyfriend and that I didn't deserve a man like him?

Pulling off my towel and throwing it onto the chair, I stepped into my shower. Crap, I hated this thing. I will say, that after the shock of what I had witnessed last night had worn off, I was annoyed I'd missed out on using Scott's lovely shower.

Oh well, be grateful for what you've got, Lizzie.

Looking forward to the feeling of hot water running over my aching body, I reached forward for the taps and found a very expensive pair of pink Victoria's Secrets panties. Just hanging there.

My hand froze and with the familiar surge of adrenaline, my eyes started darting around the yard. Could he be here watching? There was no black sedan in the street when I looked about ten minutes ago. I'd been checking about every half hour or so, and so far there'd been no sign of him. I suppose he could have parked in the next street over and walked here. Maybe he'd visited through the night. I'd managed to doze off for a few minutes here and there and it's possible I hadn't heard him even if I'd been awake.

"Riley! Would you mind coming out here?" I called. Riley must have been in the kitchen because his head appeared out the door.

"What's up?"

What should I say? *Hey look what turned up* and show him the knickers? Just then the doorbell rang.

Ducking his head back inside, he yelled out to me, "The police have arrived. I'll go and let them in."

Okay, a quick shower it was going to be. Surely if Sedan Man was watching, he would leave with the police here. When I'd finished, I put the panties in the back pocket of my jeans and walked into the house. Riley sat at the table with two uniformed police officers, all drinking cups of coffee. Jumping up and pouring another cup, Riley handed it to me and introduced me.

"Lizzie, this is Officer Lucy Wilkins and Officer Ed Helms."

Officer Lucy Wilkins was not what I expected in a female police officer. She was petite, with shiny blonde hair pulled back into a bun and had a girl-next-door look about her. Her partner, Officer Helms, was completely opposite at about six-foot tall, gorgeous dark skin and was muscle from head to glorious toe.

"Pleased to meet you," I said, shaking their hands in turn, my palms going a little sweaty when I touched Officer Helms's.

"Lizzie, you wanted to talk to us about the break-in you had here a few weeks ago," said Officer Wilkins, who was obviously trying to take charge and almost seemed to be doing the peacock thing, fluffing out her beautiful feathers. I'm not sure if this was for Riley's benefit or her sidekick's. Either way, there were an awful lot of pheromones floating around this room right now.

"Yes, a few things have happened since then. I didn't really think they were related until last night."

They listened intently as I recalled the events that had happened since I'd spoken to them last—leaving out the part where I visited Scott—taking notes where appropriate. I watched Riley's jaw tighten and his eyes go hard when I mentioned the panty incident in the car.

"Are you certain they were yours?" asked Officer Helms.

"I'm pretty sure. I mean, I didn't pick them up and have an inspection but I'm certain he was letting me know they were mine," I replied. "Anyway, when I got in the shower this morning, they were hanging on the tap."

I pulled the panties out of my back pocket and held them out for all to see. The most embarrassing part of all of this was that the knickers hadn't been washed since I'd last worn them.

Officer Wilkins pulled a plastic bag out of her pocket and using her pen, dropped the panties into it. I guess I wasn't getting those back in a hurry. Fine by me, I'd probably burn them now anyway.

After taking a few more details, questioning me about every boyfriend I'd ever had and every man I'd ever had contact with, they promised they would look into it and left, leaving me with a particularly quiet Riley.

"I think I might go for a walk. I need some fresh air to clear my head," I said, walking toward the stairs.

"I'll come with you. We can stop at my place on the way to the river and I'll get changed. In fact, why don't you pack a bag while you're upstairs and you can stay with me until they catch this guy?"

"Riley, that's silly. It could take them forever to catch him. Who knows, maybe he's given up anyway." I shrugged.

"Don't argue with me, Lizzie. Either you come and stay at my place or I'm moving in here. But the good shower is at my place."

Gee, he really knew how to put up a good argument. "Okay fine, I'll go pack."

Yeah, I know I didn't exactly put up a fight about it, but after last night, the thought of staying here another night on my own did *not* appeal to me. Besides, Riley was right. A good shower would win every time.

HALF AN HOUR later we were at Riley's. I'd never been there before and I have to say his house was gorgeous. The garden was basic, backing onto the river, with beautiful green grass and a couple of large old trees that shaded the house. It was an old

Presbyterian Church built in the early eighteen hundreds and looked like it would have only held about a hundred people.

Riley had done a wonderful job converting it, putting in a mezzanine floor over the back half of the room that held his bedroom and small bathroom. Downstairs was a small, open-plan lounge-cum-dining room and a small kitchen. Lots of timber flooring and white walls, but he had kept and restored the old leaded windows in the side walls. These at present were throwing a rainbow of color around the room as the sun shone through them. Interesting that I only counted one bedroom. Where was I going to sleep?

Reading my mind again, Riley looked at me and gave me a wicked smile. "As you are spoken for, I will do the honorable thing and sleep on the couch."

He smiled as he placed Cat on the floor. I couldn't leave Cat behind in case something happened to him. Admittedly, the major threat would probably come from my neighbor, Hazel. Looking at Riley, my heart did this flippy thing it was prone to do around him. I hadn't mentioned my break up with Scott at all to him, and now didn't seem like the appropriate time.

Changing the subject, I said, "Well, are you getting changed for this walk or what?"

"Sure. I'll just be a minute," he said, heading up the stairs.

I had a good look around while I waited for him. The house actually looked like an interior designer had helped with the decorating. The neutral color palette used was very sophisticated, yet masculine. Unlike Scott's apartment though, this house looked and felt like a home. Riley had a dirty cup and bowl in the kitchen sink, obviously left over from this morning's breakfast. There was a pile of dirt bike magazines on the floor next to the couch, DVD's next to the TV, and the whole place looked and smelled like Riley. I'd already fallen in love with it.

"Are you ready?" he asked.

I'd been so engrossed checking out his home, I hadn't heard him walk up behind me. Embarrassment burned my cheeks at being caught. I quickly turned toward him and tripped over Cat. Riley reached out to stop me from falling, but momentum had the better of me and I fell straight in to him, making him lose balance. We crashed to the floor.

I heard him grunt as my body slammed into his. I lay there trying to catch my breath, my full body weight on top of him. Every nerve-ending was on full alert as my body aligned with his. I tingled from head to toe, but mostly in places I shouldn't mention. Let's just say these places hadn't tingled like that in a very long time. If my cheeks were burning with embarrassment before, now they were in full flame. God, I hoped Riley couldn't read my mind. The images I had going through it were pretty X-rated.

Looking at him under me, my face only inches from his nipples, I thought how I could happily stay there for the rest of the day.

I noticed the look on his face and can't actually describe what emotion I saw. He definitely looked like I had taken the wind out of him. I'll remind you that I'm not the skinniest girl on the planet, so that didn't surprise me. I probably should get up and let him catch his breath.

Riley was not a small man and I could feel every hard muscle as I contemplated the best way to get off him. He didn't look like he was about to help me anytime soon, so I started to wriggle my way backward in an attempt to get my feet on the floor.

Riley suddenly put his arms around me and held me very tight, preventing any movement at all. "Please, don't move like that," he almost pleaded, looking me in the eyes.

I noticed the outer ring of his irises had turned a darker blue and the intensity of the color almost winded me as much as the fall. I watched as he took a deep shuddery breath and rolled me over to the floor. Wow, was the only thought I could conjure, as he looked down at me.

I lay there trying to catch my breath as Riley stood and held out his hand. I knew I should apologize for knocking him over, but to be honest, I wasn't sorry at all.

CHAPTER 21

$\mathcal{W}$e spent the rest of the day at Riley's, curled up on the couch watching DVDs.

I had so much work to get done I really should be at home, locked in the office, but somehow sitting here next to Riley seemed like the better option. Go figure. By the time we'd worked our way through every Jason Bourne movie released, night had descended, my eyes were stinging and my yawning was getting more obvious. Reaching for my phone to check the time I realized I had a missed call.

"I didn't even hear that ring," I whined, swiping the screen and pressing the voicemail button.

"Had you turned the volume down?"

As voicemail connected, I quickly checked, noting I had accidentally switched my phone to silent. I sighed.

"Hi Lizzie. This is Brian Hogan, the jeweler. I'm sorry I've missed you, but wanted to let you know that I have some information for you about the ring you brought in. Could you all come in tomorrow morning so we could have a chat about it? Say ten-ish. I look forward to hearing from you."

Ending the recording I turned to Riley, unable to hide my

smile. "Did you hear that? The jeweler has some information for us about the ring."

He nodded. "Hopefully he has some answers, and the mystery can be solved."

"Fingers crossed."

"Did you want to watch another movie?" Riley held up the latest James Bond DVD.

Daniel Craig was pretty tempting, but as I stifled another yawn, I declined. "Do you mind if I go to bed?"

"Sure. I'll grab some clean sheets and change them for you."

"That's okay. I can do that," I said, standing. "Just show me where to get them from."

Riley stood up and walked toward the stairs. I followed him up to his bedroom and waited while he pulled clean sheets out of the closet. Walking over to the bed, he started pulling off sheets. Just looking at his bed had my girl bits tingling again. I started to wonder how many women he'd entertained here, but that thought didn't sit well in my stomach, so I quickly busied myself helping him put the clean sheets on.

We were completely silent throughout this process, and occasionally I looked over to Riley to see if I could figure out what he was thinking. The only light in the room was coming from downstairs and the adjoining bathroom, so I couldn't see enough of his features for his thoughts to be given away. When we'd finished, he finally looked at me and smiled.

"If there's anything else you need, just let me know. Goodnight." He turned his back and walked back down the stairs.

What sort of a statement was that? Was there anything else I need? Well, how about you naked? No, I didn't think he'd respond to that too well, so I decided a cold shower would be the better option.

Riley had thought to leave a clean towel in the bathroom for me, so after stripping off I stepped into his walk-in shower. The whole time I was in there I desperately tried not to think of all the times Riley had stood naked in this very spot.

Turning the cold water up even higher, I stuck my head under the showerhead and closed my eyes. These thoughts were doing me no good what so ever. I really needed to get a grip. I sighed. This was not helping.

Getting out of the shower and away from my fantasies, I put on the least sexy pajama's I owned and got into bed. I must say Riley's bed was pretty inviting, even without him in it. It was much bigger than mine and crawling under the sheets felt like heaven. It was soft and comfortable and even though we'd changed the sheets, I could still smell Riley on the pillow. Lying there, I could hear him moving around downstairs, probably making up the couch to sleep on. He had the television on low and the soundtrack to the late night news drifted up the stairs. I heard him reach over, the lights went out and the TV was zapped off. Darkness and silence descended.

It always fascinates me how all the noises are magnified in the dark. I heard the rustle of his sheets and him fluffing up his pillow. After a few minutes of straining, I could even hear him breathing. I really hoped he didn't snore but I suppose I could forgive him one flaw.

Now it was dark, I didn't feel anywhere near as tired as I had before. Probably the cold shower woke me up. I lay there for what felt like ages thinking about Riley on the couch and started to feel a bit guilty. If it weren't for me, he'd be the one laying in this comfy bed.

Getting up, I walked downstairs and moved toward the couch. I think Riley must have dozed off because I could hear his breathing slow and become more even. A streetlight shone through the stained glass windows and I could see just enough of him to stop me in my tracks. Standing over the couch, I looked down at him lying flat on his back, head to the side and all his features totally relaxed. Wow.

I don't know how long I stood there watching him, but he woke with a start, obviously feeling my presence.

"Are you okay?" he asked.

"Yes thanks," I answered, grateful he couldn't see my glowing face. Sitting on the edge of the couch, I felt Riley move his leg for me and then roll onto his side. "I think we should change spots."

"What do you mean? Aren't you comfortable up there?"

"No, no, it's amazingly comfy. It's just that if it weren't for me, you'd be the one having the comfy sleep. So I think you should take the bed and I'll sleep on the couch. I'm shorter than you anyway so it won't matter to me." Sitting here in the dark with Riley so close had me feeling very fluttery and shaky. I just hoped he couldn't sense what I was feeling.

"I'm not taking the bed." I could feel him smile.

"Please don't argue with me, Riley. You have been so kind to me ever since we met and what have I done for you? Dragged you into some sort of mess I don't even understand, and kicked you out of your bed. No, please, the least I can do is to be the one to sleep on the couch." I could feel tears start to prick the back of my eyelids. What were they about? I don't really know. Maybe my period was due. Yeah, that'd be it.

Riley sat up, probably hearing my wobbly voice and knowing I was about to cry. "Lizzie, come here." He reached over and pulled me in close.

I'm sure he did this as a gesture to soothe me and I have to say it did take my mind off from my troubles. Tucked under his arm, my cheek resting on his naked chest, I could feel his chest hair tickle my nose. I took a deep breath in and could smell a mixture of his aftershave, deodorant and what I can only describe as Riley's smell. Believe me, when I say that any thoughts I'd been having were long forgotten. Lust was rising up in me at speeds that could break records. In fact, between you and me, I think I just had a little orgasm.

"If you remember, I was the one who insisted you stay here.

There was no way I could have slept tonight thinking of you alone in that house. I don't know why this guy is stalking you, whether it's connected to the house or not, but I do not want you alone until this is over." I felt him rest his chin on my head. Not daring to move for fear this would be over all too soon, I sat silently taking some deep shuddery breaths.

"Thank you," was all I could say.

We stayed like this for ages, so long in fact I fell asleep. I mean, it wasn't hard. There I was snuggled into warm, sexy Riley, feeling safe and protected—would you have moved?

When I did wake up, I found myself still lying on him and thankfully hadn't drooled on him in my sleep. Sitting up and looking around, I could see the display on the microwave read five-thirty. No wonder my back was cramped. I'd slept most of the night half sitting up and half lying on Riley.

Wow. That was so worth a sore back.

Hoping I could sneak off for a shower, I slowly tried to stand without disturbing him. Looking down at him, enjoying the view, my heart did its little trippy thing. Overnight whiskers had appeared on his face giving him an extremely sexy five o'clock shadow, his hair was messed just enough to be sexy and the blankets had dropped from his waist just enough that I could get a slight view of the top of his boxers. I enjoyed how the hair on his chest and abdomen trailed their way toward the unknown.

Riley stirred under my gaze, so I took a deep shuddery breath and quickly ran for the stairs. I think you understand by now I am not that sexy first thing in the morning and unless I wanted to scare the hell out of him, I felt I should jump in the shower and at least tame the hair.

By the time I got out, Riley was sitting on the bed waiting. Standing and pushing past me, he smiled and shut the door. It was only when I heard the toilet flush I remembered this was the only toilet in the house. Poor guy must have been busting.

WE DECIDED to go out for breakfast to try to fill in time before our appointment at the jeweler, so we found a nice café about two blocks from the shopping center and sat down to enjoy our bacon and egg burgers. Well, I enjoyed my bacon and egg burger, Riley enjoyed his bowl of muesli. That's probably why he was so fit-looking and I needed to lose some weight.

Sitting in a companionable silence, we watched as a few fire engines drove past, lights flashing, followed by a couple of police cars, all heading in the direction of the shopping center. Wondering what was going on, we paid for our meal and decided walking was the best option. It wasn't that far and we still had a good three quarters of an hour to kill. A couple of minutes into our walk, we saw the smoke rising high into the sky.

"That doesn't look good for someone," said Riley.

"No, I hope no-one's hurt." Just as I said this, an ambulance flew past, siren blaring.

Picking up our pace we arrived at the shopping center to see the car park empty of shoppers and filled with reporters, fire engines, police cars and ambulances, all with their lights flashing. The police had taped off the entrance to the shops and were ushering people out of a door further down the building. We stood watching as smoke billowed out of the open doors, all the while hearing people scream and shout as they pushed to be the first out.

The loud screeching of smoke detectors was blaring through the air, mixing with these panicked screams, and emergency radios squawking out instructions. A couple of ambulance officers were attending to a few elderly and even though this looked like chaos from my point of view, the police and firemen seemed to be calm and in control. It didn't look like we were going to make our appointment with Brian Hogan.

Standing back and watching for the next few minutes, I

noticed Officer Lucy Wilkins standing near one of the police cars filling out paperwork. She noticed me and gave me a small wave of acknowledgment.

I felt Riley walk up behind me as a wave of sadness hit me for the destruction from the fire and the lives it would touch. Not being able to do anything to help, we decided to leave. Watching a disaster unfold just wasn't the right thing to do.

On the drive back to Riley's, my thoughts strayed from the fire and onto all the work I had to get done if I wanted to be paid this week.

"You know Riley, I need to go home and get some work done. Surely, it'll be safe through the day, won't it?"

Riley looked at me, indecision in his eyes. Finally, he said, "I suppose it will be. How about we go over there and check it out. If the black car is in the street, we'll call the police."

"Sounds like a plan."

The closer we got the more restless I felt, but gave a sigh of relief when we arrived and there was no black car stalking my house today. He probably realized he was watching an empty house and gave up. How long he'd stay away for was yet to be seen.

Riley walked ahead of me as we approached the front door and put out his hand for me to give him the keys. Fine by me, let him go and see if anyone was hiding in there. I followed him in through the front door and let out the breath I'd been holding when all looked normal. Everything was just the way I'd left it. Riley walked upstairs to check everything up there and I headed to the kitchen to put a pot of coffee on.

Hmm, that's strange. I could smell coffee. Walking over to the coffee pot, I reached out and touched the glass jug.

It was hot.

I didn't think I'd left it on yesterday, but maybe I did. I hadn't had much sleep the night before and I wasn't thinking straight. Picking it up to make a fresh pot, I heard Riley walk into the room. Turning to look at him, I noticed he looked a bit paler than usual as he looked at me, his features hard.

"Um, Lizzie, I know this is a personal question, but...umm...has Scott slept over here recently?" Uncertainty played on the edge to his voice.

"That's not a personal question, that's a weird question. The answer to which is no. Why?" I asked, filling the pot with water.

"Okay. Has any man slept over here recently?" I watched as he swallowed down whatever was sitting in his throat.

"Riley, what's this about?"

"Maybe you'd better come and see for yourself." He sighed.

I followed him up the stairs. Reaching my bedroom door, he stopped and motioned for me to enter first.

The first thing I noticed was my bed was unmade. Strange, I knew I'd made it yesterday. I'd been up early and trying to fill in time. Approaching the bed with caution, I pulled back the sheets and looked down...and suddenly understood all the personal questions.

"Is that what I think it is?" I whispered, bile rising in my throat.

"Yes."

Nausea swamped me as I pushed past Riley and ran for the bathroom. Damn, still no toilet. Holding my hand over my mouth and fighting the gagging reflex, I ran for the upstairs toilet, making it just in time. So much for the lovely egg and bacon burger I'd had for breakfast.

I could hear Riley on his phone, probably calling the police and after a few minutes, there was a small knock on the door. I sat on the floor next to the toilet bowl, back to the wall, trying to control the shaking that had taken over my body.

Riley came and sat next to me, pulling me into him for a hug. His hold was tight as he kissed the top of my head, letting out a long sigh. When my shaking finally stopped, the anger rolled in. Standing up, I started to pace the room.

"Why the hell is this happening?" I asked, more to myself than to Riley. He was still sitting on the floor, head in his hands.

"I don't know," he answered quietly.

"I don't know what I've done to encourage this guy. I don't even know who he is!" My breath was fast, my pacing even faster.

Hearing a car pull up out the front, I walked over to the window and looked out to see a police car in my drive.

"The police are here. I'd better let them in."

By the time I reached the bottom of the stairs, Officer Wilkins and Officer Helms stood on the doorstep. Opening the door, I guided them into the kitchen and sat down heavily at my little table. Riley quickly filled them in on what had happened.

"Was there any sign of forced entry?" asked Officer Wilkins. Riley shook his head.

"Not that I could find. I checked every window and door and all were locked, just the way we left it."

"If this is the same person who broke in the first time, could he have taken a spare key you keep lying around?"

"No. After the first break-in, I changed all the locks in the house, so even if he did take a key it wouldn't work now anyway," explained Riley, rubbing his eyes with his palms.

"We'll take the linen in as evidence and start our investigation," said Officer Helms, "but this isn't like TV. We don't have a big forensic lab that will test it and give us an answer in a hurry. Unless we catch this guy, it's not likely we'll find him. I suggest you don't stay here alone until this is over," he said, looking at me.

"She isn't staying here at all. Is it okay for us to take anything Lizzie may need?"

"Yes. You can do whatever you want."

"I think I'll start by burning the bed," I said, nausea swirling in the stomach.

I knew the police were doing their best, but I wanted them to come in and solve this within the hour, just like on NCIS. Officer Wilkins gave me a small smile.

"Lizzie, this is my phone number. If you're worried at all, just call that number and I'll come right over, whether I'm on duty or not. If it's life threatening I'd still advise you to call emergency services first. They can get here faster than I can. Phone me second though."

She reached out and touched my arm. It was only a small gesture, but one I appreciated. Looking into her eyes, I felt like someone really understood how I was feeling.

"Thank you," I said taking the card and holding it like it would be my lifesaver.

After they left I gathered up some more clothes, my laptop and got Riley to help me with some client files. I felt extremely guilty carting it all into Riley's home. It looked and felt like I'd taken over his space.

CHAPTER 22

Things were pretty quiet between us for the rest of the afternoon. I'd tried to get some work done, which was difficult on Riley's kitchen table. The particular file I was working on involved lots of little receipts I had spread in piles everywhere—on the table, on the chairs, on the floor—you get the picture. Riley was doing his best to accommodate me, but by six o'clock I could tell I was getting under his feet.

"I'm ordering Chinese for dinner. What would you like?" he asked.

"That sounds nice. I'll have the lemon chicken please. Oh, and some fried rice with those prawn cracker things. I love them."

"I didn't think anybody loved them," said Riley with a shrug, his face reminding me of a brewing storm.

While we were waiting for dinner to be delivered, I cleared away all my crap and tried to hide it out of sight as much as possible.

"I might have a quick shower now, if that's okay?" I said to Riley. He'd sat down and had the evening news on TV, waiting for some information on the shopping center fire. Looking over his shoulder, he gave me a small smile. "Yeah, whatever. Knock yourself out."

I still was having trouble shaking the events of this morning from my mind, and along with the Scott debacle, I was feeling quite grotty. On the one hand I had a man who I thought cared about me, sleeping with an older woman because I was so unattractive, and on the other hand, I had a complete stranger, breaking into my house and tossing off in my bed. What did that say about me? Maybe if I cleaned myself up a bit and put on my nice jeans and top for dinner, I might feel a bit better about myself.

By the time I emerged from the bathroom, dinner had arrived. I'd spent a bit of time applying make-up and fixing my hair, so I should feel pretty good about myself. But I didn't. Still, not to be one to dwell on unpleasantries, I pushed all thoughts of Scott to the back of my mind where I would deal with it later. There were a few other issues back there that needed to be dealt with as well, but all in good time.

Riley had poured two glasses of wine and handed one to me as I walked into the kitchen. The TV had been turned off and his iPod was playing a mix of current hits and some oldies. Sitting down to eat, Riley's mood improved greatly as we chatted for hours about our childhood memories, about our families and about what we hoped to do in the future. Sitting here with Riley, it was easy to forget all the crap that had been happening lately. Billy Joel's *This Night* started playing, Riley stood up and held out his hand to me.

"Could I have the pleasure of this dance?" he asked, laughter playing on his voice.

We'd finished the bottle of wine and my senses were not what they should be. "I'm not a very good dancer," I said, the room spinning slightly as I stood.

"That's okay. I am, according to Gran, so I can lead you," he said, laughing.

He had a wonderful laugh, and a wonderful smile, oh and wonderful eyes, oh and a wonderful body. Actually, thinking about it I couldn't really pick a fault. Sighing, I allowed him to pull me in so close I could feel his heart beating through his shirt. I felt the warmth of his hand on my waist and the heat seeped right into my skin. His other hand took mine as he started to lead me in a slow waltz.

His Gran was right. He was an excellent dancer. The music seemed to fill the room as the world consisted only of Riley and me. I felt like my heart was about to jump out of my chest, it was beating so hard.

What was happening here? Looking up at him, I could see his eyelids had gotten heavier and as we spun around the room, his eyes never left mine. As the song reached its climax, Riley spun me around and dropped me into a dip, supporting me the whole time so I felt completely safe. His face was so close to mine, if I moved, just slightly, our lips would touch. Riley's gaze dropped to my mouth and my palpitations kicked up a notch. If he was ever going to kiss me, it would be now.

But I never found out. My phone started ringing. Crap. Crap and double crapping crap.

I felt Riley sigh. The moment broken, he pulled me up to standing and turned his face away. God help the person on the other end of the phone. This had better be life threatening.

Pulling my phone out of my bag, I saw the caller was Molly. For a brief moment, panic ran through me. Looking at the time, I saw it was after eleven and Molly never rang me this late. Pressing the answer button, I said, "Molly, what's wrong?"

"Oh my God, Lizzie. Have you seen the late night news?"

"No, why?" What on earth could be on the news that would be so urgent?

"What's wrong with your voice? You sound all husky." I could hear suspicion in her voice.

Clearing my throat, I said, "That better?"

"Hmm. Well, someone died in that fire today and they just named who it was." Her voice was now void of the panic I'd heard when she first spoke. Now she was just curious.

"Really? Who was it?" I asked, not really caring.

I mean, there I was just about to be kissed by Riley, when she phoned to tell me about something on the news? What could be that important? Looking at Riley, I kept thinking about what could have happened. He still had his back to me so I couldn't see his face. Maybe he was regretting ever asking me to stay.

"It was Brian Hogan. The jeweler. Wasn't he the one you took the ring to?"

I felt my blood run cold. "Are you kidding me?" I asked, even though I knew there was no way Molly would joke about a thing like that. "Did they say what happened?" Molly now had my full attention.

"Only that a fire broke out in the jewelry store this morning. They evacuated pretty quickly but he must have been overcome with smoke."

"How come he didn't get out?" I asked. Riley had turned around and had his head close to mine, trying to listen to the conversation. "Hang on, Molly. I'll put you on speaker." Putting the phone on the table, we both leaned in so we could hear properly.

"I don't know. I just thought it was an interesting coincidence, don't you? Where are you anyway?"

I hadn't told my family about my run-in with Sedan Man. The last Molly knew was when he followed me through town the other day.

"Umm…I'm staying with Riley for a few days." There was silence on the other end of the phone. I could just imagine what was going through her mind right about now. I just prayed she censored it before it came out of her mouth.

"O…kay," was all I got back.

I also hadn't told anyone about my break up with Scott either, so I knew what she was thinking.

"It's okay, Molly. Riley is putting me up for a few days, while we sort a few things out with the house." Well this wasn't a total lie. I did need to sort a few things out and it did happen at the house.

"Yep. Whatever you say. Well, I'll let you get back to it then, shall I?"

Hanging up, I looked at Riley. There was nothing to get back too. In fact, whatever there was, it was now filled with awkwardness.

AFTER A NIGHT of tossing and turning and not getting much sleep, I decided at five-thirty in the morning to give up. Getting up, I completed the usual morning routine and emerged from the bathroom to find Riley sound asleep on the bed. Tiptoeing down the stairs, I made a pot of coffee and sat on the couch, waiting for the caffeine to kick in and do its thing. The couch had Riley's sheets on it and they were still warm. Picking up his pillow, I put it to my nose and took a deep breath. It smelled of his aftershave.

"Morning," Riley said from behind me, his voice husky from sleep. I jumped so high I spilled coffee all over his pillow. Damn. How the hell I was going to explain that had me stuffed. I looked around to see him smiling at me, still wearing his boxer shorts and nothing else.

"Morning," I mumbled, jumping up, dropping his pillow and thinking I may be able to clean it later without him noticing.

"Sorry, I didn't mean to startle you. You're up early."

"Yeah, I had trouble sleeping. I kept thinking of Brian Hogan."

Riley looked a bit dark under the eyes this morning and I wondered if he'd had trouble sleeping too.

"Me too. Sorry I fell asleep up there. I was waiting for the bathroom but must have been more tired than I thought." He smiled, walking into the kitchen.

"Why don't you go back to bed and get a few more hours sleep?" I suggested. "You look exhausted."

"No, I'm fine. I'll admit the couch isn't the most comfortable thing I've ever slept on, but I'm okay." I watched as he poured himself a cup of coffee.

"Riley, do you think the fire yesterday was really an accident?"

I didn't want to know the answer to this but it was a question which had been on my mind all night. I didn't need to wait for his answer though, as *no* was written all over his face.

"I don't know what to think," he said with a shrug. "It's a pretty big coincidence if it isn't."

"I think so too. But I just can't figure out how." The caffeine hadn't kicked in yet and my sleep-deprived brain was having a hard time piecing this together. I just wished Brian Hogan had told me the story of the ring in his message, and hoped his death was not connected to our search for its owner.

"Me either. Maybe we should tell the police about our conversation with Brian and leave them to do their job. If there's any connection, surely they'll figure it out."

"Yeah, you're probably right," I said, putting my cup in the sink. "What are your plans for today?" I was amazed at how fast my mind could change gears.

"Well, I really need to get back to your house and finish the tiling. The bath should be ready early next week and I had a call yesterday about a big renovation job I need to quote for," Riley said, not meeting my eyes. "How about you? What are your plans?"

The thought of Riley moving on was another issue I'd pushed into the *To Be Sorted* bin in the back of my mind, all to be dealt with at a later date. It's funny how these things can force their way back out again, just when you least expected it.

"Oh! Well, I guess I need to go into the office and give some of these files back. Where is the job you have to quote?"

"It's in Loganville."

"But that's hours away. You wouldn't be able to drive there every day."

"No. I know. I'm thinking if I get the job, I'll move there for six months and rent this place out for a while."

Any thoughts I'd been having of breakfast had suddenly vanished. My appetite just deserted me.

"It'll be worth quite a bit of money and it'll be great for my business to get such a big job," he continued in way of explaining.

"What about your family? Won't they miss you? And what about Ruby?" I asked, a familiar lump forming in the back of my throat. Riley just shrugged.

"I don't know. I guess I'll just see what happens."

To say I was apprehensive to go back home was an understatement. I was physically dreading what I might find. I was also regretting having too much to drink last night and my headache was a constant reminder of it. On the drive I kept replaying our evening and hoped I hadn't said or done anything to upset Riley. His mood had been odd this morning. It seemed he was avoiding me as much as possible, and when he was around, he wasn't making much eye contact. I know our near kiss may have left him uncomfortable and I wanted to tell him I was sorry, I didn't mean to make him feel that way, but I just didn't know how to start. Pulling up in my driveway, he turned to me.

"I'm sorry about last night, Lizzie. I'd had a few too many drinks and I was really out of line." He stopped and took a deep breath, looking at the roof of the truck as if it would give him the right words to say. "I enjoy your friendship and I don't want to do anything to make you uncomfortable." He shifted in his seat, looking out the side window and avoiding me altogether.

"Yeah, me too," was all I could say, feeling like someone had dumped a bucket of cold water over my head. The whole *I enjoy your friendship* bit really stung. I couldn't help it. I'd fallen for this guy and to hear he valued my friendship sucked. Well, I valued his friendship too, obviously, but I wanted so much more than that. Riley turned and looked at me for a minute then got out of the truck, slamming the door behind him.

Okay, I could understand he was uncomfortable, but angry? What was that about? "Riley!" I called, stumbling out of the truck and running after him. "What's wrong?"

I caught up with him at the front door. Lucky for me it was locked or I don't think I would ever have caught him. I looked up at him and could see the anger simmering in his eyes.

"Nothing!" He took a deep breath and finally looked me in the eye. I counted the seconds, waiting to see what happened next. "Life just sucks, that's all. No matter what they tell you, the jerks always win."

He unlocked the door and slammed it open. Personally, I had no idea what he was talking about, but I decided it was best to stay out of his way for a while.

Thankfully it looked like no one had been for a sleepover while I was away, so finding some rubber gloves from under the kitchen sink, I headed to my bedroom with a large garbage bag to strip what was left on my bed. What sucked was, I really liked this linen and now it was going to have to go. Stripping the bed bare, I kept thinking today wasn't a good one. And it was only going to get worse when I got to the office and had to face Scott and Belinda.

Filling the garbage bag, I took it all down to the skip and threw it in. Looking back at the house, I stood for a while and thought how much my life had changed since I made the decision to buy it. Riley was definitely a positive change, even though he just wanted to be friends. Our friendship was new though and I wondered how it would go after him being away for six months. Probably not great.

―――――――――

By the time I'd driven into the city, my mood was definitely black. It had started to rain, and I'd had to park two blocks from the office and make three trips to get all the damn files inside. Riley had wanted to come with me but I convinced him I would be safe. It was daylight after all and I would be in the office most of the time. His mood hadn't been any better than mine, so I thought a bit of space would do us both good.

Taking the elevator to the third floor, I took a deep breath and prepared myself for what I'd find. All sorts of images flashed through my mind. Like, did everyone in the office know what was happening? Were they all talking and laughing at me behind my back? How many times had Scott and Belinda done it in the office, maybe even on his desk? True, that didn't sound like something Scott would do, but I obviously didn't know him as well as I thought I had.

The closer I moved toward his office, the more I could feel people's eyes on me as I walked past. They knew. That I'm sure of. It seems I was the only person who didn't have a clue. My footsteps slowed the closer I got to his outer office but I knew this was like taking off a Band-Aid. I had to do it quickly.

Belinda was sitting at her desk when I walked in and I know that anger should be high on my list of emotions when I thought of her, but it wasn't. Humiliation and embarrassment was. To be honest, I was almost relieved the relationship was over. I just wish it had been on my terms and I didn't have to face the humiliation of telling all my family and friends I was so stupid and clueless that I didn't know what was happening under my own nose.

Looking at Belinda, sitting up tall, with her blonde hair perfectly smooth, not a frizz in sight—how the hell she managed that on a day like today had me beat—her make-up perfect, I couldn't help but think even though she was the same age as my mother, she didn't look it. Seeing how perfectly she presented herself, I could see why Scott was attracted to her.

"Lizzie. Let me help you," she said, jumping up when she saw me struggling in the door carrying three boxes of files.

"No! I'm fine thank you. I don't need your help. You've done enough for me already, thanks very much."

"Lizzie, please don't be like that. Let's go somewhere and talk." She almost seemed to be pleading with me.

"There's nothing I want to say to you, Belinda," I said, turning away from her.

That was a total lie. I had heaps I wanted to say, none of which was polite, so I thought keeping it to myself was probably the better option. Dumping the boxes on her desk, I was about to walk out of the room when Scott's office door opened and out he walked, completely unaware I was there.

For a couple of seconds the world stood still, none of us knowing what to do. I used the time to have a good look at them both. Looking at Scott through new eyes, I wondered what I'd ever seen in him. True, he wasn't bad looking, and he did look good in a suit, but compared to Riley, he was downright ordinary. Add to that, he'd never treated me that well. Sure when we first started dating, he'd treated me like royalty but after we officially became an item, he never bothered about me much. At one point I thought I loved him though, and that he at least cared about me.

How stupid was I?

Scott was the first to move, turning around, walking back into his office and closing his door. Disgust rolled over my tongue. After nearly three years, I meant so little to him he couldn't even say he was sorry. Turning away, I walked straight to Human Resources and quit my job.

I know, I know—I shouldn't make hasty decisions when I'm emotional and about an hour later I started to panic a bit. But the thought of having to see him again required more strength than I had.

Walking aimlessly through the city, it didn't take long before I realized I was at the shops. They held so much appeal today, I couldn't resist. They contained absolutely everything I needed to be whoever the hell I felt like being. Scott had left me, Riley was leaving me and a bald-headed crazy freak was the only man attracted to me. I looked tired, dull and frizzy. I also felt about ten years older than I really was. Can you see my point?

Yeah, yeah, I know I really should have been saving my money. I was unemployed after all, but right now I didn't like myself very much. At least I didn't like what I saw in the mirror. Maybe a complete transformation was what I needed. I'd worry about money next month. I still had a few savings, which I had originally kept to be spent on my kitchen, but hey, I'd just have to live with the old one until I got a new job. Surely it couldn't be that hard.

BY THE TIME I got home, it was getting dark. Riley's truck was still in my driveway and the downstairs lights were on, so picking up my bags, I walked inside. I think I got carried away with all the shopping I'd done. It was one of those days where everything I tried on looked good. Maybe because it was all quite different to what I would usually buy and I was so open to change. I don't know, but I wasn't looking forward to the credit card bill next month.

Stepping into the kitchen, I looked at Riley sitting at the kitchen table, beer in hand, barely moving a muscle. Seeing me, a mixture of emotions passed over his face. If I had to list them, I would say the first was relief, the second was disbelief looking at my bags, and last was anger. Seeing this last one, I stopped not quite knowing what to do. He seemed to go from calm to angry in less than a second as he looked down at his beer, shakily shredding the label. Slowly putting my bags on the floor, I walked into the room and sat silently at the table.

"Did you bother to think about anybody other than yourself today?" he asked, his voice quiet.

"What?" I asked, confused.

"I've been sitting here for the last three hours, trying to call you to see if you were okay." His voice was now getting louder. "Thinking that asshole had caught up with you and was doing who the *fuck* knows what to you. And you were *shopping!*"

He was full on yelling by now, leaning over the table and looking down on me. From where I was sitting, it was a pretty scary place to be. In all honesty, I hadn't given a single thought to the maniac following me. My whole day was consumed with Riley leaving, Scott cheating and my whole crappy self-esteem.

Pulling my phone out of my bag, I looked to see I had seventeen missed calls from Riley. I'd put my phone on silent when I was in HR filling out all the necessary paperwork it required to resign and had forgotten to switch it back again.

"I had no idea where to even start looking!" he yelled. "I phoned Belinda and she told me you had left hours ago. I asked to speak to Scott but he wasn't in the office. I was just praying you were with him, can you believe that. Because if you were with him, at least you'd be safe!"

He paced around the room, eyes blazing. Actually, he had really amazing eyes when he was angry. The outside rim of them had gone that deep blue again. Not that I was noticing it, of course. I was actually feeling bad for worrying him so much.

"I'm sorry. You're right. I should have called to let you know I was okay. I put my phone on silent and forgot about it."

He stopped pacing and ran his hands through his hair, as frustrated as hell. I hadn't moved a muscle, too afraid of what would happen. The silence seemed to go on forever.

"I lost track of time. Riley, I'm really sorry. I had a crappy day and thought a bit of shopping would take my mind off of things. I didn't mean to worry you," I added quietly.

He turned his back and walked out of the room. I felt my stomach cramp as panic ran through me.

Oh my God. What have I done?

I could see him visibly shaking as he walked past me, so I got up and ran after him, ready to beg forgiveness. I don't normally like upsetting people, but the thought that I had upset Riley almost broke my heart. He was the last person on earth I would want to hurt especially since it was my own self-pity that caused it.

"Riley, please," I begged. "Please, don't be mad at me."

I grabbed his arm, forcing him to stop. Panicking he would leave for good, I walked in front of him and forced him to look at me. It was then I saw the tears welling in his eyes.

Suddenly, I couldn't breathe. I mean, I really couldn't breathe. It felt like something was constricting my chest so tight I couldn't get a breath in or out. What the hell had I done to him?

I gulped, trying to force air into my lungs, but I couldn't get it in. I tried again, but still I was unable to breathe. I could hear the loud wheezing coming out of my chest and let the tears I'd been holding back fall down my cheeks. Squeezing Riley's arm tighter, I put my head down and dropped to my knees, fighting for breath.

Riley pushed my arm off his, turned and walked away.

"I'm sorr—" I wanted him to hear my apology and forgive me, but I couldn't get any oxygen, so how I thought I could talk was beyond me. Right now though, coherent thoughts were not happening. I looked up and saw Riley's back disappearing and felt my heart shatter into a thousand pieces. If only I could turn back the clock, I would do it all completely differently. Please God, if you are listening, don't let Riley leave me. Please, *please*.

Thankfully, God was listening. Riley quickly returned with a kitchen chair and with very little effort, lifted me into it.

"Put your head between your knees, Lizzie."

What? What did he tell me to do? I could hear his voice, shaky with emotion, but I was still gasping for air and couldn't understand what he was saying. The next thing I knew, Riley had pushed my head down between my knees and was holding it there, one hand pushing me down between my shoulder blades.

Slowly, I could feel the air return to my lungs and when I had calmed down enough and my breathing had started to even out, I sat back in the chair and cried. Riley sunk onto the floor next to me. Looking over at him, his head hanging low, I suddenly forgot about breathing at all. Sinking to the floor, I grabbed onto his arm as if my life depended on it.

"Riley, please believe me. I'm sorry. Please don't leave," I begged. Looking back at me, all anger now gone, he just seemed tired.

"It's okay, Lizzie. I'm not going anywhere."

CHAPTER 23

*R*iley had decided this week we would have Friday night get-together at his house. It didn't feel odd at all that Riley had seamlessly slid into our group, everyone feeling like he belonged there. So after spending the morning finishing off some client files, I decided the least I could do for staying here was to clean his house for him.

I found the vacuum and mop, and set about my cleaning chores. Riley's dad had called and he'd left me alone to go and help him on a construction job for the afternoon. He hadn't mentioned anything else about the quote he'd done for the job in Loganville, and I for one, hadn't brought it up. We were also silent on the subject of my meltdown, which I was thankful for. Looking back on it, it was pretty embarrassing.

I was in the bathroom, scrubbing the shower when I thought I heard a noise outside. I wondered if it was Cat getting into mischief, so putting down my cloth, I wandered out to investigate. Cat had adapted quite well to his new quarters and was behaving himself very nicely, which was a relief. When he first got here, I had visions of him tearing up Riley's furniture with his claws, trying to fight boredom. Right now, he was sound asleep on the bed, so I figured I must be imagining the noises.

Walking back into the bathroom, I resumed my cleaning when I heard it again. Looking at the clock, I saw it was five-thirty. Riley would probably be home soon. It may even be him outside. I put my cloth down and moved to the stairs. As I did, a shadow passed the colored window on the side of the house. If it *was* Riley, it was strange I hadn't heard his truck pull up, but who knows, I was in the shower with the door shut.

I moved down the stairs and checked the lock on the front door. I hadn't seen Sedan Man for a few days now, but the thought of him still creeped me out. I'd just stepped toward the back door, ready to check it, when I saw the doorknob slowly turn.

"Riley, is that you?" I called.

No answer.

From where I stood, I could see the deadlock was firmly in position. Riley had this really weird deadlock system on both his doors, so I waited to hear him inserting his key. No key.

As I stepped back into the shadow under the stairs, I heard someone walk around to the front of the house, and watched as the same thing happened on the front door. I searched my pockets for my phone and I realized I'd left it upstairs. Damn.

Creeping back up to get it, I waited and watched. Whoever it was went window by window, checking if they would open. My heart moved into my throat as Cat woke up, the hair on his back raised.

I grabbed my bag, my hands shaking, and pulled out everything but what I was looking for. I found a notebook, receipts, my credit card I'd thrown back into my bag in a hurry, tampons, I even found a half-eaten chocolate bar, but no phone. Damn. Where the hell had I left it?

With my eyes keeping watch on the windows and doors, I strained to hear what was going on out there, all the while racking my brain to think where Riley's cordless phone would be. I know in my house it's never where it's supposed to be and I usually have to call it to find it.

I remembered seeing Riley with it last night in the kitchen, so I hoped against hope it was still there. I crept back down the stairs, trying my hardest to be silent. I would never have made a secret agent. I'm clumsy on a good day.

Yes. There it was, sitting on the bench, like a lifeline. With shaking hands, I dialed the numbers that would connect me to Riley.

Holding my breath, I listened to it ring.

Come on, come on, pick up. Finally.

"Hello, Lizzie?"

I let out the breath I was holding.

"Riley. Where are you?" I whispered. I was hoping he was going to say the backyard and my over-active imagination was just at play.

"I'm still at Dad's. Is everything okay?"

Shit. It wasn't him creeping around then. I suddenly became really unsure of what to tell him. I didn't want to freak him out again and worry him.

"Yes, yes. All's good." I was going to have to get brave and sort this out on my own. "Just making sure you'd be back in time for tonight."

"Yeah. I'll be leaving shortly. I'll stop at the bottle shop and pick up a few things and then I'll be there."

"No! Why don't you come straight home? I can get Danny to pick up whatever you need. I'm sure you've had a hard day and just want to get home to put your feet up."

I'd started to babble. That's what happens when I'm nervous. After assuring me he would come straight home, I hung up the phone and contemplated my next move. I needed a weapon. I was *not* going to sit here and be scared any longer. Time to be proactive.

In the kitchen, I looked through the drawers and picked up a carving knife. It looked scary enough and would definitely cause some damage. When I was a kid, I did a little Jujitsu and I remembered my Sensei telling us to never pick a weapon we weren't prepared to defend ourselves against. Could I defend myself against a carving knife? I didn't think so. In fact, the thought of being faced with a knife terrified me.

Looking further, I found lots of things that would be totally useless but finally came up with the bug spray. A good squirt to the eyes and he'd be crying for weeks. Also, this didn't terrify me anywhere near as much as the knife.

Okay, I was armed. I crept over to the front door, put my ear to it and listened. I had no idea whether or not anyone was still there. I'd been making quite a bit of noise searching for my weapon. After a few minutes, my ears adjusted and I could hear a faint voice.

"Lizzie, Lizzie. I know you're in there," a male voice taunted me. "Let me in. I know you want to." I heard a soft chuckle.

Fear ran through me and my blood pumped at a million miles an hour. I slowly lowered myself to the floor for fear of my knees giving out on me. So much for bravery.

I don't know how long I sat there—straining to hear, listening for the slightest sounds—but it felt like an eternity. I heard a car door and footsteps, and let out a God Almighty scream when someone pounded on the door I leaned against.

"What the hell?" I heard from the other side of the door. "Lizzie, is that you?"

It was Danny. *Thank God.*

Standing up and looking through the peephole, I saw Danny and Andrew looking at each other, alarmed. Unlocking the door and opening it, I let them in.

"Geez, you scared me girl. What the hell was the scream for?" Danny looked annoyed as he walked in. That's how he handles fear. He gets annoyed. Or cries. Whichever. "I nearly wet myself."

"Sorry. I thought I saw a bug," I said, holding up the can of spray, trying my hardest not to let them see my hand shaking.

I had a good look around outside before l closed and relocked the door.

———

AFTER GETTING US ALL A DRINK, I decided to get ready for the evening. As I was drying my hair, I heard Riley knock on the door.

"Hey Lizzie. How long are you going to be? I really need the loo."

I wrapped my towel tightly around myself and opened the door.

"You can have it now if you like. I can get dressed in the bedroom," I said noticing how dirty he was. "I think you should use the shower while you're there." I smiled and stepped through the door, allowing Riley to pass.

"Thanks. I think I'd have to sit outside otherwise."

Waiting until I heard the water start, I thought I'd try some of my new clothes. They were a bit different from what I usually wore so it would be interesting to see everybody's reaction.

I'd been talked into buying a new pair of jeans that sat low on my hips and gave everyone a good view of my new belly button ring. The top I'd chosen didn't fit me as tightly as Molly's fitted her. Instead, it hung just low enough on my chest to give everyone a hint of my assets. These, of course, were boosted with a beautiful new Elle McPherson bra. The top fell loose from beneath my breasts to my waist, with just a peek at my skin underneath.

I felt a little uncomfortable, but hid behind lots of make-up and fluffed up hair. As I walked into the lounge room, everyone stopped what they were doing and stared.

"Do I look that bad?" I asked.

I was about to turn and run back upstairs to get changed when Danny let out a low whistle.

"Right now, I may consider going straight for you," said Andrew, coming over and kissing me on the cheek. "You look absolutely incredible."

I looked to Molly. It was funny, but out of everybody, her approval meant the most.

"Wow," she said, walking toward me and pulling me into a big hug.

Holding tightly, not wanting to let go, I said, "I love you, Molly."

"What's going on?" I heard Riley's voice behind us. Letting go of Molly and turning, I heard Danny say, "Lizzie's been shopping, thank goodness. She now has nice clothes."

I saw Riley look from Danny to me and heard him let out a long sigh. Looking me up and down, sadness in his eyes, he silently walked past me into the kitchen. Not quite the reaction I was looking for, but really, what did I expect?

"Don't think he's impressed, Lizzie," whispered Danny. "He obviously never understood just how awful your old wardrobe was."

Picking up the nearest pillow, I threw it at him and laughed. "My clothes were not that bad."

"Yes. They were."

AFTER DINNER, we sat around talking. I knew I would have to tell everybody about Scott, and now with a few drinks in me, I felt a whole lot stronger. Molly, bless her, gave me the perfect segue into it by asking me how Scott was and had I seen him much lately.

"Um...Scott and I actually broke up." Silence filled the room. Nobody moved.

Then all at once everybody started talking.

"How?"

"When?"

"What happened?"

The only person not saying anything was Riley.

"This is reason to celebrate. Break out the champers," yelled Danny.

"What happened?" asked Molly.

Everyone quietened down while I told them the story. I didn't leave anything out, including what happened yesterday and how I quit my job. This was my family and they had to know the truth. The whole, humiliating truth.

When I'd finished, I looked down at myself and said, "If Scott preferred a woman my mother's age over me, what does it say about me?"

"It doesn't say anything about you, but it screams a whole lot about Scott," said Danny, totally disgusted.

I wasn't able to look at Riley to gauge his reaction. Andrew walked over and took my hand.

"I know how you feel. Someone I cared about played up on me once. But you will get over it and you will find someone who values you."

"But that's just it. I'm not upset the relationship is over. It's just that it confirms what Scott always told me. I wasn't good enough for him, and if I wasn't good enough for him—the low-life, cheating, scum-bastard—then who am I good enough for?"

The tears were running now, messing up all the lovely make-up I'd spent ages perfecting. I was starting to think my mum was right. My eyes were too close to my bladder. I had never spent as much time crying as I had in the last few weeks. Andrew pulled me close and held me until the tears subsided. Molly handed me the tissues, after offering one to Danny and taking one herself.

"Let me tell you something, Lizzie," she said, kneeling down in front of me. "You are, and always were, too good for that prick of an asshole. If he said you weren't good enough for him, then he is not only a low-life, cheating, scum-bastard, but he's also a liar. And I, for one, am going to kick him in the balls so hard he will never be able to reproduce any little liars like himself."

I noticed Danny, Riley and Andrew all cross their legs at this last statement. I had to laugh. Trust Molly to put it like that.

"I have to tell Mum yet," I said.

"That one, you're on your own with."

We all laughed. It felt so good to be with my family. I can't imagine my life without them. Finally getting up the courage to look over at Riley, I found him looking down, peeling the label off his beer bottle. I had no idea what he was thinking right now.

CHAPTER 24

*L*ater that night, lying in Riley's bed, lights out, I let the events of the evening play through my mind. I felt a whole lot better now that everyone—well almost everyone—knew about Scott. I felt like a huge weight had been lifted off my shoulders. Once I told Mum and Dad, I could get on with my life and put Scott behind me. Listening closely, I could hear Riley moving around on the couch.

"Riley? Are you awake?" I called out quietly.

"Yep. I'm awake."

"Are you okay? You haven't said much tonight."

"Yeah…I've just got a bit on my mind, that's all."

"I was thinking I'm going to move back home tomorrow. There's not much point to staying here now he knows I'm here."

I heard Riley sit up. "Who knows you're here?"

"Sedan Man. He was here today."

I quickly filled Riley in on my visitor that afternoon and by the time I'd finished, he was sitting beside me on the bed, taking up way too much air space.

"I really appreciate everything you've done for me, but it's time for you to have your life back."

Walking away from Riley would be the hardest thing I've ever had to do, but it was getting too painful to be so close to him all the time.

"I promise you, Lizzie, if you move back to your house then I will be moving in there with you. At least until this is over."

"But that's not fair to you. This is my messy life and I need to learn to sort it out for myself."

"How do you think I would feel if I stayed here and something happened to you? I would never forgive myself."

I have to admit I did sleep a lot better when Riley was around. I felt him shift his weight on the mattress. "Why didn't you tell me about Scott?"

The answer to that was easy. Telling Riley about it was a whole lot harder.

"Riley, you don't have to feel responsible for me," I said, trying my hardest to ignore his last question. "Take tonight for example —you could have been out dating some gorgeous woman, instead you're stuck here with me and my crazy family and all the dramas that come with the package."

"I'm not stuck with you, Lizzie," Riley said, patiently. "And I happen to like your family. Life's never dull with you all around." I could feel him smile in the darkness. Geez, this was torture. I could not only smell him, but I could feel him too. "And you didn't answer my question. Why didn't you tell me about Scott? If I'd known about it, I would have handled things a whole lot differently."

"It's humiliating," I said in a small voice. "I just want to pretend the last two and a half years never happened and hide in a hole for a while."

I couldn't bear it any longer. Thank goodness the lights were out and I didn't have to see the look of pity in Riley's eyes. Slinking down in the bed, I pulled the sheets up over my head and hid. I felt Riley move, obviously unsure of how to handle me. After a while, he took the hint and left me alone to sulk.

SUNDAY NIGHT CAME around way too quickly for my liking. It was time to tell Mum and Dad about Scott. I couldn't put it off any longer. To make matters worse—Lord only knows how—Riley had scored an invite. He'd worked on my house all day and had been playfully teasing me that tomorrow my newly renovated bath and shower would be fitted.

We hadn't spoken anymore about me moving back home, but my mind was made up. With the bathroom in, I no longer had any excuses to stay at his house. I suspected Riley had accepted the job in Loganville and wanted my place finished so he could move on and not have any loose ends. Working at the house all weekend, we'd only spotted the black sedan once, yesterday. Riley went running out to try to grab the driver. He'd quickly driven off as Riley approached and we haven't seen him since.

Walking into Mum's, we found everyone in the lounge and heard Molly squealing.

"Eew. That's disgusting! Andrew has been drinking from that glass," she squirmed. Looking over at Danny, I could see he was drinking out of Andrew's glass.

"So?" asked Danny, looking at her.

Personally, I didn't see the problem with it, but I knew Scott had pretty much the same reaction when I drank from his glass once.

"Why is that so gross? He sticks his tongue in my mouth when he kisses me, so what's different about it?"

Good point. One to which Molly had no response as she picked up her own glass and drank, all the while glaring at Danny.

"If you have a problem with that, lucky you weren't at the party Andrew and I went to the other night. It wasn't just drinks people were sharing," Danny chuckled at Molly's reaction.

I looked over to Dad and could see he'd gone very still, not quite sure what Danny was talking about.

"Everybody went dressed as the opposite sex. I went in my high heels, red G-string and little black dress. Andrew was hysterical. He went dressed as a sexy granny, with the knitted cardigan and long socks under a sexy little dress."

This image made me smile. I could not picture Andrew, who always dressed very conservatively, dressed as a sexy granny. To prove his point, Danny pulled out his mobile phone and started showing us all the photos.

"Ha," laughed Grandma. "That reminds me of a fella when I was younger. Well, maybe I shouldn't call him a fella. It was really a girl. She used to dress as a man all the time so people wouldn't know she and her partner were lesbians. Of course we all knew. Even though, she was a very convincing man. She certainly wasn't the prettiest girl I've ever seen."

Danny passed the phone to Grandma. She took one look at Andrew in the photo and burst out laughing. She laughed so hard her teeth flew out of her mouth, across the room and landed at Molly's feet. In one fast movement, Grandma was out of her chair, raced over to Molly, picked her teeth up and popped them back in her mouth. Looking around the room at us, she smiled as if nothing had happened.

The look on Molly's face was priceless. She was so grossed out that Grandma's teeth came within a millimeter of her, she was almost frozen in place. Danny and I burst out laughing, while Andrew was slightly more composed, managing to discreetly cover his laugh. Riley just had the full-on smile. Mum looked horrified. I'm not sure what horrified her more, Grandma's teeth flying across the lounge room or the fact Grandma put them back in her mouth without washing them.

Riley leaned over and whispered in my ear, "See, I told you it was never boring when your family's around."

AFTER WE'D ALL EATEN, I volunteered to help Mum with the dishes

"So, what did you want to talk to me about that couldn't be said in front of everyone else?"

I hadn't said a word about needing to talk to her. "Can't I help with the dishes without having a reason?"

"Yes, you can. But usually you don't," she said, staring me down.

"Okay!" Taking a deep breath, I continued on. "Scott and I broke up." Holding my breath, I waited for her to respond.

"What did you do?"

Why did everyone always think it was me? "I didn't *do* anything! Scott was playing up and I caught him." The familiar lump sat in the back of my throat again. Looking down at the ground, I saw Mum's big toe start to tap. This was a habit she had when she was getting angry. As kids, it was our cue to run.

"Well, Karma will get him. What goes around comes around." She turned to face the sink and started on the washing up. Molly, who'd been standing in the wings, came over and put her arm around my shoulder.

"Karma sometimes gets a bit of help," she said with a smile.

Oh no. I can only imagine what little plan she'd been concocting. "It's okay. I'm not bothered by it. I just want to move on and forget all about him."

"But what about work? You'll have to see him there," snapped Mum. She was obviously upset about my news.

"Yeah, about that."

Let's just say the conversation that followed was not a pleasant one.

LATER THAT NIGHT, lying in the dark and listening to Riley breathing, I started to think about the party Danny and Andrew went to. The photo of Danny in his red G-string had been the most disturbing. Danny was way too hairy to be a convincing girl. Before long, my brain started on a path that led me to thinking about the gender neutral person I see on my walks, which led me to think about Avis and Will and the photo I'd once owned of the two of them standing on my front porch.

All of a sudden the pieces clicked into place. How Avis's letters had read that they couldn't be together, how people didn't understand them and how Will had said he had changed for Avis. Of course, he'd changed. Will was a girl.

Jumping out of bed, I ran down the stairs and stood in front of Riley. Looking at him in the semi-darkness, lying there asleep, naked from the waist up, I almost forgot what I'd come down for. Oh, yes, that's it. Putting my hand on his shoulder, I gently shook him until he woke up.

"Riley. Riley. Wake up."

"What's wrong?" he asked, sitting up and rubbing his eyes.

"I've figured it out! All this time the answer was right in front of us."

"What are you talking about, Lizzie?"

"Avis and Will. I know why they couldn't be together."

I sat on the lounge next to him, my hand touching his leg in my excitement. Riley leaned around and turned the lamp on. Blinking in the bright light, it took me a minute for my eyes to adjust. Wow, that's an improvement, I can see his muscles a whole lot better now. Gee, I'd really like to trace the hair on his stomach right down to where it disappeared into his pajama pants.

"Why couldn't they be together?"

"Hmm? What?" I asked. Feeling a bit flushed, I looked up at Riley and wondered what the hell he was talking about.

"Avis and Will. Why couldn't they be together? You just woke me up to tell me."

"Oh! That's right." Getting my thoughts back to where they should be, I said, "Will was a woman."

Riley didn't say much to this, he just sat and stared at me, then rubbed his eyes a little more.

"I must be really tired, because I thought you just said Will was a woman."

"I did. Think about it. All the things written in the letters, the fact their families didn't approve of them," I said, ticking off my fingers as I spoke. "And remember that photo I had? That day at the library, when we saw the photo of Avis with that lady, I said to you I thought she looked familiar. I just couldn't figure out why. Well, it's because she was the same person in the photo I had. Only in the one I had…she was dressed as a man."

Riley didn't look as convinced about this as I was. "But why would she dress as a man?"

"Remember what Grandma Mabel was telling us? About the woman who pretended to be a man so the community would think they were just your everyday couple. But how they were really gay? They weren't accepted back then like they are now, so they had to hide. I mean, we are talking about fifty-something years ago, remember."

"So you think Will gave the ring to Avis so they would appear to be an engaged couple and then their families found out and disapproved?"

"Yes…something like that."

"But it still doesn't tell us who Will was." This was true. Feeling slightly deflated, I sat back and tried to think this through.

"I wonder if Brian Hogan knew who he was. He did say he had an interesting story to tell us."

"Well, we'll never know the answer to that."

"Well, it's more than we knew this morning," I said.

"If we're being honest here, we don't know anything for a fact."

I thought about this for a minute. "I think we should go back to the library and take a look at those old photos again. I just wish I hadn't lost the one I had, then we could compare them properly."

"Do you think you'd remember it enough to be able to know if it's the same person?"

"I don't really know. The photo was old and wasn't the clearest photo I've ever seen. Only one way to find out though. Tomorrow, we're going back to the library."

CHAPTER 25

J woke up the next morning ready to drive straight to the library, but Riley reminded me he had to be at the house for the delivery of the bath. I argued I could go alone but as Riley had been a part of this since it started, it was only fair he got to be there, too. So, I sat in my kitchen with a cup of coffee and my thoughts, waiting for the delivery van.

At some point that *To Be Sorted* file in the back of my mind would have to be dealt with, but today I didn't feel like I had the energy for that. I did wonder about Sedan Man though, and how he fitted into my life. I'd gone over it a thousand times and could not come up with any logical reason why he would be following me. I mean, if he was some weirdo stalker, how did I meet him? I'd never been one to frequent bars or nightclubs, so it's not like I acquired an admirer there without realizing. I couldn't ever recall meeting him through work. The only time I could remember seeing him was after I moved in here. But according to Hazel, he'd never been here before I moved in. A memory stirred of the day I purchased the house and the events that led to it.

Closing my eyes, I drifted back to that day and how the agent had told me her boss had wanted the house for himself and was prepared to stop at nothing to get it. People had died, mum told me that the house had bad karma, and I'd had to fight to even bid.

But later she'd been arrested for playing her part in it, and it had all ended when the gavel came down and I was announced the new owner, right? So Sedan Man couldn't be connected.

Getting up, I looked out of the window to check for his car. We hadn't seen him since Saturday, but I wasn't convinced we'd seen the last of him.

Thankfully the street was clear. Even though, if I was him I probably would have changed cars by now. We could pick his black sedan a mile away. Hearing an engine coming down the road, I looked over and saw the delivery van we'd been waiting for driving up the street. Yay. Hopefully the unloading wouldn't take long and we could get on our way.

I was feeling really antsy about seeing the photos again. Last night my theory had seemed sound, but this morning, in the cold hard light of day, I was wondering if I was plain crazy.

Once the van had expertly reversed into my little drive, just narrowly missing the fence posts, Riley ran outside and along with three other men—geez, how heavy was that thing—they unloaded my beautifully restored bath and managed to get it upstairs and into place.

It looked so nice. The old rust stains and watermarks were gone, the inside of the bath now gleamed, shiny and white. The outside of the old cast iron bath was painted a high gloss black. If I hadn't known the truth, I would have thought it was a brand-new bath.

"We've re-enameled the inside of the bath and the outside has been painted with a high-quality marine paint. Look after it and it will outlast you," smiled the deliveryman. Yeah, with creepy Sedan Man following me around, I didn't think outlasting me would be all that hard.

Handing me the invoice, the three men got back in their van

and drove away. Looking at the figure at the bottom of the page, I nearly passed out.

"Shit, no wonder it looks so bloody good. What did they do? Coat it in gold first?" I could have bought three baths for that amount.

Riley, choosing to ignore my last comment, casually walked back upstairs, over to the bath and started fitting the plumbing to it.

"What are you doing?" I asked, following him.

"Making it hold water. At the moment there is a reasonable sized hole where the plug goes. I need to get it fitted and sealed so the bath won't leak."

"Do you have to do that now?"

"Yes. I have to seal it with silicone, which needs to dry. If I do it now, it can dry while we're out."

"How long will it take?" Geez, how long did a girl have to wait?

Seeing my impatience, Riley smiled and got to work. Watching him was quite mesmerizing. He was wearing a black T-shirt and jeans today and as he moved I could see the T-shirt pull tight across his back and see the outline of his muscles. I watched as his jeans rode low on his backside every time he bent forward.

"On second thoughts, there's no need to hurry. Take your time." I smiled and enjoyed the view.

WE FINALLY MADE it to the library after lunch. We'd had another stop on our way there to grab something to eat—I'm starting my diet tomorrow, okay?—so you can imagine how impatient I was. Barely able to wait for him to find a park, I fidgeted in my seat, willing the lady whose park we were waiting for, to hurry up and reverse out.

"Maybe I should tap on her window and ask her if she'd like me to do it for her," I suggested.

"Patience, Lizzie. The library isn't going anywhere."

"Neither are we at this rate."

When we finally made it into the library, we made our way straight to the section upstairs that held the photos. We both remembered where they'd been filed, so it didn't take us long to find them. Well, we found where they should have been. All the photos seemed to be there except for the ones we were looking for.

"Look again in case they've been misfiled," I suggested. I watched as Riley flipped his way through the photos again. Still not there.

"Why don't you have a look and I'll see if I can find someone to help," he suggested, standing up and handing the box of photos to me.

I too flipped through them, but couldn't find any of the photos we were looking for. Within a couple of minutes Riley was back with the pretty lady, who had helped us the first time, in tow. She too flipped through the photos and looked a bit puzzled.

"Well, we didn't realize they were missing. I have to say, these old photos have been popular though. You're not the only ones who have been in to see them."

"Really? Can I ask who else has been to look at them?"

"Well, I don't know their names of course, but the day after you were here, two men came in and asked for them. I only remember because I was working in this section at the time. Of course, I don't know if they were the exact same photos you looked for, but this section of the library hardly ever gets anybody interested in it." She sighed. "I'll have to report them missing." She walked back down the stairs.

Waiting for her to be out of earshot, I leaned forward and whispered, "Riley, do you think it's strange that every time we get somewhere with finding out who Will might be, the evidence keeps going missing? I mean, first my bag gets stolen with the one and only photo I had, then when we may have information from Brian Hogan, he gets killed in a fire, and now the photos are missing too."

"Yeah, I know." Riley sat back in his chair and ran his fingers through his hair. "I've been wondering for a while if the guy in the black car may be connected to this."

"Really?"

"Think about it, Lizzie. You said you'd never seen him before you moved into the house and Hazel said she'd never seen him before you moved into the house. What if he's looking for something? Your house did have a break-in, remember?"

"Yeah, but the house was cleared out before I bought it. Sure, one other bidder at the auction caused a lot of drama wanting to own the house, but I figured he just thought it was a great buy. And the only thing that went missing in the break-in was my underwear."

"Okay. How about this? What if whoever cleared the house didn't find what they were looking for and then you started to do the renovations? If it were me, I'd be wondering if you had found it when you were ripping things apart."

"But the only thing we found was the ring and the letters. Why would anybody be after those so badly? I mean couldn't they have just asked Avis for them when she was alive?"

"Maybe Avis didn't hide them. Maybe her mother did. Avis may never have known where they were."

This was something I'd never thought about. Sitting quietly for a few minutes, I processed what Riley had said.

"Well then, if Sedan Man is looking for the ring and letters, why is he stalking me the way he is? Tossing off in my bed isn't going to make me hand them over."

"I don't know. It's just a theory. We don't know anything for sure."

Just then my phone rang, gaining me a few death stares from other library patrons. Oops. Oh well, shit happens, I thought, quickly reaching into my bag and turning it to silent. Looking at the caller ID, I saw it was Molly. Getting up, I walked outside to answer it.

"Hi, Molly, what's up?"

"Hey, I was wondering if you're still living with Riley or are you back at your house yet?"

Looking back to see if Riley had followed me, I said, "I'm going home today. I just have to get my stuff from Riley's. Why?"

"Could you have Harper for me tonight? I've just got a call about a job in Loganville and I need to stay there overnight. I don't want to leave him alone."

"Yeah, that's okay. I just have to keep him away from Cat, that's all. When are you dropping him over?"

"Well, I was hoping to come over soon because I really need to get on the road."

"Okay, I'm not there at the moment but I'll head home and see you soon."

I went inside to fill Riley in on what was happening. We got back in his truck and headed to my place.

WALKING TO THE FRONT DOOR, we immediately saw the familiar signs someone had been there while we were out. Riley turned to me and handed me his car keys.

"Take these and wait in the car. Lock the doors. If he comes out before me, drive as far away from here as possible and phone the police," he whispered.

Grabbing his arm to stop him heading up the stairs, nausea gripped my stomach. When was this ever going to end?

"Let's just phone the police and wait in the car until they get here."

"No. I don't think he's here anymore, but if he is I don't want to give him the time to get away again. Now please, do as I ask." Riley looked at me, his eyes pleading.

"Nope. I'm sorry, but if you are going up there, so am I. Two against one is far better odds anyway." Determination was rigid on my face.

Riley sighed, turned and headed for the stairs, motioning for me to stay behind him. I was more than happy to follow his instruction. I may be acting brave, but believe me, I was not feeling it.

Reaching the top of the stairs, Riley decided to look in the bedroom first. I could feel his body ready to respond, as he slowly pushed the door open and scanned the room. From where I was standing, it all looked normal, but I felt Riley tense as he entered the room. It was as I followed him, my hand holding onto the back of his shirt, I noticed the photo that had been placed on the bed. I let go of Riley and silently watched as he picked the photo up and examined it.

With a sigh of disgust, he passed it to me and whispered, "I'm going to finish searching the house."

My hands trembled as I took the photo and looked at the close-up image of me sleeping. I can't tell you how creeped out and horrified I was that someone had been that close to me and I never knew. All sorts of horrible thoughts started to run through my mind...like...had he touched me? Surely I would've known if he had. I could feel the anger and resentment build.

I'm the kind of person who doesn't really lose their temper quickly. Usually I have to be pushed and pushed until one day I'm pushed too far. Today, I was getting close to breaking point. I heard Riley walk back into the room.

"He's not here anymore," he said, walking up behind me and placing his hand on the small of my back.

"*Ah!* This is so frustrating!" I yelled, close to tears. "What the hell does he want from me?"

"I think he's just taunting you."

"I want this to be over. I want to know why this is all happening and I want it to stop. I've had enough!"

"Do you have any idea when that may have been taken?" asked Riley, his voice steely as he nodded toward the photo.

"No. It's definitely been taken here though. I only bought these sheets when I moved in."

I watched as Riley pulled out his phone and dialed the police. After a few minutes, he hung up.

"They are on their way," he sighed.

Walking back down the stairs, ready for their arrival, I saw a silhouette at the door and realized Molly had arrived.

CHAPTER 26

"*H*i Liz. Thanks for having Harper for me. I felt so bad leaving him on his own."

"He's no problem. So long as I hide Cat." I walked into the kitchen and put the coffee on. I really needed something much stronger, but it was still too early in the day for alcohol. Although, maybe I could sneak some in my coffee.

"I've got something for you too," said Molly, following me into the kitchen. Harper had gone, nose to the ground, looking for any signs of Cat.

Lifting her large canvas bag on to the table, she pulled out a framed photo about the size of an A3 sheet of paper. It was a beautiful black and white image of my house. The house still looked sad and broken in its state of disrepair, but the light Molly had captured it in, made it look haunting and beautiful.

"Oh, Molly. It's incredible," I cried, walking over and taking the photo from her.

"Yeah, I'm doing a before and after shot. If ever you get it finished, that is. I thought they'd look nice hanging together."

Looking closer at the photo, I could see it was taken from the opposite side of the street, slightly sideways on to the house. It had a full shot of the tree in the front yard, without obstructing the view of the house.

"I had to Photoshop it a bit. Because of the angle I took it on, I got a lot of the cars in the street as well. I took a second photo one day when the street was nearly empty and edited them together."

Wow, Molly had put quite a bit of effort into this. "Hang on a minute. Do you still have the original?"

"Of course I do. I don't delete anything. You just never know when you may need it." Yeah, like now for instance. "Why?"

"Did you happen to notice if a black sedan was in the street on the original photo?"

"No, I didn't notice. But I'll check my laptop when I get to Loganville. What do you want to know for?"

"If it's in the photo, can you see if you can get the license plate number? I'll give it to Riley and see if his brother Jared can track down the owner. Maybe then I can get my life back."

"Is that guy still following you?" Molly still didn't know the extent of what had been happening and I wanted to keep it that way.

"Yeah. The police think he may be the one who broke in here. I'd like to be able to catch him so I can sleep better at night."

"Well, if that's why you've been staying at Riley's, why are you moving back now?"

Good question. I could hear Riley moving around in the bathroom upstairs and knew now was not a good time to get into the whole explanation of how having him so close was torturing me. My hormones couldn't take much more.

"It's complicated," I sighed.

"Are you struggling having him so close?" God…another mind reader.

"Am I that transparent?"

"Yes. You just have to take one look at your face when you look at him, to know how you feel."

Sighing, I handed Molly her coffee and sat at the table. "I just need some space to get control again, that's all."

"If it helps, he has the same look in his eye when he looks at you."

"It doesn't matter," I said, shaking my head. "He's moving away, probably as far from me as possible." The all too familiar lump formed in my throat again.

"Well then, strike while the iron is hot. Don't just sit here feeling sorry for yourself. If you want him, go and get him."

"That's easy for you to say, Molly. You are extremely confident about who you are. And after Scott, I'm not even sure if I would recognize that look from someone else. And if I did recognize it, how do I know it's real?" I could feel the tears prickling the back of my eyes. Looking up, I willed my body to reabsorb them before Molly noticed.

Molly reached over and placed her hand over mine. "You'll know it, Lizzie."

Hearing Riley running down the stairs, I quickly rubbed my eyes with the back of my hand, while Molly looked at me as if to say *well, what are you waiting for?*

"Hey, guess what?" Riley asked without really waiting for an answer. "Jared just phoned to say Shelly had the baby. She had a little girl, Mia Ruby."

His face was glowing with pride and happiness, and Molly and I sat back to bask in his glow. In fact, I'm pretty sure for a moment there I could see moisture around those beautiful eyes. Molly was the first to move, getting up and walking over to Riley, pulling him in for a huge Fuller hug, pushing her ample breast into him as hard as she could. I think she was just doing this to make me jealous and to prove her point. Well, I must admit, it was working.

Humph.

Pulling away and turning to look at me, she gave me a very

calculating little smile. Not to be outdone, I got up, took a deep breath and moved toward Riley.

"Congratulations, Uncle Riley," I said, moving to him with my arms outstretched. All of a sudden, he reached out and pulled me to him, surrounding me with those gorgeously toned arms. Lifting me off the ground, so my nose was snuggled into his neck, he pulled me tighter. Geez, he smelled good. His aftershave mixed with his shampoo and body wash was a complete aphrodisiac as far as I was concerned. Places started to tingle that had absolutely no right to tingle here, in my kitchen, with my sister watching.

On second thoughts, who cares where we are and who's watching. Taking a few deep breaths and inhaling every bit of his scent, I enjoyed the feel of his breath against my ear.

After holding on just a little bit longer than necessary, I let go and stepped back. Feeling slightly dizzy, I held onto the kitchen chair for support, wishing with everything I had he would reach down and kiss me. I'm not sure what was going through his mind, but he looked from me to Molly and then back again, running his hands through his hair as he did so. I'd noticed this was a habit he had when he seemed to be frustrated.

"Hey, I'd like to go and visit them as soon as possible. Jared said the family's allowed to visit this afternoon. Do you think that would be okay?"

"Why are you asking me? Of course it's okay. Go. Enjoy seeing your newest family member for the first time," I said, smiling.

"But I don't want to leave you alone."

"I won't be alone. I'll go over to Mum's for a visit." I could see Riley weigh this up before saying, "Okay. I'll call the police back and see if they can talk to you at your mum's. But please Lizzie, stay away from here until I get back."

"Oh, Riley, would it be okay if I got your house key from you. I just want to get some things before I go to Mum's." I wasn't telling him these things were all my belongings that had made their way to his house over the last week or so. I knew I was going to have a fight on my hands. I will admit my heart was not in the move home, but I also knew I couldn't do this anymore. Having Riley sleeping only meters away from me, with absolutely no walls or doors or locks to prevent me from getting to him, and knowing I couldn't touch him, was just way too hard. Distance is what I needed.

"Why don't you follow me over there now? I want to get changed before I head off anyway."

So that's what we did. Molly left, I locked Harper inside with a bone Molly had kindly supplied, and I followed Riley back to his house. Waiting while he had a shower and left, promising I would lock the door behind me, I packed my clothes, laptop and Cat in the car and dropped them all off at the house. Harper was still in the kitchen eating his bone, so I felt pretty confident the house had not been violated while I was away. Sneaking Cat upstairs, I locked him in the bedroom, along with all the rest of my crap and then headed over to Mum's.

THINGS WERE PRETTY quiet in the Fuller household when I got there, which meant Grandma must either be out or having an afternoon nap. Finding Mum in front of the television, watching Judge Judy while she knitted, I felt a feeling of safety envelope me. It was like when you were a kid and the school bully had chased you all the way home, and as soon as you opened the front door and smelled the dinner Mum was preparing, you knew nothing could hurt you anymore. That was exactly how I felt now. Sitting on the couch, I looked over to see Mum smiling at me.

"It's very quiet here, Mum. Where's Grandma?"

"I know. Isn't it lovely? She's gone out to the seniors club.

They're having another get-together today, so I dropped her down at the Global Church, down the road."

"At least it keeps her active and out of your hair for a while."

"Yes. I can watch Judge Judy without her constant interruptions. She even boos them, and shouts at them, raising her fist in the air. If you can believe that," said Mum, a frown forming between her eyebrows. She obviously disapproved of Grandma's right to heckle.

"Something smells good. What are you cooking?"

"It's a new recipe I found while watching *Ready, Steady, Cook*," she said, her frown turning into a smile. "It's a chocolate brownie recipe but it's really different to the one I've been using. As I say, you're never too old to learn something new, so I thought I'd give it a go. What are you doing here, anyway, Love?"

"Oh…not much. Riley's brother's wife had their baby, so he's gone to the city for a look."

"Ooh…how lovely! What did they have?"

"A girl, Mia Ruby." I smiled. I hoped Riley took lots of photos of her because I couldn't wait to see what she looked like. Mum and I were a lot alike in that way. We both loved babies. I'm not too keen on children, however, which seems to be a bit of a problem because from what I gather, they don't stay babies very long.

"Oh, Love. I've just finished this lovely little pink cardigan and bonnet set. I was going to give it to the hospital for the baby ward, but do you think they would like it?" asked Mum, pulling a tiny pink jumper out of her knitting bag. Taking it off her and holding it up, I wondered how a whole person could ever be that small.

"I think they'd love it, Mum." Seriously, I don't know if they would, I had never met Shelly actually, but the thought that Mum was so kind and caring made my heart all warm and fuzzy. Getting up and walking over to her, I gave her a hug.

"Are you alright?" she asked.

"Yes. I'm just a bit tired. I haven't been sleeping very well, lately."

"Well that's probably because you've been sleeping with Riley and not all that concerned about sleep," she scolded.

"First of all, I am not sleeping with Riley. Geez, I wish. I've been staying at his house while my bathroom is getting fixed but he's been sleeping on the couch. Second of all, who told you?" I know I hadn't mentioned it. "Let me guess, Danny, right?"

The blush creeping up Mum's cheeks was a complete give-away. "He may have let it slip, but I wasn't supposed to let you know he told me."

"Secrets don't last very long in this family," I huffed. "Anyway, what have you got against Riley? You were always telling me to get naughty with Scott."

"Yes, I know and look where that led," she said, a look of regret dancing in her eyes.

Sighing, I said, "It's not your fault, Mum. None of us knew what an ass he was."

"That's not true. Danny kept telling me he wasn't a nice person, but I thought if you married him, you would be looked after. You were always the one who needed to be looked after, Lizzie. Molly was the strong one who looked out for you when you were little, but now you live alone, I've been worried about you."

"There's nothing to worry about, Mum, I can look after myself."

"But that's such an old house and you're all alone in it. What if there is some maniac out there looking for a beautiful young lady like you?"

If only she knew. "No one is going to hurt me, so relax. I'm okay."

Yeah, great speech, Lizzie. If only I felt half as confident about that as I sounded.

Hearing the phone ring, Mum put her knitting down and

went to answer it. I heard a few oohs and ahhs, and the familiar click of Mum hanging up the phone, and then she walked back into the room.

"Grandma needs to be picked up early. Apparently she's up to no good and the Minister has asked her to leave." I heard the heaviest sigh I had ever heard, escape her. "Would you mind getting her for me? I just can't leave my brownies in the oven and you probably won't know when to take it out."

"Sure, Mum. No problem," I replied, forgetting all about my visit from the police.

CHAPTER 27

$\mathcal{I}$t was a quick drive to the Global Ministry from Mum's. It took me about five minutes and I was there.

Driving in, I was amazed how big this place was. The car park alone was the size of a football field. The front of the building was almost triangular in shape, a cross standing proud on the top, overseeing everybody who walked through the doors. There were two separate entrances, both with canvas canopies, reminding me of a very expensive 1960's hotel.

The building stood about three stories high at its highest point and was glass from floor to ceiling. Huge palm trees flanked the entranceway with a wide circular drive drawing worshippers toward the doors.

It was immaculate. Not a single blade of grass on the lawn was out of place or a single leaf daring to drop and mar the perfect landscape. This building was so far removed from Riley's, it was hard to comprehend they were both built for the same purpose.

Finding a park, I walked up to one of the entrance doors, pulled on the oversized chrome handle and walked into the air-conditioned hall. Inside lots of double doors opened onto the foyer, allowing hundreds of people to enter or exit, whatever the need may be. Walking down the hall, I saw the nameplate of Pastor David Thornton attached to the last door on my left. The door was open but no-one was inside. I walked back up the hall on the plush carpet and looked around for somebody to help me. Wondering if they might be in the stadium, I quietly walked to one of the doors and slowly opened it.

Wow can be the only word used to describe the inside of the room. It was huge. If I had to guess, I would think it would hold a couple of thousand people, with a raised stage in the center, looking down over the—at present—empty chairs. The largest monitors I've ever seen were suspended over each side of the square stage. There was no way you could miss anything if they had a live video feed running to those during the show.

At present though, the arena was empty. Turning to leave, I walked into a lady so small she made my mum look tall.

"Can I help you?" she asked.

It was hard to pick her age, probably in her sixties. Yet she was dressed to perfection. Her tiny frame was clothed in an expensive Chanel suit, her hair was pulled back in a rather severe bun and she wore Prada glasses, with immaculate make-up. All-in-all, she reeked of money.

"Oh, I'm so sorry," I said, stumbling backward, putting my hand on my heart as if that would stop it racing. "I'm looking for my grandma. Mabel Philips? She was here today with a seniors group and I was asked to come and pick her up early."

For such a small lady, she was really formidable, reminding me of an expensively dressed headmistress. "Of course, follow me, please."

She led me back out of the arena and toward the rear of the building. Reaching David Thornton's office, she held the door open for me to enter and I felt my pulse pick up again. This was almost like being sent to the headmaster's office, and I hadn't even done anything wrong.

"Please take a seat. I'll find somebody who can help you." She left, leaving me alone in the room.

I took the seat as directed, but soon found myself feeling restless. These chairs were actually bloody uncomfortable. They may look lovely and expensive, but damn they were hard. Oops. Sorry God. I was in a church so I probably shouldn't curse.

Getting up, I took a good look at the room. It was reasonable size, with a large stainless steel and glass desk in front of me. Apart from the latest computer sitting on the corner of it, it was pretty well clear of anything. Behind it was a large, black leather, high-backed chair. I could visualize the good pastor sitting there, passing judgment on all who sat before him.

On the wall behind it, was a huge portrait of a rather superior looking man and woman, with two small children sitting at their feet. The photo looked quite old and I suspected it was David Thornton's grandparents with his father and aunt sitting beneath them. Remembering the documentary I'd seen on TV, the little boy—who looked about ten in this photo—would be Charles and the girl his younger sister, Mina.

Old photos fascinated me. I loved looking at the way people used to dress and the way they posed for photos. There was absolutely nothing natural about any of it. I wanted to take a closer look at it, but the door opened and Pastor Thornton walked in with Grandma Mabel. As he offered a seat to Grandma, I sat down and waited to find out what was going on.

"Hello. I'm David Thornton," he said, extending his hand for me to shake. This was the first time I got a good look at him. Our last meeting in the hospital was a bit blurry and wasn't really a meeting, as such. He wasn't as tall as I remembered, maybe about five foot seven, his dark hair cut to perfection, dressed immaculately in a well-cut suit, minus the jacket which was on a hanger near the door, a dark blue shirt and tie. Taking his hand, I noticed he also got a regular manicure, as his nails were shaped to perfection.

"Hello. I'm Lizzie. Mabel's granddaughter," I said, quickly retracting my hand before he got to have a look at my manicure, or should I say, lack of.

"I'm very pleased to meet you, Lizzie." His voice was just as smooth as I remembered it. "Thank you for coming down here early to collect Mabel. There has been an incident this afternoon and I felt it was best she go home," he said, sitting in the large chair behind the desk. "In fact, it saddens me to say, but I would rather Mabel never return. Her behavior will not be tolerated here at the Global Ministry."

Looking at Grandma, I wondered what the heck she'd done to get thrown out of a church. I mean, didn't they forgive everyone here?

"Well," I hesitated, "What happened?" I looked at Grandma. She'd been quiet up to this point, which was unusual to say the least.

"Without going into too much detail, let's just say she was found in a compromising position with one of the other patrons."

"Grandma, you weren't with Ben Willett again, were you?" I asked turning to her.

"Well, he'd taken a blue tablet this time and I thought what a waste if I didn't make use of it." She actually had the good grace to blush.

At this point, there was a quiet knock on the door and the small headmistress lady poked her head around the door. "Excuse me, David, but Mr. Willett's family is here for him."

"Oh, of course. Would you ladies please excuse me for one moment while I get them settled?" Not waiting for our reply, he got up and followed the small lady from the room.

"Grandma, you are eighty-two and we're in a church!" I said as soon as Pastor Thornton was out of earshot.

"Well, at least if I carked it, you wouldn't have to take me too far."

"You're lucky I'm the one to come and get you and not Mum.

She'd be giving you a good old lecture right now." I couldn't help but smile. You had to love Grandma's spirit.

"Yeah, I know. You'd think she was the mother and not the daughter, wouldn't you?"

After a few minutes of silence, I wondered how long we were going to have to wait. Maybe Grandma and I could sneak out while the good pastor was busy. Trying to decide what to do, I continued my look around the room, but my attention kept going to the photo on the wall behind the desk. Something about it was yelling out to me, but I couldn't figure what it was. Just then, the door opened and David Thornton walked back in.

"I apologize for the interruption," he said, sitting down. "Now, I can assure you, Mabel, Ben Willett has had the same punishment as yourself. He will not be invited back here again either. I know you are both elderly and that the natural urges of youth don't just disappear, but the Bible clearly does not condone sex outside of marriage."

Listening to him lecture Grandma and thankfully not me, my eyes went back to the picture behind him. And that's when I saw it. Sitting on the third finger of the lady's left hand, sat Avis's engagement ring. There was no mistaking it. The ring was far too unique to be any other.

"Is everything alright, Ms. Fuller?" he asked me, concern marring his perfectly smooth face.

"Um, yes!" I said a bit over brightly. "I was just thinking how awful Grandma's behavior is and I'm sure Mum will chastise her suitably." I grabbed Grandma's arm and almost dragged her from her chair. "Come on, Grandma, we're going home to talk to Mum."

Grandma looked at me as if I was crazy, but I didn't care, I just wanted to get out of there as fast as possible. My brain was working way too fast and I just couldn't connect the dots. What was the ring doing on the finger of old lady Thornton? How had it got from her, to Will and then to Avis?

Standing, David Thornton reached over to shake my hand. "Thank you for your understanding, Lizzie. I'm sorry it had come to this," he said, holding my hand a second longer than necessary.

Had he realized what I saw? Panic surged through me now. I wanted to run away and hide until I'd figured this all out. Surprisingly, Grandma managed to keep up with the pace as we almost sprinted to the car. Well, Grandma was actually doing more of a fast shuffle. I had just beeped the doors open, when I felt a hand on my arm, preventing me from moving any further. Spinning around, I expected it to be David Thornton and prepared myself for the worst.

But the man who stood in front of me was definitely not David Thornton. Instead, he was about my height and my age, had what looked like premature baldness creeping in, and was dressed really badly in old jeans and a T-shirt a couple of sizes too big for him. I don't think he'd got the memo involving the dress code around here. But he was completely unnerving in the way he looked at me, never blinking once.

"Can I help you, please?" he asked.

I had no idea who he was or what he was doing. Hardly daring to breathe, I waited to see what his next move would be, adrenaline at the ready, prepared to run or fight. Opening my car door for me, he aided me into my seat and pushed a piece of folded paper into my palm. With a small, almost imperceptive nod of his head, he moved around to Grandma and helped her into the car as well.

"Have a good day, ladies," he said with a small salute as he turned and walked back toward the building. I didn't take the time to look at the paper, I just got in my little car and drove away from there as fast as my wheels would take me.

"What a lovely young man," said Grandma Mabel.

"Really? You don't think he was a bit strange? The way he showed up out of thin air?"

"Did he? I never noticed."

Five minutes later, we were pulling into Mum's driveway when my phone rang. Looking at the caller ID I saw it was Molly.

"Hi, Lizzie, I found that photo and you're in luck. The license plate of the car was just visible. Are you ready?"

"Hang on, let me grab a pen." Looking through my bag I finally found what I was looking for, turned over the note the strange man had given me and prepared myself for the number that would hopefully link all this together and solve this damned mystery. "Okay. Fire away."

Molly read off the number, and after thanking her, I rang Riley. Mum, meanwhile, had run out to the car to help Grandma inside.

Taking Grandma's arm, Mum turned to me. "Can you explain to me why the police were knocking on my door looking for you?" she asked, obviously unsure who she should be the most upset with.

Oops. I'd forgotten about them.

"I'll be there in a minute, Mum," I called out, dialing Riley's number. "I'll explain everything." Would I? I had about two minutes to come up with a good excuse.

When my call finally connected it went to message bank, so I left Riley a message with the license plate number and hung up. Then I went inside to face Mum and see how Grandma would explain this afternoon's antics. Not well, as it turned out.

Mum had Grandma sitting at the kitchen table and she was standing over her and trying to get Grandma to talk. Grandma had obviously thought the best way to deal with this was silence. Looking at me, Mum raised her eyebrows and waited for me to explain.

"Grandma was making out with Ben Willett and the church frowned upon it," I said, shrugging my shoulders and feeling a lot calmer now I was in mum's house.

"What do you mean, *making out*?"

"You know, doing the deed? Hiding the sausage? Doing the nasty?"

"Really, Lizzie! Do you have to be so crude?"

"Well you asked."

"I'm going for a lie down," said Grandma, finally finding her voice and shuffling off in the direction of her bedroom.

"I can't believe she got thrown out of a church!" said Mum after Grandma had disappeared.

"Well, at least she's not a boring old lady like Dad's mum."

"I just wish she could be a normal senior citizen, who sits and crochets doilies...or something equally normal."

I didn't know what to say to this. I mean, I could understand Mum's frustration, but I have to admit that when I'm old, I'd rather be like Grandma Mabel than boring and stagnant like Grandma Carol. Mum obviously preferred the latter, I thought, wondering how the heck she had come from Grandma. They were so different.

Suddenly remembering the piece of paper I'd been given at the church, I ran back out to my car. This also gave me an escape before Mum realized she hadn't interrogated me yet. I collected it off the floor where I had thrown it, turned it over, and read:

PLEASE MEET me at *The Future Care Nursing Facility*
  1024 Meadows Road, Ackwood at four o'clock this afternoon.
  I know someone who can answer all your questions.
  John Smith

MY HEART SKIPPED a beat when I read the name. This was the same person who had visited Avis at Allora Lodge. Switching the ignition on and pulling up my GPS, I typed in the address and waited for it to calculate the journey.

Hmm...forty-five minutes. Looking at my watch I saw it was

already two thirty-five, so I still had enough time to find the place and meet John Smith. I was feeling a bit uneasy about going alone though. After my visit to the church today, I wasn't sure if this could be some sort of trap. Calling Riley again to see if he would make the trip with me, I waited for the call to connect. But once again I got his message bank.

I hung up, and tried to decide what to do. I knew it would be stupid to go alone, but Riley was unavailable, Molly was away, and Mum and Grandma were busy. That left Danny and Andrew.

On the second ring, Andrew answered.

"Hello, Andrew speaking."

"Hi Andrew. It's me, Lizzie."

"Hello, Sweetheart. What are you doing?"

"Well, I was wondering how busy you guys were this afternoon and if you're free for a road trip."

"I'm sorry, but we're completely booked up. We finish at six this evening. We could come with you then. Where are we going, Poppet?"

"Just over to Ackwood to visit someone. I feel a bit weird going alone, that's all."

"Then we'll come with you. Can it wait until then?"

"No, sorry. My appointment is at four. It's okay, though. I'll go on my own. I'm sure I'll be fine."

Damn. I knew this was a really stupid move. But what could I do? I couldn't let this opportunity pass me by. It may just answer all my questions. But what if it was a trap? What if David Thornton figured out I knew it was his family who owned the ring? So what if he did?

Did he have anything to hide? For all I knew, the ring may have been stolen from his family or lost even. It may not even be connected to what's been happening lately. I decided then and there I had to go, and ran back inside to tell Mum I was off.

CHAPTER 28

*I*t turned out my GPS underestimated the traffic. It took well over an hour to get to the nursing facility. Driving up the long, tree-lined drive that led me to the main administration building, I had butterflies the size of birds flying around in my stomach. Surely meeting somebody in a place as populated as this should be safe?

Reaching the building, I locked my car and walked inside. The exterior of the building looked Tudor in style with its white-washed walls and black beams running across the front. The interior was totally opposite to what I expected. It was modern, with wide halls and white-washed timber flooring, white walls and lots of colorful prints, adding much-needed color to the sterile-looking area. Along one wall, ran a reception desk—also white—with two women behind the counter.

I wasn't sure if I was supposed to ask them for John Smith or what, but looking around I figured that was my only option, so I walked toward the counter and waited to be served. Geez, you had to be tall to work around here. The top of the counter came to my shoulders, making me feel like one of the dwarves as the woman on the other side looked down at me.

"Can I help you?"

"Yes, please. I'm looking for John Smith."

"John Smith? Is he a resident here?"

"Well, I don't really know, sorry. I was just asked to meet him here."

I saw the incredulous look pass over her face before she quickly put her public face back on. "I'm very sorry, but I can't help you. The exit is that way," she said, pointing toward the door I had just come in from.

I could kind of understand where she was coming from, but did she have to be so rude about it? Turning around and feeling totally pissed off, I watched as a man stepped out of the shadows. My heart skipped a couple of beats before I realized it was the man from the church.

"Lizzie Fuller." It was said more as a statement than a question.

"Yes?" We totally had this question answer thing the wrong way around.

"I should probably introduce myself. I'm John Buckner, also known as John Smith. Would you walk with me?" he asked, gesturing toward the corridor to my right.

I wasn't really sure about the answer to this. I was thinking I was probably safer in here with Rude Britches over there watching us, but I didn't think I would be any the wiser if we stayed.

"Okay. But you need to tell me why you got me here."

"There's somebody I'd like you to meet."

Following him up the corridor and making several turns into other corridors, all of which looked exactly the same as the last, I was completely lost by the time we stopped and knocked on one of the doors. Waiting a beat, he opened the door and motioned for me to enter first.

I felt the sudden wave of panic hit me. Being here was a bad idea.

"Nobody's going to hurt you, but you do have a lot to gain if you stay," he said.

Looking into his eyes, I tried to get an indication if he was telling me the truth or not, but in the end, this was way too mysterious for me.

"Who's in there and why won't you tell me what's going on?" I demanded.

"Please, if you just go in and let me introduce you, it will all become very clear."

Now I could turn and run and never solve the mystery, or I could grow a set of balls and enter the room. Turning on my heel, I briskly walked into the room before those balls shrank again.

It was a small room, rather like that of a hospital ward. Maybe that's why I had the heebee jeebies. A television was mounted high on the wall, with an ensuite bathroom off to the side and a bed in the center of the room. Lying in that bed was a particularly small, fragile looking lady, who if I had to guess her age, would put her in her late eighties, dressed in a cream-colored nightgown and white fluffy slippers. Hardly a killer in waiting, I thought, feeling much more relaxed now I was actually in the room.

"Nana, I'd like you to meet Lizzie Fuller," said John as he walked toward the lady.

The lady looked over at me, her eyes cloudy with cataracts. I wasn't really sure how much she could see, so I tentatively walked closer to the bed. Reaching out her hand, she waved it around for me to move closer still. Once I was within her reach, she grasped my hand and held it tightly. I don't know why, but I could feel that lump in my throat once again.

"Lizzie, this is my grandmother, Wilhelmina Buckner, nee Thornton. Mina to her family." So this was David Thornton's Aunt. "And Will to all her friends," John continued.

Looking between John and Wilhelmina, I thought I'd misheard. I could feel the cogs in my brain turning as all the pieces of the puzzle finally fell into place. I was too shocked to speak.

When finally I regained control, I asked, "Is this the Will who knew Avis Miller?" I needed to make sure I had this right.

John nodded.

Feeling Wilhelmina's grip tighten, I looked down at her aged hand holding mine as if her life depended on it. "Oh my God, I don't believe it! Can...can...she speak?" I asked, looking back at John.

"Yes, but it is a bit of an effort. She has emphysema and breathing's difficult a lot of the time." He stopped and looked at his Nana, and I could feel his love and compassion for her. "I've been watching and listening at the church and have overheard conversations I don't think I was supposed to overhear. Most of them involved you and your house," he said, finally looking up at me. "You've really had my cousin on the hop since you bought it. He's been so afraid you would find the ring and connect it to our family."

"Are you the one who put Sedan Man onto me?" I asked, suddenly feeling on edge and defensive.

"Who?"

"The big, bald guy who drives the black sedan. He's been following me for weeks."

"No, but I know who you're talking about. I've heard my cousin talking and I know he's afraid. When the house was cleared out, they couldn't find the ring. Then the house had to be auctioned and he wanted to buy it to demolish it, hoping to eradicate all evidence. Avis always told him it would come back to haunt him one day."

"You are talking about David Thornton, aren't you?"

"Yes, the one and only," he snarled.

"So he knew Avis as well?"

"I wouldn't say he knew her, but he visited a couple of times to try to get the ring back. My Uncle Charles had tried many times over the years and, before he died, he told David all about Nana and how important it was the public never knew the real story."

"Why? What's so important about it?"

"Don't you see? I'm sure you've figured out by now Nana was in love with a woman?"

"Yes, and I also found the letters and a photo, so I pretty well understand that side of it."

"Well, if the church congregation found out the great Thornton family had a lesbian in their midst, that wouldn't sit well with them, would it?"

"I think they underestimate people."

Looking back at the lady lying in the bed, her eyes half closed, I wondered how anybody could hide her.

"That's because you aren't a member of the Global Ministry. They consider homosexuality to be a sin and they condemn sinners. Plus…there are a lot of other things that go on that they may start to question as well. My cousin is not a good Christian, Lizzie."

Wilhelmina started to move in an attempt to sit up, and was coughing and struggling for breath. John quickly moved forward, pushing me out of the way and placed the oxygen mask on her mouth and nose. After a few minutes of listening to nothing but the whirring of the motor and Wilhelmina's labored breathing, she removed the mask with shaky hands and tried to speak.

"Move closer. I think she wants to tell you something," said John, putting his hand on my shoulder and encouraging me forward.

Her eyes moved to mine as she held the mask in her wrinkled hand and I saw the tears well up as she gave me a weak smile.

"I gave the ring to Avis when we'd been together a year," she wheezed, her voice weak. "I knew we could never get married, but the ring could be a symbol of our own union." I watched as the tears in her cloudy eyes disappeared and a light took their place as she remembered the love she shared with Avis. "She loved it, she was so happy." She smiled. "That didn't last long though. Her mother walked in and saw it. The look on her face as she looked at Avis was one of pure disgust." Wilhelmina stopped for a coughing fit, but as John tried to put the mask back on her, she shooed him away. "I even changed myself to look like a man and went by the name Will thinking people wouldn't know the truth and then we could be together. But Avis knew and she couldn't live with her mother's hatred." Stopping to inhale some more oxygen from the mask, the sadness returned to her eyes. "But she couldn't abandon her. I know Avis loved me, but she couldn't really accept who she was. I gave up, but I never stopped loving her. I never found that kind of happiness again. I love my son and my grandson of course, but I never loved another person the way I loved her." The memory was obviously painful. I watched tears run down her wrinkled cheeks.

"What do you want me to do with the ring, Ms. Buckner?" I had to know. It was only right she decided what to do with it.

"You have it? Avis kept it?" she wheezed, her eyes suddenly bright.

"Well, I don't have it with me, but it's in a safe place. I can get it to you tomorrow, if that's okay?"

Her cough kicked up a gear as she shook her head. She took my hand and said, "No, no, no. Do not give the ring back to them. It was my mother's and I don't want them to have it. They don't deserve it. My brother spent his whole life hating me and what I stood for, and now so does his son. You take the ring and do whatever you want with it. It's yours now," she said in-between coughs.

"But I don't want it. I feel really strongly that you should have it back."

"Then sell it," she said, putting the mask back on and turning her head slightly away from me, her body language telling me in no uncertain terms this was the end of the discussion.

"How about I sell it and use the money to buy Avis a headstone." Turning back toward me, her smile hidden by the oxygen mask, she squeezed my hand tighter.

Feeling at peace with my decision, I said goodbye and left her to rest as John walked me back to the front reception area.

"Thank you, Lizzie. I think you've made Nana a very happy woman."

"She obviously married then?" I asked, curiosity about her whole story getting the better of me.

"Yes, she already knew my granddad. He was a family friend and her father pretty much arranged the marriage. It was important to them that everything looked proper and correct to the congregation. It's still the same now. I mean, if the truth was told about what happens behind closed doors in that place, people would flee from it in droves." I could hear the hatred in his voice as he spoke. "My granddad treated her well though, right up until he died, and they did have my dad. He passed away a few years ago from cancer, so I'm all she's got now." Hearing buzzers going crazy at the nurses' station, John looked up and said, "Well, I'd better get back to her. I don't like leaving her alone for very long. The doctors have told me she doesn't have much more time and I want to be there for her as much as I can." I could feel his sadness as he looked at me and shook my hand. "Goodbye Lizzie."

WALKING to my car with a heavy feeling in my chest, I knew I should be happy that the mystery was finally solved. I knew who Will was and who had owned the ring. But all I could think about was how their families had kept them apart. I thought of Danny and Andrew, my mum and dad, and of Riley's gran and grandpop.

It didn't matter who you loved...just that you loved. There was no excuse for anybody to stand in the way of it. Avis and

Wilhelmina would never get another chance; it was too late for them now.

I crossed the car park toward my car feeling frustrated by the situation, knowing there was no way I could change anything.

Discrimination is wrong. I believe everyone is entitled to their own opinion. We're all different. What's right for me may not be right for you. I also believe that we should all love, respect and honor one another. Only God can judge, and when Judgment Day arrives, He will. In the meantime, I think the whole world would be a better place if we all respected our right to an opinion and not to force our own beliefs on each other.

I couldn't imagine my family doing that to Danny and Andrew. Even though I knew Dad still wasn't one hundred percent okay with Danny's sexual orientation, he loved him far too much to see him unhappy. So he put his personal opinion aside and accepted him for who he was.

The more I thought about this, the angrier I became. So much so, I was totally unaware of the large, bald-headed figure stepping up as I walked between the cars. My scream was stifled as he put his hand over my mouth and a large, shiny blade to my throat.

CHAPTER 29

The feel of the cold, hard blade against my skin terrified me, so much so I felt paralyzed. My knees buckled under me. I felt the man pull me up and drag me toward the waiting car. Still holding the knife to my throat, he unlocked the car doors with his remote.

"Get in," he demanded.

"No, I don't want to," I squeaked, fear sending my voice into the stratosphere. The blade grazed across my skin and a trickle of warm blood flowed down my neck. I decided that until I had a better plan, I should probably do what he said.

He forced me in through the driver's door. I had to climb over the center console to get to the opposite seat. Wondering if I had a chance to open the door and escape, I checked the lock and saw it firmly in place. No hope there. Baldy was already behind me and starting the car. My heart sank as we pulled out of the car park, leaving any chance of escape behind and panic closing my throat.

I watched hopelessly as we passed my little Mini and drove off into the unknown. I could feel my neck stinging and put my hand to my throat. I looked down and saw it was covered in blood. Nausea and fear rolled through my stomach.

"I'm going to throw up!" I said, looking around desperately, pushing the switch for the window to go down. It wasn't working. He must have them locked.

Alarm registered in his eyes and he waved the knife in my direction again. "Don't you dare," he snarled.

Too bad, I thought, as I turned my head in his direction and threw up the entire contents of my stomach—which I may add was quite a bit after I'd stopped on my way here to have a thick shake, burger and chips.

The car swerved across the road, as he attempted to protect himself from the barrage coming his way. It didn't help though. It was dripping off his arm, sliding down the side of his face and hanging off his earring. I could see his gag reflex kick in and quickly winding down his window, he stuck his head outside and took some deep breaths.

Once he gained control, he turned to me, raised his fist and struck. "*Bitch!*"

My head hit the window hard, everything turned black as I said a quick goodbye to the world.

IT WAS the sound of a dog barking that pulled me from the darkness. I pried my eyes open. My head throbbed and I struggled to remember what had happened. Blinking several times, I begged my eyes to adjust to the light faster than they were. I saw I was on the floor in my kitchen and the dog I could hear was Harper.

I have no idea how long I was unconscious for, but judging by the gloom in the room, I'd say it had been a while. The blinds were closed, adding to the shadowy darkness. I tried to sit up and realized one hand was handcuffed to my refrigerator. No wonder my wrist hurt so much. I raised myself onto my knees to take the pressure off my wrist and tried to figure out what was going on.

"Hello, again," I heard a familiar, smooth voice say.

Struggling to my feet, I hoped my legs weren't quite as jelly-like as they felt. I turned around as far as the handcuffs would allow and came face to face with David Thornton.

"We meet again," he crooned. My voice hadn't caught up with the rest of me yet, so I glared at him instead.

"You're probably wondering what I'm doing here? Well, it turns out it's quite a story. One you can blame Avis Miller completely for," he said, pointing at me.

I'm not sure why, but I felt compelled to defend her, even though we'd never actually met.

"Don't blame other people for your choices," I said, my wobbly voice deciding to join in on the proceedings.

"Oh, I would never do that, Lizzie. I hope you don't mind that I use your Christian name. I do feel we are quite connected now. Don't you?"

"The only part of me that I would like to be connected to you is my fist," I mumbled, trying to shake the grogginess that I was feeling.

He gave a throaty chuckle. "Now, now, please don't be like that. You will soon be standing in front of St Peter, and if you want to spend eternity with our Lord, then you will need to be repentant."

He'd moved closer and was now standing only a few feet away. Shaking my head, I felt the sluggishness start to fade and my desire to fight kick in as I thought of all the bad things he'd done. Surely, God would forgive me one little punch right about now. Bugger it, I'd worry about that when I met St Peter.

It only took me a second, but in that second my fist connected with his jaw nicely. He staggered backward as the shock registered on his face. He'd not been expecting that. Recovering quickly, he rubbed his chin and moved closer. The look in his eyes was so chilling, I saw the real man behind the facade. He was no Christian. His heart was full of hatred.

I watched as he raised his arm and backhanded me across the face. It was such a hard blow that, had my hand not been handcuffed to the fridge, I would have been knocked across the kitchen. Stars flitted in front of my eyes and pain shot up my handcuffed arm but I struggled to clear my head and remain conscious. Feeling my lip, I felt the blood oozing its way toward my chin.

"Don't *ever* raise your hand to me again. Do you understand me?"

His voice was low and menacing, his face forward, inches from mine, but even though he'd told me I was about to meet my Maker, I wasn't as scared as I thought I'd be. Sure, my legs resembled jelly and I could do with a really good cry, but I was prepared to go down fighting. My heart rate was so high I'd probably die from cardiac arrest long before he had the chance to kill me anyway. Getting back onto my feet, I looked up at him and met his gaze.

"What do you want from me?" I demanded.

"All I ever wanted was to get the ring back and protect not just my family, but my congregation."

"What are you protecting them from? The truth? Surely they deserve to know how evil you really are?" This gained me another strike. Thankfully this one wasn't as hard, but if I survived this I was going to look awful.

"My aunt was the sinner, Elizabeth, not me!"

"Really? How do you figure that?" I asked, pulling myself back up and desperately fighting tears. "Your aunt fell in love and you can't choose who that will be with. But you did choose to hurt people and lie to them. Surely that's a bigger sin?"

"I pray for forgiveness for my sins. She did not."

"How did you know I found the ring anyway?" He looked thoughtful, but chose to answer my question.

"Patrick Johns, Ms. Miller's solicitor, is a member of my congregation. I'd asked him to talk to Ms. Miller and find out what happened to it. If this gets out into the community, our church could be destroyed. The whole foundation of who we are as a family and what we represent would be shattered. My whole life is in that church. What would happen to me if it fell apart?" I could see the agitation in his eyes.

"You're an evil person," I said, not really caring anymore. It pretty much looked like today was D-day for me so I may as well go down in a blaze of glory, as they say. "They deserve to know who you really are." Drawing his hand back, he struck me across the face and the stars appeared. My head felt like it was going to explode...again.

"Now I have to go and pray. I need to ask for forgiveness. All because of you," he said, pushing his face close to mine.

"Well I hope God says *no*. You don't deserve it." This gained me an extra strike. I wasn't sure how many more of those I could take. Struggling to get back on my feet, my whole body shaking, I gave into my tears, as bald-head entered the room. He looked like he'd just got out of the shower.

"What are you wearing?" David Thornton demanded, turning to look at him, disdain dripping from every word.

"She vomited on me, I had to find clean clothes."

I noticed he was wearing an old oversized T-shirt of mine I used for sleeping in and a pair of my sweatpants he'd stretched to their absolute max. They stopped short just below his knees. If he hadn't been polishing a very large knife, I may have laughed at how absurd he looked.

Turning back toward me, David Thornton asked, "Where is the ring, Lizzie?"

"I don't have it."

"Do not lie."

"I'm not lying. I gave it to the jeweler."

Okay, maybe that bit was a lie.

Turning to look at Sedan Man, David said, "You said he didn't have it."

"He told me he didn't. He only had a photo."

"How did you even know that I took it to the jeweler?" I asked. I shouldn't have. I should have just kept quiet.

"We've been following you," he replied, a sick look of glee shining back at me.

I gulped down the bile that had risen in my throat.

Anger flashed in David Thornton's eyes.

"So where's the ring, Lizzie?"

"It probably burned in the shop fire," I said, putting my head down, hoping he wouldn't see my lie.

"I checked before I started the fire, Sir. It wasn't there." I could hear the fear in Sedan Man's voice. He needed the pastor to believe him.

"I don't know who to believe, you or the idiot over there!" he yelled, looking at me.

"You know if you'd just asked for the ring in the first place, I would probably have given it to you," I said, wiping my running nose with the back of my free hand.

"You..." he said, thrusting his finger in my face, "...are a liar! Though I have given you fair warning, you are going to hell, Elizabeth Fuller." He turned to Sedan Man. "You know what to do."

He turned his back on me and walked out of the room.

Waiting, we heard the front door close and a car engine turn over before it roared out of my driveway. We sat in silence for what felt like an eternity. Sedan Man stared at me, a sadistic smile plastered all over his ugly face. I noticed how dark his eyes were. I noticed the scar that ran from his lip to chin, and I noticed how crooked his nose was. Finally, he broke the silence.

"Did you like the photo I left you?" he chuckled. I felt the cold chill sweep over my skin as goose-bumps broke out by the millions.

"Did you ever wonder why your bedroom door was always

open in the morning? I'm very good at picking locks, you know. I thought by leaving the door open you would at least know I'd been there. I wanted you to know. This last week has been torture for me, watching you from afar but not being able to get close to you." He silently crossed the room, closing the gap between us.

"I was only supposed to watch your house for a short while, but once I had seen you, I couldn't help but keep coming back. I was hooked." He stopped, looking down at me. "You really are the most beautiful woman I have ever seen." Grabbing a handful of my hair, he curled it around his fingers. "I love your hair," he whispered, pulling me hard against him. "I love its softness, but most of all I love the way it smells." I heard a low, almost primeval growl, low in his throat, as he put his nose to my scalp. "You're probably wondering how I know what it smells like?" He was pulling hard, forcing me to stretch upwards to ease the pain. "I've smelled it while you were asleep," he whispered, his lips touching my ear as he gently rubbed the blade of his knife against my cheek. "You look so peaceful when you sleep, never knowing I was watching you. It's such a shame I have to kill you, because I think I may have fallen in love with you."

His lips were just millimeters away from my cheek as his tongue trailed its way to my mouth. The stench of stale cigarette smoke, made me want to gag, but before I even had a chance to breathe, he forced his mouth over mine and kissed me.

The rough stubble on his jaw scraped my tender skin and he forced my lips apart with his tongue. The taste of fear and cigarettes swirled in the back of my throat as his mouth drowned my screams. I started to make all sorts of promises to God, that if he could please get me out of this, I would be a much better girl and visit him in church more often.

Thankfully, he seemed to be listening.

Sedan Man let go of me, stood back and grinned. "I just can't decide whether I should make love to you before or after I kill you."

Okay, God wasn't listening properly. My stomach dove south and darkness threatened to consume me. This man was certifiably crazy and I couldn't see any way out. At least if he killed me first, I wouldn't have to know what it felt like to be raped. The kiss violated me enough.

"It's okay, Lizzie," he said, reaching out and cradling my face in his hand. "It won't hurt. I would never allow you to feel pain. I'm going to give you lots of sleeping pills and a large glass of vodka, that way you won't feel anything when I push you down the stairs and break your neck." I could hear sympathy and compassion in his voice. He honestly believed he was helping me. "I thought about doing the same for Avis, but decided in the end that pushing her down the stairs just seemed easier. The stupid old woman didn't die though, did she?" He stepped away from me and started to pace the room, agitation building with every step.

"Brian Hogan was different though. I had to make sure he was dead. Couldn't make the same mistake twice." He laughed.

My legs buckled and I wanted to pass out as I slowly sank to the floor. Nausea rolled around my stomach as I thought about Brian Hogan. He'd still be alive today if I hadn't asked him to help identify the owner of the ring. The bravery I felt before had gone and what was left was pure, paralyzing fear. Maybe if I kept him talking, I'd have time to ask for a miracle.

"Why did you kill him?" I asked, impressing myself with how steady my voice sounded, considering I now sat on the floor, my knees hugged to my chest, using all the self-control I could find not to cry.

"I had to. He knew the truth. His father remembered who he made the ring for. I should have killed him as well but I don't enjoy it, you know. I try very hard to be a good person and only ever kill when I have to. I need you to believe that, Lizzie. I really don't want to kill you." He looked at me, almost pleading for me to understand and give him my forgiveness. "I wanted to find that ring so badly," he said, kneeling in front of me, his open palm running across my cheek, his thumb trailing behind in a soft caress. "I looked and looked for it the day I broke in here. I even had a mate steal your bag to try to find it." He paused and took a large breath. "This would have been so much simpler if you'd just left the ring lying around. Do you understand that? We would have had a chance Lizzie," he said, agitation making his voice louder. He sat back on his heels and the knife glinted under the kitchen lights as he started to twist it around in his free hand. I watched as his eyes hardened and anger flashed.

"But no—just when I was happy and trying to work out how we would make this work, you moved in with him," he spat, grabbing my arm and pulling me toward him. "It should have been me you were making love to," he whispered dangerously, squeezing my arm painfully tight. If I had any chance of getting out of this alive, I knew I had to keep him calm. I'd watched a lot of crime television and knew an agitated killer was an unpredictable killer.

"I...I...I don't even know your name," I stammered, trying hard to settle the hysteria raging inside me.

"Joe. My name is Joe," he said, letting go of my arm and moving away from me. "You should tell me, you know."

"Tell you what?" I asked, my voice giving up the pretense and wobbling.

"Tell me how you made love to him. Tell me what he did to you and if you liked it." He sat down on one of my kitchen chairs, placing the knife on the table and waited for an explanation.

I had no idea what to do next. I could tell him the truth, but I don't think he would believe me. I could lie and probably piss him off even more. Weighing up my options, I noticed Harper walk into the room. I'm not sure where he had been hiding up till now, but if I was looking for a hero, he was not it. He took one look at Sedan Man and came running to hide behind me. I felt Joe tense as he picked the knife up and looked at Harper, obviously trying to decide if he was a threat or not.

"It's okay. He won't hurt you!" I said, putting myself between Harper and Joe. "Please, don't hurt him," I begged.

I could count my heartbeats as I sat, barely able to breathe, watching for Joe to put the knife down.

Slowly he did, only briefly taking his eyes off Harper as he got up, walked to the cupboard above the sink and removed a glass. As he walked toward the kitchen table, he lifted his jacket from the back of the chair and pulled a small flask from the pocket. He emptied the contents into the glass and pulled out a small pill bottle. Lifting the glass to his lips, he took a swig and stood watching me.

What I saw was the sick look of pleasure sit happily in his eyes.

"ow, I'm going to undo your handcuffs. I've imagined our love making many times and I want our first time to be magical. It will be more exquisite if you can use both of your hands." He reached back into the jacket pocket and pulled out a small key. As he walked toward me, I felt a tingle of hope. If I was released from the refrigerator at least I had a chance to get away from him.

"Oops, almost forgot." He smiled, turning back toward the table he picked up his knife. "If you do anything stupid, I will kill you. I would much prefer you to be alive when we make love, but it's not a necessity."

I felt my knees buckle as any hope I may have had flew straight out the window. As he reached out and lifted my wrist, I felt the sharp pain run up my arm and winced. Joe gently caressed it as he released the handcuff.

"Is it hurting you, Lizzie?"

"Yes," I answered, my wrist throbbing.

"I'll give you something for that in a moment. It won't be much longer and you won't feel any pain. I promise," he said, as he gently kissed the top of my head.

I could feel Harper trembling at my feet so I reached down and gave him a pat as Joe walked back to the table and upended the pill container. About fifty tablets fell out, some hitting the table while others rolled to the floor. If I took all those I really would be entering an eternal sleep. Grabbing a handful of them and picking up the glass, Joe started his walk back toward me.

Meow!

My attention, momentarily, turned to Cat. Thinking it was suppertime, Cat walked into the room and stood for a moment assessing the situation. I felt Harper's body tense. Cat was totally oblivious to the danger of the situation and sauntered over to Joe. He started to wind himself around his legs, obviously thinking Joe was probably his best option at getting food. Joe didn't even seem to notice Cat as he walked toward me.

Fear stopped me from thinking clearly. I needed to stop it but images of what Joe wanted to do to me kept flashing in my mind. I knew I wanted escape and the pills, alcohol and death would definitely be the easiest way out, but there was a part of me that couldn't go through that without a fight. Fighting though could lead to getting my throat cut. That was not something I wanted to experience in a hurry. The closer he got, the faster my heart raced. I had to make a decision and fast.

"When all of this is over, I'm going to find that boyfriend of yours and slit his throat. I hate him. I hate that he has violated you. I'm going to enjoy watching the blood drain from his body." Joe was so close now, the saliva from his mouth sprayed across my face as he spat those last words.

"Excuse me? What did you just say?" I asked, wiping his spit away with my hand.

"I said I'm going to enjoy killing Riley."

I felt myself snap. A conscious decision on what I should do was no longer an option. Common sense flew out the window taking the fear with it as anger took over. There was no way in hell I was letting him anywhere near Riley while I still had breath in me.

"What's wrong with you? What are you doing?" he asked.

All conscious thoughts gone, I made my Sensei proud and remembered everything he had ever taught me. Pulling my hand backward, I palm-heeled Joe's nose with all the strength I had. Somehow, adrenaline made me ten times stronger than normal, as blood gushed from his now broken nose and he flew backward. I heard the glass shatter as it hit the floor and took the opportunity of his limited vision to jump on him, gouging his eyes as I did so. As he stumbled backward, me clinging to him, I felt him trip over Cat and fall. Somehow, I managed to keep my hold.

Joe, too stunned to react straight away, howled in pain as I grabbed his ears and started smashing his head into the floor. He recovered all too quickly and threw me off him like a rag doll. My back smashed into the cupboard.

I screamed in frustration, got back to my feet and ran at his back. Jumping up, I wrapped my legs around his body and held on tight as he thrashed around trying to shake me off. I felt the pain rip through my back when he body-slammed me backward against the wall. My breath whooshed out as I crumpled to the floor again.

Harper barked madly as I watched Joe stagger around the kitchen looking for his knife, blood still oozing from his nose. I tried to catch my breath, and took the opportunity to open the cupboard door and pull out whatever could help me. Feeling around in the dark cupboard, my hands closed around a spray can of what I hoped to be my trusty old bug spray. Now Sensei always told me that unless you were far enough away from your attacker to run, you needed to get in close because you could do more damage from there.

I slowed my breathing and waited until Joe walked back toward me. I had my finger on the trigger ready and waited for

Joe to get close enough. Hearing his steps echo across the wooden floor, I counted to three and pressed that trigger for all it was worth.

It was like killing a cockroach. You don't stop spraying until the bug is dead or you run out of spray.

Joe dropped the knife and screamed as the spray made precision contact with his eyes. With my finger on the trigger, I followed him around as he screamed in pain.

Harper will forever be my hero for what happened next. He ran across the room, his few teeth bared, as he lunged at Joe and bit down hard, locking on and not letting go.

The scream that emerged from Joe will be a noise I will never forget. He dropped to the floor, powerless to even swat Harper away.

Suddenly noise filled the room, as the back door was kicked in and the room filled with police officers, including Officer Wilkins and Helms, and Riley's brother Jared.

I stood frozen as they rushed in, guns first and descended on Joe. I have to admit breathing was difficult with all the spray in the air and I succumbed to the fumes, dropping to my hands and knees. From this position I looked over and noticed Harper had latched onto Joe's privates and even with a room full of people with guns, he was not letting go.

"Harper! Come here, boy," I called, coughing.

I figured the police had this under control now and didn't like the idea of Harper being in the line of fire. He immediately came running to me, tongue out, licking my face in his attempt to make sure I was okay.

Once Joe was secured and no longer a threat, and the guns were holstered, Officer Wilkins stepped over to me.

"Lizzie, can you stand?" she asked.

I looked up at her and nodded my head. Holding out her hand, she helped me to my feet.

Watching as Joe was handcuffed and almost dragged out of

the room, I saw the blood seeping through his pants, leaving a big red stain as it soaked into the fabric. I should be feeling elation, but honestly, I wasn't feeling anything.

Sure, relief was in there somewhere, but all I felt was numb. It was as if I was having an out of body experience, where my soul floated somewhere around the ceiling, observing everything from a third-party point of view.

"Lizzie, this is Tom, a paramedic. He's going to help you," said Officer Wilkins as another man in uniform approached me.

Tom sat me down on a chair he'd pulled toward me and wrapped a silver foil blanket around my shoulders. He took my pulse and my blood pressure, hooked me up to various mobile machines and determined I would live. Apparently though, my wrist needed an x-ray and it was probably a good idea to have a brain scan, as it appeared my head had taken a few knocks. Humph, he was telling me.

A gurney was wheeled in and another paramedic tried to help me onto it. Harper however, was not leaving my side. A younger officer stepped up and reached out to Harper, the trepidation showing on his face. I looked down at Harper and gave him a reassuring pat.

"Good boy, Harpie. You're a good dog." I smiled. This seemed to be enough for Harper as I could see his body physically relax. A lead miraculously appeared from somewhere and was clipped onto his collar, as he was led out of the room. Watching Harper's disappearing back, I felt the numbness start to wear off. The void was now being filled with that many different emotions, I didn't know what would surface first.

"I don't want to go to the hospital," I said, turning back to Tom. "Can't it wait till morning and I'll go to the x-ray place? Please?" Okay, anxiety seemed to be topping the list. This would have to have been the worst day of my life, and to finish it off I had to go to the hospital?

"Sorry love. It's for the best. They'll get you through nice and quickly and then you can go home for a good sleep." Tom seemed like a nice man, but honestly, he had no idea.

"This is my home and I'm not sure I ever want to come back here again," I whispered.

"Well then, let's get you sorted and see how you feel tomorrow."

Looking around the room, I recognized no-one. Even Jared, who I'd only met once, had disappeared. I felt desperate, and lonely. I knew if I started to cry, I would never stop, so I tried my hardest to bite the tears down. Slowly climbing onto the gurney, I felt about a hundred years old as the paramedics then wheeled me outside.

Outside, blue and red lights flashed, casting strange shadows over my neighbors who filled the street, eager to know what was going on. Police tape was strung across my driveway, preventing any unauthorized entry. I could see Joe being wheeled into another ambulance, closely followed by two police officers.

Lying back, I closed my eyes and wished for this to all be over. I wanted to be anywhere but here.

A hand touched mine. I briefly opened my eyes and came face to face with Riley. He was the one person I really wanted to see and suddenly, everything seemed all right.

I was safe.

I could no longer hold them back. The tears ran down my cheeks and I struggled to keep control of my emotions as the shock registered on his face.

God only knows what I looked like. I'd had countless hits across the face, dried blood on my throat, congealed blood oozing from my swollen lip, my left eye was swelling shut and I had stubble rash on my chin from where Joe had kissed me. Oh, and my wrist could possibly be broken and I'm sure I had tufts of hair missing. Holding my breath for the thousandth time tonight, I waited for his reaction.

The paramedics had stopped my gurney just short of the

vehicle and were running around doing goodness knows what, but I was completely unaware of any of them as I waited. Riley's face was illuminated from the light coming from the inside of the ambulance and I could see the torture in those beautiful blue eyes.

"What did he do to you?" he whispered as tears wet those gorgeous lashes.

That was all it took. Sobs escaped me and I no longer had control over my emotions whatsoever. Riley leaned closer as I sat up and he held me against his chest.

Geez I loved this man. I clung to his shirt as I felt him start to shake. I don't know how long the paramedics allowed us to sit like that, but before long Riley's shirt was soaking and I struggled to control my breathing. The sobbing would not subside.

Riley only let go when the paramedic forced the oxygen mask over my face and patiently told me to try to take deep breaths and slow my breathing. Within a few minutes, I'd regained some control. Let me tell you, if I looked bad before, now both eyes were swollen from all the crying and my nose was pouring snot by the barrel load. Riley was obviously a very brave man, as he seemed undeterred by it all.

THE PARAMEDICS kindly allowed Riley to stay with me on the way to the hospital along with a uniformed police officer. On the ride, I'd tried to recount the events of the day with as much clarity as I could find. I had a monster headache and IV catheters poked into both arms, so my ability to recall events were not at its best, but I tried. Trying does not however, imply succeeding so by the time we got to emergency, I'd merely confused the poor rookie police officer who was taking my statement.

"Why don't you allow Lizzie some time to be looked after and when she's feeling better, I'm sure she'll be able to give a statement," Paramedic Tom suggested.

Sighing, I watched the young officer close his notebook.

"Okay. I'll be staying close though. Don't worry, you're safe now, Lizzie. Joe Woods has been brought to the same hospital, but he is heavily guarded." He smiled reassuringly, his voice official.

Inside, Riley never left my side, except when I was taken to x-ray and imaging when I was accompanied by Officer Rookie who, even though he looked too young to be a police officer, the sight of his gun did reassure me quite a bit. By the time I was wheeled back to emergency, my family had arrived.

Oh dear God, would this night never end? I know I should be grateful for their love and concern, but all I wanted was some sleeping tablets and a comfy bed where I would be safe and could forget everything that had happened.

Looking at the clock as I was pushed back into my cubicle, I saw it was two thirty in the morning and everyone looked exhausted. Mum was the first with the hugs, holding on tightly as everybody else looked too shocked by the sight of me. I still didn't have the bravery to look in a mirror, but judging by how white they'd all turned, I must look horrific.

Wiping her eyes, Mum stepped back and allowed Dad near. I heard the sob in his throat as he pulled me toward him and even though I thought I was all cried out, the tears started all over again. Cradled in his arms, I held on tight, feeling like a child. Maybe Mum was right. I would always need someone to look out for me.

Danny was next to step up once Dad let go and as he held me, he whispered, "You've got to have one serious makeover when you get out of here, girl." Laughing, I punched him playfully in the arm.

As I looked at Grandma Mabel, I noticed how for the first time, she actually looked her eighty-two years. Emotion burned bright in her eyes as she swished her teeth backward and forwards.

Molly was the last to approach. Andrew had been holding her, her eyes swollen from crying, she looked like the one who'd been punched.

"I missed my big job in Loganville because of you," she scolded. I knew this was just a cover. Sometimes Molly acts brave to cover her vulnerability.

"Love you, Moll." I smiled.

Officer Rookie was standing back carefully watching to make sure nobody hurt me, when Danny finally noticed him. He took one look at him in his perfectly pressed uniform and asked, "Well, honey. Do I look like a bad guy? Because you can frisk me if you like."

The color drained from Officer Rookie's face. He either took his job way too seriously or it was too early in the morning for jokes.

"Daniel, have some respect for the law!" scolded Mum.

"I do have respect and I'm just saying I'm not as good as I look, if you know what I mean." Looking over at Andrew, I saw him roll his eyes. "Don't roll your eyes at me, Andrew. You know how bad I can be." Danny laughed.

Dad groaned.

Grandma just kept rolling her teeth around.

It certainly seemed like everyone was back to normal.

After the doctor had given me the all clear—no, my wrist wasn't broken and my brain was still intact—I was patched up as best they could and sent on my way. There was a small kafuffle as everyone argued over who I was staying with until Riley said I was staying with him. Officer Rookie was to stand guard until David Thornton had been arrested for his part in the crimes.

Honestly, I didn't care. The lovely doctor had given me something pretty strong for my headache and to help me sleep. Apparently counseling was a good place to start, but until then denial and sleeping tablets seemed the way to go.

THE NEXT DAY arrived bright and sunny. I stretched luxuriously in Riley's bed—he disappointingly seemed to be absent—then lay back with my head on the pillow, relaxed and content. Looking at the clock, I saw it was already twelve thirty in the afternoon. Crap, those tablets must have been good. I'd slept like a log without any dreams.

A few things had to be sorted today, like my statement I still had to give to the police. I also had to look in the mirror. When we got back here last night, I walked straight to the shower, stripped off naked and scrubbed every inch of my body, avoiding the mirror altogether. I needed to be strong before I could do that. Caffeine would be a good help. I moved to get out of bed, wincing at my sore body.

Riley was already up and sitting at his computer by the time I made it down that stairs.

"Hey, how are you feeling?" he asked.

"Sore. And still a bit groggy. I'm hoping coffee will help." I forgot my wrist was weak as I picked up the coffee pot and winced.

Riley, not missing a beat, jumped up and poured the cup for me. "You just need to give it time. The doctor said it would be sore for a few days, maybe even a week." His hand had brushed mine as he handed me my cup and I felt the jolt of electricity run up my arm. I looked up at him and smiled.

"What are you up to?" I asked, nodding in the direction of the computer.

"Just sending a few emails and finishing off a few quotes."

Damn, that's right. I'd forgotten about that.

"Did you get the job in Loganville?" I asked, turning away and walking to the table so he couldn't see how this thought upset me.

"Yeah. That's the email I'm sending now," he said, with a sheepish smile. "The police officer has gone. They arrested David Thornton this morning and are holding him until he gets in front of a judge for his bail hearing."

I let out a sigh. "That's good. Hopefully they will take a very careful look at that family and uncover all the evil things they've done. I'm sure Avis isn't the only person they've hurt to cover up indiscretions."

"When you're ready, I'll take you to the station and you can give your statement," said Riley, walking to the table and placing his cup on it.

"How did the police know to come to the house last night?"

"Jared called them. When I got out of the hospital from visiting Mia, I got your messages. I gave the license plate to Jared and he phoned it in. As soon as I heard who the car belonged to, I tried to call you but it kept going to message bank. You were supposed to be at your mum's, so I called her. She told me how you'd picked Mabel up from the church and left. The fact that you wouldn't answer your phone made me panic, so I spoke to Jared and we came straight to the house. Seeing the black sedan and the lights on, we knew he was there but I didn't know you were there until I crept up to the window and looked in." Riley looked down at me, the intensity in his eye blazing. "When I saw you handcuffed to the refrigerator I wanted to break the door down and get you out. Jared convinced me to wait two minutes while back up arrived."

"So you overheard what was happening inside?" I asked, uncertainty causing my stomach to clench.

"Yes. The first thing I saw was him kissing you." I saw the muscles in Riley's jaw tensed at the memory.

"Yeah, that reminds me, I need to get some acid to rinse my mouth out with." I tried to smile to lighten the mood and show

Riley I was okay, but it was harder than I thought. I was desperately shoving the emotions from last night into the *To Be Sorted* file in the back of my mind. Hopefully, they would soon be buried by all the other *To Be Sorted* crap and I would never have to actually visit them again.

"Lizzie, when you're feeling better, we really need to talk," said Riley, in a voice barely above a whisper.

"We can talk now," I suggested, hoping against hope he was going to say the words I desperately wanted to hear. Of course, we didn't get to talk because as it always is with Murphy's Law, my phone started to ring.

"Why don't you go and get dressed and I'll answer that," nodded Riley.

"Okay. Thanks." Damn, I hate phones. I think I might take it and drown it. Better yet, maybe smashing it with a very big hammer would be better.

Stomping my way to the bathroom door, I took a deep breath, opened it and approached the mirror with my eyes closed. *You can do this, Lizzie.* Everybody else had seen my face, it was time to man up and look for myself. Slowly I opened my eyes.

Okay, internally, I was screaming the house down, but all that could come out of my mouth was a quiet little *eek*. My throat constricted. What looked back at me from the mirror was a black and purple face I hardly recognized. My eye and lip were swollen and a clump of hair missing from the back of my scalp. No amount of make-up in the world would cover this.

I decided the only thing I could do was have a shower and wash my hair, styling it as best I could to cover my face. Thankfully I always have some make-up in my handbag, so I gently brushed on mineral foundation and sprayed myself with perfume. Finding some clothes I'd left in Riley's laundry pile, I pushed my D-cups up as far as they would go, hoping that with this distraction, nobody would be paying too much attention to my face. With my best heels on, I was ready to face the world. It wasn't great, but I did feel a whole lot better than I had thirty minutes ago.

Riley smiled when I got back downstairs, his eyes only momentarily lingering on my cleavage. "It was your mum on the phone. She wants us all there for dinner tonight. She's celebrating Harper's heroism."

CHAPTER 31

*A*fter spending the rest of the afternoon at the police station recounting every detail I could remember from the events of the day before, I drove with Riley to Mum's. I felt a familiar tug on my heartstrings as I watched him concentrating on the road, deep in thought.

I knew I'd fallen in love with him and I kind of had a feeling he felt something for me, but there was no use kidding myself. He was leaving soon.

"Are you okay?" he asked, concern causing his eyebrows to knit together.

"Yes. Why?"

"You just groaned." Oops. I really need a filter between my brain and my mouth.

"I have to go back to Ackwood and get my car," I said, quickly thinking on my feet. "I remember having the keys in my hand as I walked through the car park yesterday, but I honestly don't know if I dropped them or put them back in my bag. I hope my car's still there," I said, crossing my fingers.

"I'll get Molly to drive with me and I'll go and pick it up."

"Oh?" Jealousy rolled and clenched my stomach. "Why Molly?"

"Because you probably shouldn't be driving just yet and I don't want it to stay there another night." Riley looked at me, a look of amusement in his eyes.

"What's so funny?" I snapped.

"Nothing. It's just, even with all those bruises, you look really cute when you're jealous." This earned me the megawatt smile.

"Who says I'm jealous? Maybe I just don't like Molly driving my car," I sulked. Gee, I really need to work on my poker face a bit more.

Pulling up outside Mum's, Riley turned to me. "Lizzie, I have to drive to Loganville in the morning to prepare for a job and I'm going to be gone for a while, but when I get back, I want to sort a few things out with you."

"Can't we sort it out before you go?"

"I'd like to, but I have to get your car tonight and I'm leaving early in the morning, so I don't think I'll have enough time," he said, a look of sorrow clouding his eyes.

"Oh, okay." I felt my heart sink.

Sitting there in Mum's driveway looking out at the darkening sky, I wondered what it was he wanted to talk about. I mean, if he was going to tell me he loved me, was crazy about me, couldn't live without me etcetera, then why couldn't he just say it? The only answer I could come up with was that he didn't feel any of these things and wanted to let me down gently. Shit, that was an emotion that hurt. Hearing Riley open his door, I blinked several times to try to clear any lingering feelings and followed him into Mum's.

Mum had gone all out. You would have thought it was Christmas with the amount of food she'd prepared. This was a feast. There were roast vegetables, roast chicken, gravy and my favorite of all, a huge chocolate mud cake. My stomach growled at the smell of it.

"Hello, Baby," she said, rushing over to me as soon as I walked in the door. Returning her hug, she stepped back to survey my face and I saw the tears well in her eyes.

"I'm all good Mum. I'll look like my old self in no time." I smiled.

"Well, come on in. We've got a few extras tonight. Your Auntie Margaret and Uncle Frank have come for dinner. I thought it was about time they met Riley."

"Really? Why do they have to meet Riley?" I asked, anxiety churning in my stomach.

Mum answered with a cluck, as if I'd just asked a stupid question. Walking into the lounge, I spotted Danny and grabbed his arm.

"Did you know Auntie M and Uncle Frank were going to be here?" I hissed.

"No. Do you think I'd be here if I did?" he answered.

"Danny, I can't do this!" I said, anxiety now running through me at warp speed. "Mum's showing him off, isn't she?"

"Looks like it," he grimaced.

"Riley and I are not an item and if there were any chance of that happening, them being here will guarantee he runs for the hills. I've scared him half to death with my appearance in the morning. He's watched me vomit in public, flash my knickers, seen me naked—which let me tell you was not a good thing at the time—and I've frightened the life out of him. Plus, he had to look at me today before I even had a chance to fix myself up. Believe me the way I look right now is good. Riley doesn't deserve this," I said, looking at Danny, desperation screaming from every pore.

Danny looked at me sympathetically. "You're right, he doesn't. I mean you look like shit now. No man deserves to see you look worse than this. But, he's got to meet them some time," he said, shrugging his shoulders.

"No, he doesn't! Did you not hear me? I said Riley and I are not an item. In fact, I think he wants to tell me he doesn't feel that way about me." My heart started to palpitate and sweat broke out on my upper lip. "Danny, please. I couldn't stand the humiliation if Mum announces we're a couple. You have to stop her."

"Okay, okay. I'll talk to her. But I don't think she'll listen. You know what she's like when she's got an idea in her head."

Yeah, I knew only too well.

"Margaret!" I heard Mum call. My heart skipped a beat. "I want you to meet Lizzie's new boyfriend, Riley."

Mum was herding Riley into the lounge and away from Dad and Andrew, who were hiding out in the kitchen. I took one look at Riley's face and wished with all my heart the ground would open up and swallow me.

"Sorry, not quick enough," whispered Danny, who judging by the grin on his face was not sorry at all. He was standing back ready to enjoy the show.

"It's no good trying to stop her now. She's been going on all afternoon about your new boyfriend," said Grandma Mabel, who'd snuck up behind me.

Riley looked like a cornered rat, eyes wide, looking for all the exits. As humiliating as this was, after all he had done for me, I had to save him.

"Mum! Riley is not my boyfriend," I hissed, grabbing Mum's arm and giving her the death stare. This didn't have the required effect as it was difficult to squint your eyes when one of them was already half shut.

"Oh, hush, Lizzie," she said, turning away from me and back to Riley. "Riley, this is my sister Margaret and her husband Frank," she said, pushing Riley forward and if I may say, under the oncoming bus.

Auntie Margaret's face was priceless though. There was unspoken competition between Mum and Auntie M to see who had the best-looking children, the smartest children, the child with the best job, etcetera, etcetera. Well, if Riley really was my boyfriend, Mum would have just won Best Looking Son-In-Law.

Auntie M looked like she'd swallowed something sour as she held out her hand to Riley. I heard Danny snigger behind me, as I watched Riley turn on the charm. I saw the look of triumph cross Mum's face as she quickly changed the subject and called everyone to the table.

"Sorry," was all I could come up with as Riley walked behind me to the dining room.

Dinner, as usual was a noisy affair, especially with the extras in the room. Auntie M held center of attention as always with her loud voice and colorful language, Harper enjoyed his bone and I enjoyed the chocolate cake. After dinner, Riley organized with Molly to go and get my car, and Danny gave me a lift home to face my demons.

Cat was happy to see me, winding himself around my legs, hoping I would feed him. Standing in the doorway to the kitchen, I took a few deep breaths and told myself it was all over now. I had Officer Wilkins' number on speed dial and I knew Mum and Dad would understand if I changed my mind and slept on their couch. I wouldn't do that, of course. I had to build a bridge and get over any lingering fear of yesterday.

After getting into bed—being extra vigilant and putting a chair under the door handle—I thought about the ring that had started it all. I knew I didn't want it and after knowing about Brian Hogan the jeweler, I didn't want the trouble of selling it either. I just wanted to get rid of it. Deciding that tomorrow I would contact John Buckner and give the ring back to him, I took one of the sleeping pills the doctor had prescribed and drifted into a deep, dreamless sleep.

THE NEXT MORNING dawned wet and stormy. I looked out into my driveway and saw my Mini had been returned. I don't know what time Riley and Molly had got back, but I hadn't heard a thing. After doing the usual shower, teeth cleaning and hair thing, I went downstairs in search of caffeine. There was a note on the table along with my car keys and fresh coffee brewing in the pot.

Hi Lizzie

I tried to wake you last night but your bedroom door was locked and I didn't want to disturb you. I picked up the last of your things from my place and left them in the lounge in case you needed them and I put a pot of coffee on. I know how much you need your morning caffeine hit.

Take care

Riley x

SO THAT WAS IT. Riley was gone. Suddenly the house felt empty. Looking around, I felt the loneliness seep back out of the walls and smother me once again. Maybe the loneliness would never leave this house. All I knew was I didn't want to be here anymore. Throwing the note back on the table, I gave Cat some biscuits, picked up my keys and stormed out of the house.

Getting in my car, I drove aimlessly. Before long I realized I was heading back to Ackwood. Jared had given the ring and the letters back to me at the hospital and I had them in my bag, so John Buckner, here I come.

An hour later, I pulled up at the nursing home and found John, but sadly not Wilhelmina. Holding back tears, John told me how Wilhelmina had passed away later in the evening of my last visit. He said she felt at peace knowing Avis's grave would be looked after and that the ring had been found. She prayed that all the awful things the Thornton family had done would be known and that justice would be served. If only she'd known.

"John, I don't want this ring," I said, handing the box over to him, along with the letters. "I'm giving it to you to do whatever you want with it. I know Wilhelmina told me to keep it or sell it, but right now, I can't deal with it."

"I'm sorry for what my family did to you, Lizzie," he said, sorrow in his eyes.

"It's okay. I'm glad he got caught and will be prosecuted for all the things he did. I'm just sorry Will wasn't here to see it."

"Yeah, but I like to think she's in Heaven and that she's happy now."

I liked to think this too.

———

A WEEK HAD PASSED since Riley left and I'd been to visit John. I paid a visit to Avis's grave and found someone had been there and left some flowers for her. Hopefully, John would do the right thing and one day, give her a headstone.

Danny, Andrew and Molly had decided a night out in the city was what we all needed to celebrate life. I hadn't heard a word from Riley since he'd left and had a sinking feeling I never would. The distance between us probably gave him the reason he needed never to contact me again. Having a major broken heart gave me no reason to celebrate life, so it was with arguments and threats that I was dragged to Danny's salon and given another makeover.

With long flowing curls, smoky eyes and the sexiest little dress I'd ever bought, I reluctantly got into Molly's car with the promise that I could consume lots of alcohol once I got there.

Danny and Andrew had chosen a popular nightclub in the heart of the city and being Friday night, it was packed. Bodies jumped around on the dance floor, jammed up against each other as they all fought for position at the bar, and the music pumped. I'll admit, that after my second drink—remembering I am not much of a drinker—I was feeling the most relaxed I had in days. The short skirt was also gaining some male attention, which was good for the ego.

After the Scott debacle and Riley running for his life, my self-esteem was at an all-time low. Molly's self-esteem, however, was not low as I watched her strut her stuff in her tight midnight blue mini dress and four-inch high heels. With her hair tied up messily on top of her head and silver dangly earrings showing the curve of her beautiful neck, two different men jostled for her attention. When the song ended, she gave them both a little finger wave and strutted back to me.

"Having fun yet?" she yelled above all the noise, as the next song started to play.

"Not really, but it's not too bad."

Okay. I was having fun. Looking around the room, I thought this place was actually all right. The bar was positioned in the middle of the room with a dance floor on one side and tables on the other. A single glass staircase worked its way around the room and up to the second level of tables for those wishing a more intimate setting. The lighting was low in the seated areas, and bright and flashy over the dance floor as the DJ mixed his stuff at the far end of the room, in his box high above the crowd.

Taking the time to crowd watch—one of my favorite pastimes —I saw Danny and Andrew grind their stuff with the best of them, laughing and enjoying each other's company. I loved them both with all my heart, but a spike of jealousy for what they had threatened to spoil my alcohol induced happiness. Thoughts of Riley and what he was doing right now flitted through my mind.

"You're not allowed any sad thoughts tonight, Lizzie," said Molly, reading my mind.

"That's easier said than done." Looking at my drink, I swirled it around in my hand and tried to think of something other than those sky blue eyes.

"Hello, Elizabeth," I heard a familiar voice say.

Looking up, any thoughts of Riley completely forgotten, I came face to face with Scott. This was the first time he'd spoken to me since I'd walked in on him and Belinda. It took me a moment to gather my thoughts and get over the shock.

"What are you doing here?" I asked, my voice several octaves higher than I'd hoped for.

"Belinda and I are having an evening out," he nodded in the direction of Belinda, who seeing Molly, had sensibly kept her distance. "I saw you standing here on your own and she convinced me to come and talk to you."

"What could you possibly have to say to me now?" I asked. Anger and bitterness dripped from my every word.

Molly stepped up behind me, ready to do battle if I needed it. Feeling her there gave me the courage to ask what I'd always wanted to know.

"All I want to hear from you, Scott, is why. Why did you do it?"

"Can we go somewhere and talk? It's noisy in here," he asked, nervously glancing around the room. Danny and Andrew had also stopped dancing and come to offer their support.

"Why don't we go outside?" suggested Andrew, probably trying to avoid a situation that could erupt in here. Nodding his head in agreement, we all followed Scott out the front door, to the footpath.

The lineup of people waiting to get in snaked its way down the side of the building, as everyone eyeing the door, waiting for their chance to get inside, turned our way. Scott was obviously nervous as he kept glancing back at Danny and Molly, his only back up Belinda. I'm not sure if that would help or hinder him.

"Do you have to have the cavalry with you?" he asked.

"Yes. You've left it this long to talk to me, so you don't get to set the terms," I snapped, stopping and turning to look at him. Standing there, shoulders hunched, he looked small and insignificant. "What did you ever want from me?"

I watched him take a deep breath and slowly let it out.

"I needed a cover. I knew Belinda was special long before anything ever happened between us, but our boss is very particular, as you know. He wouldn't have given me the promotion I desired if he didn't think my personal life was up to his standard. As much as Belinda is a magnificent woman, she is divorced and quite older than me. I'm sure you could see my predicament."

"No, but keep going."

"When you started at the office, all the men were talking about you. You caused quite a stir you know." He smiled at the memory. "I noticed you straight away and you seemed to have the qualities I was looking for. I thought I could help you transform yourself into the beautiful person you're capable of being. With some guidance, you could have had it all."

"I never wanted it all, Scott. You would know that if you ever listened."

"Oh, I listened, Elizabeth. And watched. The problem with you is you're lazy. You could have been perfect if you'd just put in some effort." His annoyance was starting to show, as his breathing became rapid and his speech faster.

"What do you mean by that?"

"I mean, I may never have continued a relationship with Belinda if you had improved yourself."

"What's wrong with me?" I yelled, hurt.

"Well, look at you now for instance. You are the most frustrating woman I have ever met. You are pretty but you refuse to make the most of yourself. Firstly, you could actually go to the gym. Secondly, your brother is a goddamn hairdresser. There is no excuse for the way you look."

Holding my chin high, I said, "Any man here would be happy

to have me." Looking around I could see several heads nodding in agreement.

"Just say the word," yelled one man. I smiled at Scott.

"See?"

"That's because he doesn't know you," said Scott, getting right up in my face.

Wow that hurt. Not that I was going to let him see that. "So I wasted two years of my life on you!" I yelled.

"No. I wasted two years of my life on you." Scott stopped, took a deep breath and looked at Belinda. She'd been quiet throughout this whole thing.

"You're just not enough, Elizabeth. You're not smart enough, you're not pretty enough, and you're definitely not sexy enough. I'm sorry, I couldn't pretend anymore."

I felt my cheeks burning as I looked around at our audience, everyone within earshot had gone quiet, listening to the drama unfolding in front of them. Suddenly the footpath didn't feel like the best place to be having this conversation.

"You had the chance to be with me and you weren't interested in trying to be what I wanted. Belinda does try. She is everything I ever want in a woman." Scott stopped for a breath, "You're just not in the same class."

I could feel the tension in the air build around me the more Scott spoke, and I felt, more than saw, Danny move toward him. He was angry, but before he had time to do anything, Riley stepped up, placing his hand on Danny's shoulder, holding him back.

I'd been so consumed with what Scott was saying I hadn't even noticed him join us. I watched as Riley moved past Danny and stepped in front of Scott. Scott flinched as Riley stood over him by a good six inches. I saw the look of satisfaction on Riley's face as he swung his arm and punched Scott on the nose.

Scott fell to the floor, blood gushing everywhere. Riley turned his back on him and walked toward me. Shocked, I looked up into his eyes as he gently took my face in his hands. The only thing I could see was his face as he gently pulled me toward him.

"He's right. You're not in the same class. You're way above anyone else," Riley said, his lips so close I could almost taste his breath. He just needed to move a little closer and he'd be kissing me. And that's exactly what he did.

I had so many emotions running through me, I didn't know what to feel, but the softness of his lips were pulling desire to the top of the list.

Dropping his hands to my waist, he pulled me hard against him, holding me up. His kiss was soft and lingering, and I heard someone give a deep blissful sigh. Pulling back, Riley looked at me with those gorgeous blue eyes and smiled.

"I've wanted to do that for a very long time," he said.

"Hit Scott or kiss me?" I asked.

He gave a small chuckle. "Both," he said, dipping his head to kiss me again as I heard the crowd erupt in a loud cheer.

Continue reading book 2 - on sale now!

https://bit.ly/442Jvr1

GIVE MURDER A HAND

$\mathcal{I}$ sat on my rotting back deck, looking at Molly as she checked the time on her new watch. Her watch matched the rest of her. Perfect. It was a designer brand and matched her designer dress, which was a bit too short, a bit too tight, and cut low enough to show everyone who cared just how ample her bosom really was.

I looked down at my T-shirt dress and wished—not for the first time—that I could just be a little more like her.

Maybe if I had her budget I'd be able to dress like that. I sighed. The truth was, even with her budget, I still couldn't pull that outfit together so effortlessly. Molly is my sister and she's beautiful. We've been told that we look very much alike, but honestly, I am a watered-down version of her.

My name is Lizzie Fuller, and I'm the tallest female member of my family, measuring in at five foot two inches. Barefoot, Molly is shorter by half an inch, but that half an inch is very important to me. Our brother Danny towers over both of us at five foot eight, but both Molly and I have a much more impressive D-sized cleavage. I am however, the only sibling to have inherited two dimples. Where from? Who knows? Grandma

Mabel was a bit of a wild card, so we have no idea what's hidden in the family gene pool.

The day had turned into a bit of a scorcher which, as it was summer, I guess should be expected. My deck was old and rotten, but it was safe if you sat on the end nearest to my neighbors, Hazel and Allen. Of course that had the disadvantage of Hazel, the quintessential busybody, being able to hear everything I said. But as long as I didn't talk about her, it wasn't really a problem.

I sighed contentedly, and pretended to listen as Molly dreamily told me about a new man she was interested in. Honestly, my attention was on her dog, a little Maltese Terrier named Harper. Every time Molly came over for a visit, Harper went out to the garden, and frantically dug in the same spot. I usually went out and shooed him away, but next visit, there he was again. I'd decided to let him go for it. I wanted to plant some trees anyway so he was saving me the trouble of digging the hole. Plus, I always looked at him with his bright eyes and his tongue hanging out, and thought how enjoyable his life was. Seriously, when it's my time to be reincarnated, I want to come back as a dog.

I turned to look at Molly, still dreaming about the new man, her eyes bright and her tongue almost hanging out, and right there and then I believed people really did look like their dogs.

Lucky for me, I owned a cat, and that rule didn't apply to cats. Did it? I was about to ask Molly when she shouted at Harper.

"Harper! Get out of there!"

I looked, wondering where he was as I couldn't see him anymore, when I realized he was in the hole he'd dug.

"Come here, boy," she called. He stuck his head up out of the hole and barked. *Woof.*

"Don't bark at me," she scolded. "Just come here."

Eventually he came, but he didn't come clean. Harper was usually white and fluffy but right then, he was brown from his shoulders down, and had dirt stuck to his snout. He also brought something from the dirt to give to Molly. I noticed her eyes bulging as the realization dawned that she had to put him back into her beautiful shiny SUV. I stifled a giggle.

"Oh, Harper! Look how *dirty* you are," she chastised as she stood and walked towards him. "And what is that?"

"Don't yell at him," I said. "He looks happy." And he did. His eyes shone brightly as he trotted up the three steps onto my wooden deck, and dropped the gift at Molly's Jimmy Choo-clad feet.

"Eww, that's disgusting!" She squirmed, moving her toes to push it back down the stairs.

I knew she was squeamish about things like that, but as she turned towards me, her complexion paled, she swayed, and then fainted...right on top of Harper's gift. Shit. *Shit.*

Running over to help her, I looked at Harper. "Good one, Harper. *Now* what am I supposed to do?"

I wasn't good in stressful situations, especially medical ones. My heart rate increased, as my heart pounded against my ribs, leaving me short of breath. Calling an ambulance would probably be a good idea, but my phone was inside the house. Years ago, I'd completed a first aid course, and a memory stirred about how to put a patient in the recovery position. I knelt down next to Molly, grabbed her shoulder and shook her. Not exactly the recovery position, but it felt like the right thing to do. She moaned. That was a good sign, right?

"Molly!" I yelled, shaking her a little more. "What the hell are you doing?"

She moaned again. At least I knew she wasn't dead.

I grabbed her shoulder and rolled her onto her back.

"You're going to be in big trouble when she wakes up," I said to Harper, my heart rate decreasing slightly as Molly's eyelids fluttered.

"Urgh," she gurgled, stirring.

"Molly!" I shook her shoulder once more. "Molly, wake up."

She opened her eyes wide and stared at me, her gaze unfocused.

"Molly, can you hear me? Molly!"

My yelling must have worked—well, either that or the shaking I gave her—because she groaned and sat up.

"Stop yelling at me," she whispered, her eyes rapidly moving about, as she tried to figure out what happened.

As she moved, a bone rolled out from under her. Harper saw his chance, grabbed it and ran straight into the house, towards my couch—my white couch.

"Harper!" I yelled. I didn't care how happy he was. I did not need a big muddy stain on my favorite chair. Leaving Molly to get herself up, I ran through the kitchen door after Harper, but he was quicker than me. I wasn't sure how though, as that bone was almost the same size as him. Before I could catch him, he'd run through the kitchen, across the hallway, and straight into the lounge room. He was settling into place as I ran through the door.

"You naughty boy!" I chastised, stepping up to him. "That couch is nearly new and I happen to like it!" As I spoke, I looked down at the bone.

As Harper nuzzled it into position, it overbalanced, rolled off the chair, onto the floor, only stopping once it was under my timber coffee table. I gave a disgusted sigh and knelt down to retrieve it, wondering what poor family pet it would once have belonged to.

Feeling around the dirty carpet, I shuddered as my hand made contact with it and I felt the cold, damp soil lodge under my fingernails. As I dug my fingers in and pulled the bone out, I looked down at my hands, nausea rolling in my stomach. A clod of dirt fell onto the mat. The world swayed slightly as I saw looking back at me...a skull. But it wasn't the skull that freaked me out, it was that I was pretty sure this one didn't belong to a dog...or a cat.

In fact, I was pretty sure this one was human.

Stomach clenching, my vision blackened, and sweat broke out on my forehead. As the sickening feeling consumed me, I dropped the skull, sank to the floor and sucked in some air. My body shook as I pulled my knees up and put my head between them. I vaguely heard Molly enter the room.

"Lizzie?" she called. "Lizzie, are you okay?"

I waited for the dizziness to stop before responding. "What do you think?" I croaked. "Your dog just dug a *skull* up from my garden!" Panic seemed the appropriate emotion for the occasion.

"Well, it's not exactly my fault," she said, falling onto the couch.

"Whose fault is it then?" I asked, my voice getting louder with every syllable.

"You bought this stupid house. I told you not to, but did you listen to me? No! Of course you bloody didn't!"

"Well, I'm sorry!" I yelled as Harper slunk off the chair and moved behind the couch, sensing that maybe some of the blame would fall on him.

"And you bought the dog. Did I ask you too?" Molly, too, seemed led by panic. Thankfully my front door opened and in walked Riley.

Riley's my boyfriend. He's six foot three, same age as me (thirty-two and I promise I'm okay with that—honestly, I am), he has blond hair and the most amazing blue eyes I have ever seen, but it was his eyelashes that undid me. They aren't overly long, but they are black and thick. To sum him up, he's sex walking.

"Is everything okay?" he asked, his deep voice having an instant calming effect on me.

"Not exactly," snapped Molly.

My eyes filled with tears, realizing that a responsible adult could now take control of the situation. Riley took one look at me, moved into the room and dropped to his knees in front of me. I put my head on his shoulder as his arms pulled me in close.

"What happened?" he asked, his voice filled with concern. Reluctantly I pulled away from him and pointed to the skull that had once again rolled under the coffee table. He moved and retrieved it, his brow creasing.

"Is it what I think it is?" I asked, my voice slightly wobbly.

"Where did it come from?"

"Harper dug it from the back garden," explained Molly, her voice barely above a whisper as she looked at the skull in Riley's hands.

I thought about those hands and how I might make him acid wash them before he ever touched me again. Then I looked into his eyes and thought, bugger it, he could touch away.

Riley placed the skull on the coffee table, stood and moved towards the kitchen. Molly and I stood and followed him, gratefully leaving the skull behind. Harper, realizing the danger had passed, stepped out of his hiding place. He stopped to sniff at the bone.

"Harper!" yelled Molly. A second later he trotted past us, his tail between his legs.

Once in the kitchen, we passed through the back door and continued to follow Riley down the steps and to the garden bed where Harper had been digging. At this point, Harper overtook us all and immediately jumped back into the hole. I heard Molly suck in her breath as he came out, another bone clenched in his jaw. For a dog with one tooth, he certainly excelled himself today.

Riley took the bone off him and moved into the dirt himself. I grabbed Molly's arm as I held my breath.

"I think we should call the police," said Riley.

"How many are there?" I asked incredulously.

"I'm not sure but there's a lot more than this."

I felt the nausea swirl as Molly sat her designer dress down on the grass before she fainted again.

IT ONLY FELT like a few minutes between Riley dialing his phone and the police and the television cameras pulling up, but in reality it had been closer to twenty. Riley took this time to move Molly and myself back into the kitchen, and gave us both a hot cup of coffee.

Even though the outside temperature still hovered in the high thirties, the hot coffee calmed the shaking that took hold of my body. It had been a good few months since I had shaken like this.

You see, at the time I bought the house, the purchase contract had omitted a few extras I apparently got for free. Like the cat, the hidden engagement ring, and the stalker. The stalker was the cause of most of my anxiety and shaking. And of course, the nightmares that followed the day he had caught up with me, but...that's a whole other story.

Right now, I sat curled in the crook of Riley's arms and held my coffee close, feeling the heat from both seep into me. Molly had settled for cuddling Harper. Not a bad second choice, I thought.

The television cameras were set up in my garden and followed every movement of the police from a distance. I was unsure how they had gotten here so quickly, but maybe they listened to police scanners...or maybe my neighbor Hazel had alerted them. I had noticed her peering through her window as Riley stood in the hole that Harper had dug, her ears flapping with every sound.

She'd since moved closer, suddenly needing to do some late afternoon gardening, right next to the fence we shared. Honestly, we didn't need the six o'clock news. Once she had hold of the story the whole town would know about it.

I heard voices coming from the back deck and Riley went to investigate.

"Oh, hi. Are you the owner of the house?" asked a male voice.

"Kind of," answered Riley. "Can I help you?"

"Oh, um...well...um, I was hoping to speak to the owner of

the house. I'm Matt. Matt Wilson. I'm a reporter with WTN news…"

"Sorry, we don't have a comment at this time," replied Riley, closing the door in Matt's face. Molly sat up straight in her chair, her eyes a bit brighter than a few seconds before. She placed Harper on the floor and smoothed her dress.

"Who was that?" she asked.

"Just a reporter."

"I might get some fresh air," she said, standing and running her fingers through her long curls in an attempt to straighten them.

I caught my reflection in the window and knew I needed more than my fingers to straighten my mess. The humidity had had its affect, and all I had was a mass of frizz.

I watched as she ran her fingertips under her lashes, removing the imaginary excess mascara. Like I said, Molly was perfect, even her make-up didn't dare run. I watched her move to the back door and step into the chaos.

Walking to the window, I looked out at Molly talking to the reporter. It didn't take long for her to start flicking her hair, a habit Molly had when she was flirting.

"Oh my God! She's chatting up that reporter!" I said to Riley.

Riley seemed uninterested in what Molly was doing but he joined me at the window. We stood together and watched as the police taped off part of my yard, making a lot of notes as they went. My neighbors had given up the pretense of gardening and were all peering over their fences, obviously wondering what the crazy woman next door was up to this time. It was only when the police knocked on the door that Riley and I moved away.

"Hello, I'm Constable Davidson," said a young officer. "I was hoping to take possession of the skull your little dog found."

Bugger. In all that had happened this afternoon, I'd forgotten it was still on my coffee table.

Riley led the way and I stood back and watched as the officer placed the skull in a bag, and stepped out the front door. I thought of that table and knew, even though it was the least of my worries, it had to go. It was bad enough I had a skeleton in the back garden. I didn't need the house contaminated with it too.

I moved to the coffee table, grabbed the opposite end of it and dragged it after the constable, stopping when it was out on the footpath. Then I moved back into the house, up the two flights of stairs to my office and got a sheet of paper. I wrote *It's yours if you want it* in big letters with a marker pen, ran back outside and taped it to the front of the table.

I turned to see Riley smiling at me. The world swayed once again, but for a whole different reason this time. Even after months of Riley and I being together, his smile still made my world stand still.

He pulled me in close and kissed the top of my head. "There's not a disinfectant in the world that can kill skeleton cooties," I explained. Luckily for me, Riley understood my hang up with germs, especially after the horrors I'd been through.

Thirty minutes later, the collection of official vehicles in my driveway had lessened, and Molly finally stepped back into the house.

"Lizzie," she called. "Would you mind coming here for a moment, please?" Geez, why was she so formal all of a sudden? I followed her voice and found her standing just inside the back door with the reporter I recognized from the six o'clock news. I noticed the dazed look in his deep brown eyes as he gazed at Molly.

"Umm...this is Matt." She smiled. Matt looked around our age with short sandy blonde hair that curled at his collar. He was a little shorter than Riley and, as far as I could tell, had no muffin top hanging over his waistband. The biggest surprise for me was the dazed look in Molly's eyes as she smiled up at him. "He would like to ask you a few questions," she explained.

"Oh, really?" I stuttered as a cameraman walked closer and pointed his equipment at me. Yes, get your mind out of the gutter —it was his camera. Even though he looked sexy—so maybe I wouldn't mind his other equipment pointing at me—I shook my head, remembering Riley and how he had all the equipment I'd ever need.

"Yes, if that's okay?" Matt extended his hand for me to shake.

My mind stuttered as the camera came closer.

"Um...this is Sam, my cameraman. You don't mind, do you," he asked uncertainly.

I looked at Molly as she mouthed 'please'. "I...I guess not," I answered quietly.

Matt dropped his hand and tried to pull his phone out of his pocket. His fingers caught on the seam of his jeans and he dropped his phone onto the timber deck. He swore quietly as he bent to retrieve it but misjudged how close he was to Molly.

As he stood, his head caught her elbow and caused her to slop her now cold coffee all over her white designer dress. Geez, her dry cleaner would be busy. She gasped and I waited for her to yell at him. Instead, she simply smiled.

"I'm...I'm so, so sorry," he stammered, using the sleeve of his shirt to wipe at her bodice. Only when he realized he was actually rubbing her ample chest, did he stop. I looked at Sam and saw his smile from behind the viewfinder. He'd caught the whole thing on camera.

Molly took Matt's hand and gently moved it away, smiling as she did so. "It's okay. No biggie. It needed dry cleaning anyway."

It was this reaction that made me realize Matt was the man Molly was telling me about earlier, the new man she had her eye on. Well, judging by the color of his cheeks, I thought he would fit in with our family very well. Maybe he could even contribute to my book, *101 Ways to Embarrass Yourself*.

"Why are you so interested in this?" asked Riley, stepping up behind me and putting a protective hand on my lower back.

"Oh...well...um, news is a bit slow in Westport today," explained Matt. "Plus not everybody digs up a whole skeleton in their back garden."

"A whole skeleton?" I asked. That was the first I'd heard exactly what the police had found.

"Yes, they think so. I don't think they have it all yet, but the unusual thing about this skeleton is...it has three hands."

Continue reading book 2 - on sale now!

https://bit.ly/442Jvr1

JUST WHEN LIZZIE **thought the only problems she had in life were her crazy family and far too many nightmares, the house reveals yet another secret. This time it's a skeleton in the back yard. And it has an extra hand.**

HAUNTED BY THE FIND, Lizzie sets out to learn the truth of how it all got there, wanting to put the secrets of the house to rest for good. But can life be that easy? If only.

NEAR MISSES WITH DEATH, a super-hot policeman, sex crazed senior citizens, and Bradley the owner of Westport Tours, all make Lizzie's life interesting to say the least.

BUT CAN she solve the mystery of the bones before the For Sale sign gets hammered into the ground? Or will the secrets of the house take Lizzie to an early grave?

GIVE **Murder A Hand is the second book in this light-hearted romantic mystery series.**

https://bit.ly/442Jvr1

MORE BOOKS

I'm offering a free e-book to everyone who signs up to my mailing list. I promise not to spam you and only send out a handful of newsletters a year!

www.bethprentice.com

Do you want to know where it all began?

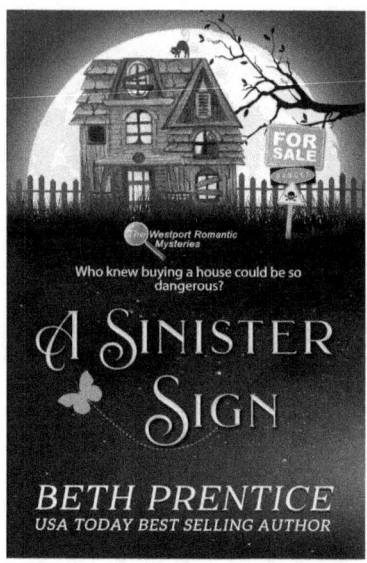

Who knew buying a house could be so dangerous?

Fed up with city life, Lizzie Fuller decides that moving home to the suburbs is just what she needs. But despite loving her family, the idea of living with them isn't all that appealing. And it doesn't take long to find the house of her dreams...or nightmares —it's really just a question of perspective.

The lonely run-down old Victorian in need of major renovations tugs on her heartstrings, and before she can stop herself, she's fallen head over heels in love with it. Unfortunately, she's not the only one who wants it, and the other bidders aren't playing nice.

Deadly accidents, missing real estate agents and a chilling stranger, are all sinister signs that this is not the house for her. Still, Lizzie is determined to rescue this fixer upper or die trying. Now all she needs to do is to win the auction and stay alive.

If only it was that easy...

A Sinister Sign is the prequel to Lizzie's adventures in Westport. If you like crazy families, cozy reads, and a sweet romance, all tied together with a ribbon of danger, then you'll love The Westport Mysteries.

www.bethprentice.com

ABOUT THE AUTHOR

Beth Prentice is the USA Today Bestselling Author of the Westport Mysteries. Killer Unleashed, her GHP debut novel, received a bronze medal in the 2016 Readers Favorite International Book Awards. Her main wish is to write books you can sit back, relax with, and escape from your everyday life...and ones that you walk away from with a smile! When she's not writing you will usually find her at the beach with a coffee in hand, pursuing her favorite pastime—people watching!